South Eight

a novel by

LARRY ATLAS

For Ann, always.

ONE

ON THE EIGHTH FLOOR of the southernmost building of the six-building campus, in this fourth county north of New York City, fourteen nurses—seven of South Eight's arriving day staff and seven of its departing night group, all women at this particular change of shift—murmur to one another in the liturgy of patient handoff. Arkin registers the treble clef of their voices as they report off, ceaseless, possibly even timeless, a moving river of sound. He stands in the middle of it, hands jammed into his pockets, the rangy slouch emphasized by the stethoscope dangling around his neck, the lab coat draped and dragged lower by the weight of his phones, pager, patient census, sign-out notes, penlight, sepsis algorithms, dosing guides. Nothing changes: the steady B-flat minor of the nurses' voices, the already sleep-bound eyes of the night staff, the anticipatory tightening in the faces of the new shift, the faint lingering scents around them all of shit, piss, and Betadine. The hallway telemetry annunciators outside the nearest block of rooms flash messages, occasionally accurate, of tachycardia within, too-slow rhythms, missed beats. Bed alarms signal motion among patients changing position, struggling with pain, struggling to awaken. Somewhere, a thready old woman's voice can be heard, "Help me," and then again, "Help me," and then again and again, metronomic and as empty of intelligence: "Help me."

––––––––––––

Arkin walks over to a computer by the chart rack, logs on, and begins confirming overnight telephone orders.

"Good morning, Dr. Arkin."

"Good morning, Nina. How was your night?"

"Quiet."—a bad-luck word never to be spoken in the hospital. Nina doesn't care, speaks it anyway. Heavyset, imperturbable, she's the night secretary for three of the hospital's twenty-four units; during the only somewhat busier day shift, her job requires six people. "Mrs. Shelton died. Dr. Williams came up and signed the death certificate."

"Okay." He's reading Williams's overnight note in one of the charts. "Did you print labs on Hammersly for his discharge?"

"I gave them to case management."

"Thanks." He scans an order for one of his new patients, an elderly man with a history of heart failure, admitted with AKI, acute kidney injury. For acidosis with an elevated potassium level on the repeat labs at midnight, the overnight doc had started him on intravenous fluids with an amp of sodium bicarbonate added. The 6:00 a.m. follow-up lab work confirms ongoing acidosis though the potassium levels are now normal, but his BNP, a measure of possible heart failure, is up significantly, worsening.

"Would you text the nurse?" He enters a new order discontinuing the fluids, which will sooner or later seriously overload the old man's circulation. This will begin with the lungs as the failing left side of his heart causes blood to back up into the pulmonary vasculature, which will in turn cause the right side of the heart to fill even less completely than it already does—leaving ounces, then cups, then pints and quarts of fluid to pool in his legs and scrotum and abdomen. Arkin has seen this so many times he doesn't think about it. Instead, he puts the old man on long-acting insulin to control his diabetes, which contributed to the acidosis, which in turn forced his cells to exchange potassium ions for hydrogen, which caused the hyperkalemia in the first place. The virtuous circle of business theory has no counterpart in medicine, only this converse spiral of decline. About the acute-on-chronic kidney failure that is contributing to the patient's broken chemistry and fluid status, Arkin can do little. He suspects the heart failure may be making its own independent contribution to the renal failure, and he selects another order to consult a nephrologist, who will recommend a change in diuretic—which Arkin has himself already ordered and which will make little difference. He orders a repeat echocardiogram and consults cardiology, who may want to consider ultrafiltration to take fluid off rather than continuing to bombard the patient and his kidneys with diuretics.

As a hospitalist physician, this is part of Arkin's role, to involve and coordinate specialist providers. In most cases, in Arkin's experience, it will not much affect outcomes with the elderly and chronically ill patients who form the majority of his patient census. Like the rest of them, this old man may improve, his acute illness coming under control, but he will still leave the hospital slightly worse off than at his previous discharge a month earlier. Even after recovery, each visit to the hospital leaves most patients, certainly the old ones, a little sicker, a little weaker, usually a little sadder. Arkin understands now that, prior to becoming a physician, he knew nothing about aging and the elderly. What he knows now is unsettling, both professionally and personally, though at thirty-three, he is one of the youngest people on the unit, younger than all the patients and half the nurses. But age rules the aging building, his aging profession, the aging Hudson River Valley city outside, of which Arkin sees little, his life revolving as it does around that of the hospital and those within.

Kate, a day shift RN on South Eight, wears a flowered scrub top over a T-shirt at the top of which Arkin can just make out the word "Relax." Because he's seen it on other nurses, he knows the rest of the message is: "I'm a nurse, I've seen worse."

"Dr. Arkin?"

He nods.

"Do you have Mrs. Warren today?"

"In 868, post-op with C. diff? I know her. What's up?"

"She doesn't look good to me. I didn't have her yesterday, but I helped out. She looks worse."

Arkin exhales, recalls some long-ago advice that when a skilled nurse tells a doctor something's wrong with their patient, or that something's changed, the doctor should pay attention. The woman in front of him, a little younger than he but with eight years as a nurse (he thinks he has heard), is newly arrived on this unit, in this hospital. Already, though, he has noticed other nurses asking her advice, has seen the newer nurses watching her at work. She stands in front of him comfortably, no more cowed by this one doctor than by the hundreds of others she's met, waiting for a response, her hair pulled back into a practical ponytail held in place by a red plastic bow. Arkin can smell the lavender in the shampoo she's used that morning and tries to remember whether he's ever seen her alarmed or angry.

"There was nothing overnight in report, but she's in a lot of pain, nausea, vomiting. Held her oral vancomycin just now, don't think she could keep it down; belly looks bad. Could you see her first?"

Arkin hesitates only a moment, the nurse watching him, her gaze steady, the eyes gray and direct. He notices her name tag, the last name in smaller letters, *Maddox*, over a picture of her, smiling into the Human Resources camera. "Let's get some fresh vitals. I'll check her labs, be right in."

The nurse, Maddox, nods and goes, and Arkin calls up Warren's chart on the computer beside him.

The patient is eighty-four, overweight, but even in pain she manages a wave as Arkin comes through the door. "Hey, handsome," she grunts.

"Hello, Sylvia. What's going on?" Arkin walks to the bed, touches her arm, soothing, familiar. Even without examining her, even through the sheet and gown, he can see the change. Her abdomen is swollen to perhaps half again its normal size, and she's spread her legs wide to accommodate it, allowing her to breathe without its bulk impeding the expansion of her lungs.

"I look like hell, that's what," the old woman says. "Why couldn't we meet when I was just seventy?"

"That would've been cruel, Sylvia—I'm already your slave."

The old lady grins then grimaces. "My belly hurts."

"I know." He gently palpates her abdomen; it's hard as a drum, a tabletop. He puts his stethoscope to it, listening in all four quadrants, hearing no bowel sounds whatever, not even the trilling, tinkling wheeze of partial obstruction. "You having any diarrhea?" he asks, though he knows the answer.

"No. Nothing since yesterday."

"Gas?"

"That's pretty personal. No."

Arkin has moved the bell of his stethoscope up to the heart, listening to the steady rhythm there, the sound of valves slamming shut, first mitral and tricuspid, then pulmonic and aortic, the tandem jazz of life—only now far too fast, around 130 beats a minute. And even without listening specifically, he can hear the lungs, too, expanding and contracting, he guesses thirty times a minute, more, the wild rapid gale of sepsis.

"Am I going to die?" she asks him. "I feel like I'm going to die today."

"We're all going to die," Arkin says gently enough, hoping the old lady will accept the cliché, the vapidity of his evasion, and spare them both not just the bad news of his diagnosis but of her prognosis.

She doesn't: "But is it today that I'm going to die?"

He takes a breath and tells her, "It could be," keeping his voice even, direct, empty of alarm; he's holding her hand. "It could be today. But, Sylvia, it could also be next week, it could be next year." Arkin catches in his own voice the shaky vibration of words repeated a hundred times before, hopes the old woman hasn't heard it too.

She just blinks at him, her expression unchanging, unsurprised.

"I'll be with you," he tells her.

"If it's today?"

"I'll be with you," he says again, and turns to Kate Maddox. "We'll start normal saline, bolus two liters, then two fifty an hour. Let's get another line in. Start Flagyl IV, give her Zosyn three point three seven five, get a blood gas and EKG now. Frequent vitals."

"Hourly?" she asks, taking notes on the back of her sign-out sheet.

"Let's do every fifteen minutes for the next couple hours, look for mean arterial pressures greater than sixty-five. Let's get a lactate, CT of the abdomen with IV contrast, don't bother with PO; noon CBC with diff, lytes—no, CMP. Blood cultures times two. Switch the NG tube to continuous suction. NPO. Low bar for ICU transfer. You can start Levophed on floor if she needs it, through a peripheral line?"

Kate nods.

"Good, then if she drops below MAP of sixty-five, we'll do that and transfer. I'll put it in the orders."

"Mm-hmm." She's still writing but takes a moment to look up from her notes, smile at the patient, relaxed and amiable, as much woman-to-woman as nurse-to-patient, Arkin thinks. To his surprise, it makes him feel, for a moment, like an outsider.

"And call Dr. Bennett—acute abdomen." He turns back to the old woman in the bed, Sylvia, a traveler in life: a mother and grandmother, a child in World War II, a bride in the 1950s, a widow for ten years, a garden club member, bridge with the girls for thirty years. He sees the lines and creases in her face, the heavy jowls, the thick quivering pads of flesh there, the puffy hands, the swollen legs and arms, the thin chain around her neck, its plain silver cross to one side and just touching the pillow, small and tarnished with the years, a gift, he thinks, of her childhood, and the stoic companion and witness to those same years, their disappointments, dreams, losses, laughter, tears, pain, grief, age. "Sylvia, it's possible we'll need to operate again."

"No," she says, barely a pause, not even a breath—or perhaps she has no breath, just the remaining conviction of *no*.

Arkin looks for a chair then thinks better of it and sits again on the bed; he again takes the old lady's hand. "Sylvia," he begins, the words forming in his mind, the points assembling themselves automatically within, as if running on ahead. "It's possible you have new problems in your belly, something called toxic mega colon. And it's even possible, likely, that you have some perforation, so that some of the contents of your gut are getting into your blood. This happens."

The old eyes, only slightly rheumy, with only the slightest glitter of fear, hold his, attentive yet somehow not, drifting off on the unfamiliar language of medicine as well as the oceanic undertow of completion.

"And when it happens, you get infected, 'sepsis' we call it, and that can kill you. We're giving you antibiotics, and that'll help, but there's a good chance if we don't find the source of the infection and repair it, we won't be able to stop it, even with the antibiotics. Do you understand?"

Sylvia nods, agreeable now, even placid.

"So we'll get a CAT scan. Is that okay?"

"I suppose."

"And we'll have Dr Bennett look at the CAT scan."

She only nods at this, minutely.

"And . . ." Arkin hesitates, hoping the air between words will soften her resistance to the final phase of his assault on her spirit. "And if we find the infection, he'll go in and fix it. He may have to take out part of your colon."

A hint of a smile, the ghost of a once-young woman who'd been cajoled, or allowed herself to be cajoled, by men before—a few, a dozen, a hundred, who would ever know?—and then, "No." Almost gently, as if sparing . . . him. "I've lived long enough. No."

Arkin looks into her face, peaceful now, almost cherubic, in contrast to the hard red furrows the nasal cannulas have dug into her plump, sagging, sweaty, cheeks, the nasogastric tube emerging from the tape abrasions on her nose.

"All right." It comes out a whisper. He tries again: "All right," though it's no stronger, just more precise, as if diction could approximate control over something likely to spin out of it. "If you don't want surgery, then I'm not putting you through the CAT scan. Is that okay? Do you understand? We'll get a plain X-ray up here."

Sheila closes her eyes now, takes a deeper breath through the nasal cannulas, centering perhaps. "And . . ." Arkin begins, pauses, says, "I'm gonna be really direct and honest. We'll focus on making you comfortable now. We'll continue antibiotics and fluids. I think that's reasonable and right, but we won't do anything aggressive. No ICU. If something should happen, if your heart should stop, we won't shock you. We won't put you on a machine if you can't breathe. If that should happen, we'll let nature take its course." Although he uses it often, Arkin hates that phrase, a cliché that diminishes nature, life, God, or whatever else his patients may happen to believe in; there should be a study to devise better. "But I'm gonna take away your pain, okay?"

The old lady just nods now, adjusts her hand in his, squeezes briefly; her grip is still surprisingly strong, a lifetime of practiced and habitual comfort in her touch, even now, comforting him.

He allows himself a smile, too, and he covers her hand with his other, presses gently in return, a slight, unmistakable, irreducible, and almost certainly unsupportable reassurance. Arkin can also feel there, at her wrist, among the plastic name ID and blood bank and Fall Risk bands, and the purple Do Not Resuscitate identifier, the racing, rampaging pulse. He stands at last, looks to the nurse, watching him from across the bed, over by the window, the Hudson River beyond, bucolic. A train rolls south on the western bank, toylike and silent at this distance.

"Then hold the CT, get the flat plate, portable; we'll do the rest, no pressors. I'll let Bennett know where we are, what Sylvia's decided. Ativan, one milligram IV q4h PRN, Dilaudid the same, q4h as needed, two milligrams now to start. No ICU. Basically comfort. Okay?"

The nurse, Kate, nods once, gray eyes as calm and steady as ever.

"Any questions?" he asks her.

She shakes her head slowly, expert, understanding the implications, and the plan.

"Good. I'll put it all in the computer. Call if you need me. Here's my cell." He scribbles his phone number on the back of a business card, hands it to the nurse, then turns back to Sylvia. "I'll come back." The old lady, eyes closed now, manages a brief wave of dismissal, half salute.

A few others of Arkin's hospitalist medical group relax around their conference room table. Some eat, almost all complain. Where earlier that morning, the nurses' conversation was B-flat minor, sad but resilient, here among the docs, it's F-sharp major, combative and clear. The talk is of billing codes and an atypical pneumonia in the Respiratory Care Unit (thoughts of COVID are ever-present); a new intravenous cephalosporin has been texted by the pharmacy, effective against MRSA infections; staff paid time off has been unilaterally cut.

Apart from all that, Arkin sits at one of the group's computers, looking up sepsis of gastrointestinal etiology, on colonic dilatation.

He wonders at the workings of memory, how reluctant it is to retain information so readily available online, obliging him to reread words read before, sapping his trust in recall. Of course, he's thinking of his patient on South Eight, but Arkin can't help recalling a similar experience from his preprofessional past: a Special Forces E6 he'd run into in Kandahar who'd returned from three weeks with his A-team at the Parrot's Beak with a perforated appendix, ashamed (as he lay gray with shock in the battalion aid station) that his team had been forced to evacuate him for this non-combat-related illness, a non-wound, trivial except for the liquid feces with its armies of bacteria pouring into his bloodstream as he tried to laugh and joke away his embarrassment and fear, and couldn't, and died. Such memories are part of what's brought him to medicine, he supposes, and for a moment, lost in them, the words on the monitor before him refuse to focus.

When the text comes, delayed as usual by a temporary overload in the hospital's Wi-Fi service, and Arkin reaches Sylvia Warren's room a few minutes later, he finds Kate Maddox still there.

"Does the family know?" Arkin asks.

"I called her daughter, the POA." Maddox sits in a chair by an open closet; inside, Arkin sees an old lady's housecoat, a pair of terrycloth slippers. A silvered heart-shaped helium balloon is tied to the closet door, its cheerily scripted "Get Well Fast!" floating anemically now, two days old and barely aloft.

"She coming in?"

Maddox just shakes her head.

At last, Arkin goes to the old lady, her body already shrinking, or seeming to, as corpses will; her eyes are open but not staring, not windows to the soul, not alight with pain or intelligence, or humor or weariness, not anything, not even sightless, as though sight had not just ceased but never was, eyes as artifacts. There's music softly playing on the patient's iPad, Arkin recognizes Billie Holiday singing a Fain and Kahal song, "I'll Be Seeing You," a tune from the deceased patient's disappearing past, the '40s of her young girlhood, Holiday singing, *"I'll always think of you that way."* Arkin shuts off the music, puts his stethoscope on the old woman's chest and listens for a long while, perfunctorily, to nothing. In his head, he can still hear Holiday: *"and when the night is new."* He straightens, looks at Maddox.

"This sucks," she says.

"I'm sorry," he says and turns to look out the window, its view of the unused and decaying piers and industrial sites along the river. "Did you put on that music for her?" he asks the nurse, although he knows she did.

She ignores the question. "You weren't here. You said you would be."

"I didn't get the text."

"I called you first. Check your phone."

Arkin pulls the phone from his lab coat pocket, thumbs through the voicemails, names of colleagues interspersed with answering service pages, along with one unidentified. "Is this you, the two-nine-six number?"

She doesn't bother answering, instead rises, begins pulling more clothes from the closet shelves, packing them into a plastic belongings bag.

Arkin realizes that his phone, jammed into his pocket, had once again self-muted. "Did you open the window?"

"What?" she says, stopping.

"Did you open the window?" The room's window is open, he has noticed, cracked open against the warm day; it wasn't earlier. "I understand . . . I know that . . . nurses sometimes open a window when a patient dies. Or they used to."

"To let the soul out," she says, almost weightless, uninflected. "Do you believe that?" he asks. "Did you do it?"

"I don't believe it," she says and hesitates, looking down at the sweater Sylvia Warren brought to the hospital three days before she died. "But I did it," Maddox says. Knit into the front of the sweater is the image of two Labradors, one brown, one yellow. Slowly, as if the stronger original impulse has abandoned her, she pushes the sweater into the plastic bag along with the dead woman's shoes, her slippers, robe, skirt, compact, hairbrush, mouthwash, cards from her children, cards from her grandchildren, her rosary. A single tear slides down the nurse's face as she turns away from Arkin and back to work.

When Arkin's phone rings, he's trying to decide on the evening's drink. Through hazed windows, past the shuttered nineteenth-century hotel across the road, and beneath the old and unused derricks over the Amtrak line, he can see the Hudson River at midsummer low. Arkin waits for his voicemail to pick up, and for the bartender, a Gulf War veteran named Harley, to come for his order. When he does, Arkin says, "Wild Turkey. Draft." The bartender nods, goes for the whiskey and beer, and after a while, Arkin's phone rings again. This time he answers. "Dr. Arkin."

"What if," the girl's voice says, "this isn't someone from the hospital?"

Arkin nods his thanks to Harley, who has brought the shot glass. Arkin drinks half the whiskey, tells his caller, "Not possible."

"Where are you?"

"The Riverside," he says, though he doesn't know why he's telling her this, having chosen a place that neither doctors nor nurses might visit after work, and see him, or speak to him. "Riverside Bar," he repeats, "on Water Street at Market." He listens for an answer, but she's silent now, waiting, it seems, for him to decide on this now too. "Where are you?"

"Five minutes away."

"Okay," he says after a moment, and then, "but it's against the rules."

"What rules?" she says.

"Yours," he answers and disconnects.

When she slides onto the stool next to his, he again smells the lavender in her hair—or is it lilac?—his whiskey and beer are gone, the bartender is drawing another, and the names of blossom are legion. Maddox looks at his boilermaker and orders herself a tequila drink.

"What did you mean, this breaks my rules?"

"I don't know, nurses' rules: doctors, bars, work and pleasure."

"You think this is fun?"

At this, Arkin smiles at last, as if into the light of some dwarf inner star, Kate Maddox thinks. "There," she says and smiles herself. "That wasn't so fucking hard."

"I'm sorry about today," Arkin manages. "My phone keeps muting itself." And then, with conviction the weight of air, "It wouldn't have made any difference."

"She was septic," Maddox says.

"Yes. And old, and DNR, and alone. But you shouldn't have been. I'm sorry."

"Other nurses were there."

"Okay," Arkin says and drinks some more of his second shot-and-beer, which Kate notes with almost clinical interest.

"I don't usually cry," she says. "But she was sweet."

Arkin merely nods.

"And you're right, I do have a rule, against dating doctors."

"This isn't a date, we're just . . ."

"What?" she asks drily. "A boy and a girl having a drink?"

Arkin understands she's quoting a line, he thinks from some Julia Roberts movie, but can't remember which. As Maddox waits for his answer, he thinks how there must have been a time, possibly in college, when such an opening would've prompted a pleasant onrush of potentiality. But he can't remember the last time such a thing happened, or for that matter had any social occasion he actually enjoyed, and so he says, "Why did you come here?"

"Why do you drink so much?"

Arkin looks out again to the river, the far bank in shadow, the sun fast-falling behind a first line of the Catskill Mountains. It makes him think of Afghanistan for at least the second time that day—of the Safed Koh range south of Kabul, where he had spent the last year of his military life, and considered the upcoming first year of college after the Army, and had also begun to drink with purpose.

"Habit," is all he can think to say.

"A lot of doctors do," she says. "A lot of nurses too. Is that why you drink? The job?"

"Well," he says and finishes his whiskey, "if I didn't drink, I couldn't do the job. But if I didn't have the job, I couldn't afford to drink. It's . . . symmetry."

"I drink"—she hesitates a moment—"so I can have sex afterwards," and then turns a gaze on him so open, so unadorned and direct, that it almost takes his breath away, for a moment wiping away the ash of burnout, the images of the hospital and its river, the Catskills beyond, or that other set of mountains and the war he'd seen among them.

———————

He has heard that during the Anaconda operation, a Canadian team made a shot from a mile and a half using .50-caliber ammunition, and he wonders if it's true. He thinks Kelly could make a shot from that distance if anyone could, but on their team, like most American teams, the shooter uses the M110 rifle, which has an effective range of only about eight hundred yards. For that matter, to spot targets for his partner, he himself uses an M49 scope, which is only 20-power, so that at a mile and a half a man would still appear to be almost 250 yards away as viewed with the naked eye. The scope on Kelly's M110 is only 10-power, so the target would look even smaller. But still, he has never seen Kelly miss, whether with a live target in the mountains of southern Afghanistan or on the practice range, even with iron sights. In fact, he wonders whether Kelly prefers not to see the target as anything other than a shape, featureless. The higher magnification of his spotting scope lets Arkin see more. In selecting Kelly's targets, it allows him to identify officers, or communications specialists, or political leaders, whatever the mission calls for, or whatever presents itself. Sometimes, Arkin really does feel he could reach out and touch these people, his enemy.

Identifying leaders among Taliban in the field can be difficult since they wear no uniforms or insignia of rank. But Arkin has developed a set of rules based on observation—that, for example, officers tend to walk ahead of their fighters, unlike American officers, who are taught to walk within the body of a patrolling formation. He knows the leader of a group of Taliban will sit while his followers remain standing; will ride beside the driver of a car or SUV, rather than in the backseat; will be the one with a cell or, often, satellite phone. He remembers surveilling a group of Taliban fighters from a distance of five hundred yards, his telescoped attention on an Iridium phone left unattended on the hood of a truck. He remembers how he watched the phone for an hour, until a young man in a black turban, the tail hanging down over his shoulder, picked it up at last—possibly it had rung, though Arkin could not hear at such a distance—and then, with a word from Arkin, was collapsed against the grill of the truck by the high velocity round from Kelly's M110. Kelly killed three more fighters before he and Arkin retreated back across the ridgeline and then down the Balkh District riverbed to where their covering squad waited for them.

Afterward, Kelly talked as the squad airlifted out, as he often did, about home and family back in the States, about girls, and sports, and cars and beers. As quiet as he could be during the mission, Kelly was that voluble after, as though a switch had been thrown on the circuit of death and life. Arkin, still only twenty, had owned just one car, had slept with only a few girls, had played two sports and bet on none, had been to no resort, had drunk no fine whiskeys, had eaten only one good restaurant meal, on the night of his senior prom, at the Bonefish Cafe in Colorado Springs, near where he had grown up and tried those first beers and known those few girls. How he had gotten to Afghanistan was not entirely clear to him, and how he had come to mark targets for death, to—in that way—know in advance who would die and when and how, was even less clear. Kelly talked on, about the whorehouses outside of Fort Bragg, about the vinegar-based sauce of Eastern Carolina barbecue, about long white Outer Banks beaches, while the blades of the helicopter drummed Arkin with insistent drowning waves of sound in a falling river of air.

Maddox awakens with no memory of sleep coming, perhaps having fallen into it, she suspects, mid-sentence, or maybe even mid-breath—the effect of a long day's work, of tequila, of the old lady's death—and of Arkin, now standing at her bedroom window. He stares out onto Route 55, quiet at this hour except for the still-bustling McDonald's, a less-bustling Subway, and an empty Card World in the strip mall across the highway. He has heard Maddox's breathing change as she awoke, as he'd noticed it deepen earlier when she'd reached across his chest to touch his cheek, run her finger along the line of his jaw as she'd whispered a soft "hmm," and then slept.

"What are you doing?" she asks from the bed, stirring now.

"Nothing," he says. "Thinking."

"You worrying about this?"

Arkin turns and looks at her, shadowed and with her head resting on one arm, pillow half hiding her face. "You're beautiful," he says.

"Make you worry less?"

"More."

"I'm not a teenager, you know. You may have noticed."

He says, "I'm a trained observer."

She rolls over onto her back, stretches, the sheet to her waist, the rest of her in the tree-dappled shadow of streetlamps, into which Arkin's own shadow slips unnoticed. "I don't really do this. I don't fuck doctors."

"You don't?"

"Well, obviously that's changed."

Arkin smiles a little, but weakly, fleeting.

She shifts a little, to see him more clearly; the bed creaks slightly, and her eyes gleam once in the streetlight. "Are you tired?" she asks, her voice low, gentle. "That way?"

"Yes. I am."

"Me too," she says, and Arkin looks at her now, away from the street outside, meeting her gaze, sober now, almost too direct. "Are you working tomorrow?"

"Yes. You?"

"Yes. You want to sleep here?"

There's a silence between them then, although to Kate it feels unlike the awkward pause around "You want to stay?" after sex. She usually doesn't, herself, but this feels different, sadder.

Arkin turns back to the window, watches a city loop bus, the last of the night, drop a passenger at the McDonald's. "We only think we know what we're doing. I was standing here thinking about the twenty things I probably did right for the woman in 68."

Kate wonders if he's already forgotten the patient's name, Sylvia.

But he goes on: "And then I came up with the five things I probably did wrong, or I didn't think about at all, or could have done differently. It happens every night. Every night I work. I wake up at three. And I think, it's okay: if you see A, B, and C, then it's this, and if it's this you do . . . and that'll work, only . . . it doesn't. Sometimes you do all the right things, and they die; or you do everything wrong, and they get better. Things don't happen for a reason."

Kate thinks about what she might say to this—"Come back to bed"?—but says nothing. Watching him, Kate realizes Arkin's hunched almost, starting intently out into the night, a dog hunting, she thinks improbably.

He straightens, exhales. "I have to change."

"I won't tell anyone," the girl says. "If you're worried about it."

"I'm not worried. I'm glad we did this." And then turns to her and adds, surprising himself, "I hope we do it again."

He more senses than sees her smile at this—skeptical, of course, perhaps a little serene. If it were earlier, and she were less tired herself, he imagines, she would laugh at him.

Instead, she pulls the covers to her chin, curls into her pillow. "Go home, Doctor. Get some rest."

TWO

ARKIN DRIVES NORTH ON Route 9, at this hour empty of all but the earliest of early morning traffic, the hardiest of overnight truckers. The hospital looms ahead on the right, an island (of a sort of antisepsis) exactly eight traffic-less minutes north of his apartment (another island of antisepsis), a drive he has made so often, often on so many days in a row, with so little to mark the days off in between, that he hardly registers the trip. The radio in his generic Honda plays generic rock, which Arkin prefers at this hour: *"standin' on the corner at midnight tryin' to get my courage up."* He wears a generic white Van Heusen shirt with a slim-striped J.Crew tie, over a pair of slim gray J.Crew cords. Somewhere in his chest, however, he feels a bright spark that the early morning chill, the gray of the car and the clothes, the shadow of the day ahead, cannot extinguish.

Arkin has suppressed the habit of regret, but he realizes—realized even as he showered and shaved and donned the gray clothes in his soulless sublet—that it would have been good to stay with her. It would have been good to awaken in the predawn quiet of her apartment, good to stop for coffee together, good to arrive for work at the same time, good to wear the previous day's clothes.

Good to watch her towel her hair dry, choose the day's scrubs. Good to see her face in the mirror noticing him watching and casually accommodating his need to share the minutiae of her morning, possibly without understanding, yet merciful.

Mercy, Arkin thinks, is a word rarely heard at the hospital. He and his colleagues talk about matters that might in other settings merit such a word. But when they speak of those matters, they do so in a jargon less categorical in tone, certainly less biblical. "It would be better," they might say, or "He would be lucky," heavily subjunctive. But not the unequivocal: "It would be merciful." He recognizes the aspect of agency involved, that mercy is granted (as Kate and he may have done for one another) whereas "better" or "lucky" merely happens. Happens as the gate rises at the entrance to the doctors' parking lot when he swipes his badge; happens as the door at the employee entrance unlocks in the same way; happens as the three-flight climb to his office happens—without exertion, anticipation, or thought.

———————

In the small doctor's cubicle off the central emergency room nurses' station, Arkin is completing his fourth admission in three hours, when one of the ER docs, Ann Hutchinson, forty, razor-thin, brutalist haircut, leans in to tell him: "There's another, fever, white count, ascites, short of breath, emphysema, possible . . ."

"All right," Arkin interrupts, "I'll see her."

"Him, and not from a nursing home. I know—it's a shock: the one thing he *doesn't* have is a UTI."

By chance, Arkin's four previous admissions have been of elderly women from nursing homes, three of them with "urosepsis, not further defined," as billing code 599.0 puts it, the other a "348.311, metabolic encephalopathy," though likely from yet another UTI.

"But he's old," says Hutchinson, "if that helps. And cirrhotic, bilirubin ten, likely SBP. I already gave him a dose of Unasyn. No surprises."

"Right, that would be bad. Where is he?"

"Room 16, chest and KUB are done, CT ordered, the ascites are impressive—I alerted IR. Hope you're okay with that."

"No, you're great, thanks for starting everything. Just that it's my fifth admission, not even two hours." Arkin is filling in for his group's deputy director, nine months pregnant and at her obstetrician's office—she'd asked him the week before—for what's turning out to be quite a long visit, Arkin thinks. No one likes their required first-call rotations in the emergency room, the sometimes torrential flow of incoming patients referred to Arkin's group, who are the hospitalists who will admit and serve as attending physicians during their stay. His director, Assam Massood, frequently notes that without these patients, the hospital would have no business and the group would have no physician jobs to fill. And the world might be a better place, it is generally felt by members of the group itself, often over the "Artisanal Cocktails and Beverage program" at a local bar on Friday night after the week's several hundred such admissions. Massood also often remarks that it's nothing like the worst of the COVID surges, with which no one can disagree and which prompts additional orders for the local organic gins and vodkas and IPAs. Arkin electronically signs and submits the eighty orders required to admit the latest urinary tract infection, committing the hospital and the group; committing the nurses to daily piggyback ceftriaxone, intravenous fluid hydration, overnight delirium, predawn lab draws; committing

Medicare to a $10,000 expenditure; committing the patient herself to days of misery.

———————————

R. Barnhardt is Med Record Number 11782485, his date of birth is June 14, 1943, and his pneumococcus, tetanus, and zoster inoculations are up-to-date. Also, even at a glance, Arkin can see that along with emphysema, age, infection, and whatever else may be going on, the patient is likely dying of end-stage cirrhosis. Arkin assumes only cirrhosis because primary liver cancers are usually admitted to the oncology service, not to the hospitalists. But liver disease is certain, because the old man is jaundiced, and not the subtle, occasionally missed jaundice of incipient disease, or of, say, a mild hemolytic anemia, but rather the fully nutlike, almost tannic ochre of dying liver. The patient's gown is stretched taut over the huge abdomen, distended by the fluid backing up into it from his blocked portal vein. Arkin guesses ten quarts of fluid at least in the peritoneum; he notes scattered petechiae on the patient's arms, small blood-freckles near-orange against the base yellow of the skin, further signs of liver failure, clotting dysfunction, minor cutaneous bleeds.

"Good afternoon, Mr. . . ." but Arkin has already forgotten the old man's name and is glancing back to his scrawled notes to search for it.

The old man opens his jaundice-yellow eyes, and says: "Arkin. You're Arkin?"

Arkin only nods, vaguely surprised. ER nurses hardly ever know who'll be admitting their patients, and even if they do are usually too busy to bother telling anyone.

This patient knows, however. "I'm Barnhardt. Can you get me the fuck out of here? To a room?"

"In a minute, Mr. Barnhardt. Can you tell me what brought you in today?" This generic one-size-fits-all time-filler earns Arkin a look so bored, and at the same time so lemony, that Arkin almost laughs.

"Possibly I came to the wrong . . . this is a *hospital*, right? And you are a *doctor*, correct?"

"Yes," Arkin says, combining an unavoidably weary smile with a glance at his watch, calculating how quickly he can start on the bare minimum physical exam he intends.

"How interesting to watch you in action." The unexpected remark, with its layers of sarcasm and amusement, catches Arkin's attention. Either he was even more transparent in his wish to get this over with than he thought, or the patient is less encephalopathic, that possibility underlined when the man offers, with a modestly self-deprecatory gesture, "Anyway, look at me. Where would you suggest I go?" The old man adjusts the nasal cannula feeding oxygen to his lungs; Arkin can the see the inevitable chafing there from long-term use. "I just didn't know I'd be in the emergency room four hours."

"I'm sorry. I just heard about you."

The man shrugs, unconcerned with Arkin's workflow.

"How long have you been sick?"

"Years. More than ten. Everything worse the last couple, breathing, belly."

"Who's been treating you?"

"Guys at Keller."

The Army hospital at West Point, Arkin knows, where area veterans are sometimes hospitalized for acute issues. "So why did you come here?"

Barnhardt hesitates, as if choosing from among a number of possible explanations before settling on, Arkin senses, a variety of truth. "They wanted to send me to Maryland. Walter Reed. I didn't want to go. I hate that fucking place." He smiles fractionally then offers a sleepily ironic, "I came to you instead." Improbably, the man manages a broader smile, accompanied by an amused repeat of his new doctor's name: "Dr. Arkin." To which the doctor himself says nothing. "Anyway, I'm worse. Breathing especially. I brought some of my records. My results."

Arkin has them open now, from a plain manila envelope clipped into the ER folder: the ultrasound report from a year earlier, plus one from a six-month-old CT scan of the abdomen with IV and oral contrast, interval liver function tests and ammonia levels, all just as Arkin supposed, detailing the measured but inevitable progression of liver disease. There had been three paracenteses over the past six months, draining fluid from the peritoneal space; an endoscopy had revealed no esophageal varices, which is somewhat surprising; a biopsy was negative for carcinoma. All the patient has brought are the imaging and lab studies, which appear to have been faxed—perhaps to the patient's home?—but no H&Ps or consult notes or discharge summaries, which Arkin thinks an interesting omission.

He looks up from his review of the data. "So why did they want to send you to Maryland?"

"Ah, that's very good, Doctor, very good."

Arkin can't imagine what was good about it, and the approval, even more than the sarcasm, is unnerving; a shimmering thrum of anxiety presents itself in Arkin's body, nerves and skin, the phrase "galvanic skin response" comes to mind.

And Barnhardt's answer, amidst the familiar instruments and educational posters and clamor of impatient voices outside the room, is even more jarring: "Security reasons."

Arkin asks anyway. "You're a veteran?"

Barnhardt pauses for a moment to focus an almost dreamy yellow-orange gaze on Arkin, as if looking past the exam room, the lab coat and medical degree, the decaying post-industrial town outside, to another place and possibly, another *Arkin*, before intoning: "Sort of. I worked for the Army, in Afghanistan, till about five years ago. Ever hear of a place called Salerno?"

A dozen more questions could occur to Arkin, but he asks none of them, most especially not the *What do you mean?* that virtually any of his colleagues would have followed with. Nor, much less, does he ask, *How do you know my name?* He doesn't ask himself why he feels a drop of sweat run down the small of his back despite the runaway air-conditioning of the emergency room. Nor, once back at his desk in the little on-call physician's office, does he think beyond the most basic of admission assessments and plans, ordering a paracentesis by interventional radiology, repeat labs, echocardiogram—while imagining which of his colleagues will be assigned the "sort of" veteran Robert Barnhardt claims to be.

———————

In the end, it's Arkin himself.

The deputy director returns from her OB appointment as Arkin is dictating the Barnhardt admission, reading word for word from the Keller hospital lab and imaging data, briefly noting additional history as "unobtainable," wanting nothing further to do with Barnhardt, and now:

"How can I ever thank you?"

"You don't have to thank me, Louise. Why don't you just pick up my group and I'll stay here and . . ."

"No, no, no, you've done enough. Just take the ones you admitted, and I'll do the rest of the day. I'm good."

"You sure?"

"Absolutely."

And she is good, Arkin thinks, not just the picture of a massively healthy pregnancy, of fading stress at the prospect of her upcoming four-month maternity leave, but of administrative competence, confidence, of satisfaction at obligations disposed of and tasks completed—which, with blithe unconcern she confirms by looking over his shoulder at Arkin's monitor, the H&P notes, and asking, "Is that your man?"

"What?"

"Barnhardt? You know him, right?"

"No. What do you mean?"

"He asked for you—or someone did, maybe registration, I wasn't paying attention. Anyway, someone called and asked if you would be here today, and I said yes, in the ER this morning, that's all. So he came in?"

"Yes," Arkin says weightlessly.

And Louise's distracted "Well, good, thanks again," signals the end of the discussion, sufficiently disinterested in a patient not her own that, for a moment, Arkin imagines none of it has happened, that Barnhardt had not sought him out, not timed his arrival, not mentioned Salerno.

"You want one?" Heather Newcomb asks Kate, holding out a pack of Parliaments. Kate remembers her mother used to smoke these when Kate was a child.

"No thanks," Kate says. "I just came out for a break. Catch my breath."

"You shouldn't be around me then," Heather says with a laugh, lighting up, stepping to one side so that the wind will blow cigarette smoke into her own pudgy face and away from Kate, who yawns and stretches.

"How long have you been here?" Kate asks.

"Six years. Came right out of nursing school. You?"

"My third job. I moved around after school. Did some travel nursing too. I like it."

"First time in the east?"

"No. I was born here," Kate says and looks away, to where a light plume of white smoke rises from the stacks of the Central Hudson generating plant on Academy Street. "I was just starting to think about Doctors Without Borders, something like that, but then my mom got sick, so I came home."

"She okay?"

"No, she died in March, lung cancer."

"Shit. Sorry." Heather waits, experienced nurse that she is, but Kate just watches the smoke from Central Hudson's chimney.

The plant is just across Route 9, close to the river and a few long blocks from the Sears house her great-grandfather built in 1911 on Loomis Street. The house had stayed in the family ever since, her mother had lived there, but Kate had not wanted to keep it after her mom's death. It was on the market now, and Kate lived across from McDonald's, an impermanent mile and a half east of her permanent past.

"Where were you last?" Heather asks.

"California. Santa Barbara—I worked in the MICU at Cottage Hospital."

"Cool. You miss it? I went to San Francisco once. You miss intensive care?"

Kate shrugs, not having considered the narrow question of nursing unit preference at the time, much less the larger one of coastal choice; she had simply come home when her mother was diagnosed, had nursed her through a fruitless few months of pointless chemo for her widespread metastases, followed by a few weeks of purposeful narcotics, and death. Kate's memories of Santa Barbara—of bike rides on the Cabrillo Path, lunch at Backyard Bowls, Shoreline Drive runs from Arroyo Burro to East Beach Park and back—populated by an innocently homogenous procession of friends from work and from her complex on Bath Street (Six Blocks to Beach! Nurse Rates!)—seem to have risen and thinned like the smoke from Central Hudson, or Heather's Parliament cigarette, blown up and out over the river, to nowhere. South Eight and the one-bedroom with the McDonald's and Subway view are her new world, East Coast edition.

"So who is he?" Heather asks, having interpreted Kate's silence—perhaps not wrongly (with Kate's recall of the distant past possibly somewhat further obscured by the more immediate memory of the previous night, what may or may not have been said, if anything of consequence had been said at all).

"He?" Kate murmurs, yawns. "No one."

"Really? 'Cause we were all wondering about you and Dr. Arkin yesterday."

"Oh great," Kate sighs, not exactly shocked but as always impressed by the observational power of half a dozen nurses in the confined space and time of the twelve-hour medical surgical shift.

"I don't even know him. What's he like?"

"He was the doc on the woman in 868 yesterday who died."

"Oh, okay." Then mildly, "He's cute. Is he married?"

Heather shakes her head, grinning. "That wouldn't stop me."

"Really? Married doctors, always *such* a good idea," and the two women laugh a little. "What's his story?"

"Oh, he's new, a few months," Heather says, watching Kate with good-natured skepticism. "I think he came from . . . North Carolina? He seems okay, doesn't flirt, doesn't hang out. No sexting. There's worse."

"God, that's true."

"Worse-looking too. I'd fuck him in a heartbeat."

Kate shrugs, helplessly overplaying it, she knows. Was there someone at the bar, she wonders, but she's determined not to give in, not gossip, not confirm, not share.

"He's smart, right?" Heather asks, not giving up.

"He's okay. Let me down yesterday, with that patient—said he didn't hear his phone."

"He gave you his cell?"

"Heather, please!"

Heather giggles and gives Kate a playful little punch on her shoulder, stubs out her cigarette, and asks brightly, "Okay, off the hook. Back to the shit pit?"

Barnhardt feels the needle enter his side not as pain, not even as a pinch, but more a nerveless puncture, as of a balloon, the fluid draining out of his swollen abdomen a pale straw-like yellow, with a wisp of blood streaming lazily into the vacuum jar, accompanied by an immediate and noticeable easing of the pressure against his diaphragm and lungs. Barnhardt sighs in relief, a faint ripple of incongruous pleasure at the surge of fluid down the catheter.

Through the big glass window separating the IR suite from its nurses' station, Arkin watches Wei Chen, their interventional radiologist, work the ultrasound probe, confirming the location of the plastic sheath in Barnhardt's belly. Chen switches to a second quart bottle, the first filled, with more to come, Arkin thinks, as Alvin Perry joins him, eyes the paracentesis in progress.

"This your guy?"

"Yep. Seventy something, end-stage liver disease, likely bacterial peritonitis, forty pack-years, bilateral pleural effusion along with the ascites, cardiomegaly, hyponatremic, bad emphysema. They'd been treating him at West Point, doesn't want to go back."

"They'll pay for him here?"

"I guess. I didn't get into it."

"And what do you want me to do?" Perry's a member of the palliative care team, so the question is understood to be a form of ironic banter—his group's main role in the hospital is consulting on end of life management. Though he wears surgeon-blue scrubs under his lab coat, his business is mostly complicated talk followed by simple medication.

He's almost a foot shorter than Arkin, who glances down to offer: "Goals of care?"

"That's easy. Unless he's a transplant candidate, comfort."

"I agree."

"Then . . . have you discussed it?"

"He just got here. I thought it might be better coming from you. I'm not sure we have much of a connection." This interests Perry, who knows hospitalist physicians almost by definition have little connection with their patients. They have minimal follow-up role after discharge, and most often, as in this case, have never seen their patients before the current admission. In fact, Perry thinks he may never have heard a hospital-based doc mention *connection*.

"Okay. I'll see him today. He with it?" Arkin nods. "Ammonia levels?"

"Seventies but doesn't seem to be an issue—he's with it." Arkin looks out at Barnhardt, who in turn now notices him behind the glass. Barnhardt's stare is unwavering, empty of pain, empty of any feeling beyond a mild, frank recognition.

"He's with it," Arkin repeats and goes.

Out in the hallway, he turns right, past the photos of the hospital's founding days, the 1920s nursing classes, women in winged collars, belted skirts, long sleeves. There are plaques, honors, awards, more fading photos, none of which Arkin sees. The corridor is newly waxed, the tracks left by the floor buffer's gleaming circles and whorls beneath the box lights, which Arkin also doesn't see.

He goes out the main entrance of the hospital into the blazing sunlight. He can't remember the last time he did this, went out of doors mid-shift, even for a moment. Cars line the circular drive beneath the portico of the main entrance, dropping off family, picking up discharged patients. A couple techs, pushing wheelchairs, eye him with mild curiosity; they never see the doctors here—perhaps he's meeting someone? But Arkin's not meeting anyone, not seeing anyone. He leans back against a column, the smooth round concreteness of it. The world swirls around him. He thinks idly that he could just walk out from under the portico, down the drive, circle round the Medical Arts building; then cross Route 9 and walk up Rinaldi to the Metro North station. He can imagine himself on the train to New York, how strange he'd look to others in his lab coat. He wonders how it would feel instead to throw it away, to throw away the stethoscope, the dosing guides and pens, to be just another passenger, the river sliding by outside the window, the big faceless city ahead. He can't see the river from where he stands. He can hear the traffic on Route 9, a security guard's walkie-talkie, the scrape of a wheelchair's handbrake.

Above and behind him, eight floors up, is the South Eight window Kate Maddox opened the day before when Sylvia Warren died. Arkin does remember the patient's name, along with her lab values, the antibiotics he ordered, the silence of her abdomen and the rush of air through her lungs as she breathed on her last morning alive. Arkin himself has never opened those windows of the dead but, without knowing quite why, has always admired the nurses for doing so. He suspects it's a lost or at least vanishing tradition, in part because windows of newer hospitals are hermetically fixed and shut. He imagines the window-transiting soul as etherous, and is amused he thinks of this word, *etherous*, rather than *ethereal*. He has never seen actual ether used, as it went out of favor long before he became a doctor; he reflects that he has never seen a soul either. He momentarily pictures vaporous creatures, half cloud, as Giotto drew them, but not with the angelic faces Giotto painted but rather the faces of patients, the idea of this disturbing him even as it surfaces. Perhaps it's not a *thing* that goes out the window but a sound, which leaves the silence of its abandoned room behind. Arkin thinks he might like to imagine—if he had time and energy to do so—what the dead would say as they departed via their nurse-opened windows.

Perhaps he will think about it tonight at the bar. Whatever they say will be more than farewell and better than goodbye. He is confident it will not be thank you; perhaps they would say, *at last*. What he says to them, which he knows well because he's said it so often, and as softly as departing souls would speak it if they were able: *I'm sorry. I failed you.* And then, improbably, and mysteriously, even to himself, *Forgive me.*

THREE

SALERNO WAS SMALL, EVEN in a country where, after Kabul, population centers of any size were few. There were three million people in Kabul; Kandahar, the next largest, had fewer than half a million, Jalalabad half that, and so on. Khost itself, near Salerno, had a population of around a hundred and fifty thousand. It also had cricket leagues and volleyball; it had a university with a medical school, an airport, and an unknown number of Taliban fighters. At its start, Forward Operating Base Salerno consisted of five hundred Italian infantryman. To honor them, it was thought, the base had been given the name of a famous landing of World War II in southern Italy. That landing had been a near-disaster for the Allies: five days into it, the Americans were in disarray and their commander considered abandoning the beachhead and evacuating his troops. In the end, naval bombardment and B-17s won the day, and the Americans stayed in Italy.

Not so the Italians at FOB Salerno. In September 2003, they handed the camp over to elements of the Eighty-Seventh Infantry Regiment, Tenth Mountain Division, to which Arkin and Kelly were later attached. Like most soldiers, Arkin had not planned his military career. He'd graduated from the community college he'd been attending and enlisted in the Army. He had not done so out of exceptional patriotism, nor out of any particular interest in fighting. Even after a year in the Army, even as part of a brigade combat team called "Warrior," he hardly felt himself to be that. He had gone from basic and AIT to jump school, all at Fort Benning, because of his pitching coach in high school. Coach King had joined the 101st Airborne Division after three disappointing years in the Dodgers' minor league organization. This interested Arkin, to whom his coach had also taught the trick of cutting a fastball. This, Arkin felt, an 88-mile-per-hour cut fastball, was his signal accomplishment in high school, unmatched by anything he later achieved at Pikes Peak Community College, and so it seemed natural to again follow the example of Coach King and become a Screaming Eagle.

Arkin had never actually made it to the 101st, though, in part because it was no longer an Airborne unit at all but also because the Army, already learning from its early mistakes in Afghanistan and rapidly expanding its numbers of sniper teams, was actively recruiting candidates out of jump school. "Active recruiting" in Arkin's case meant that, on his drunken graduation night following his fifth and final jump, he was offered a training slot for the following Monday by an equally drunken first sergeant from the 197th Infantry Brigade, which ran the Sniper School. The Army, then as always, was run by NCOs, drunk or sober, and months of application review and orders processing could be streamlined in the right bar on the right night, with the right number of drinks. So the next day, Arkin was not reassigned to Fort Campbell in Kentucky, home of the no-longer-Airborne 101st, or to Fort Bragg, North Carolina, home of the still-Airborne 82nd. Instead, he hitched a ride across Benning, from the headquarters of the 507th Parachute Infantry Regiment to those of the 197th, and to the five-week sniper course it operated. There, Arkin rediscovered his fastball.

Sometimes at FOB Salerno, or in the surrounding mountains, or gazing down on the endless series of raggedly vertical peaks and valleys from the door of a CH-47 transporting his squad, Arkin wondered what would have become of him had he not been able to hit a man-size target ten out of ten times from a distance of six hundred yards. Arkin had never done anything so well in his life. He'd never learned to dependably control his cutter, hard as it was. His interest in school, at Pikes Peak or before, and despite various counselors' excitement about his SAT scores, was desultory. Perhaps *aimless* was a better word, for what he discovered with the M24 he trained on was *aim*, so crystalline and precise that it sometimes took his breath away. Some nights, during his five weeks of sniper training, he'd lie awake and think of new challenges, corrections, conceal-ment. On training maneuvers, he could sit silently for hours—a skill he'd never mastered as a student—yet be ready to fire in an instant, unerringly. He liked to think he was the best shot anyone had ever seen; he thought this right up until the moment he was teamed with Kelly and saw his new partner shoot at the range outside Kandahar. Kelly had a lightness, almost an ease, with the act of firing that made it seem casual, even graceful. Kelly shot in a way that made killing the enemy at a distance not so much an act of violence, or even of war, but of art: a brushstroke, a pirouette.

Most men, in most such cases, confronted by such a talent and thwarted thereby in the fulfillment of their own, might have felt overwhelmed, defeated by the impossibly sudden withdrawal of fortune. Fortune, however, turned yet again for Arkin, who now, as Kelly's spotter, found in himself a newer, even more unexpected and mysterious talent than the first. Because in the months ahead, he came to understand that in the identification of targets, he truly had no equal: where others saw, Arkin felt; where others only thought, Arkin *knew*. It was a perfect match for the mission of their team: Kelly was the better shooter, Arkin the better seeker. Out of an innocent dozen, he could select the fated *one*; he could divine the path his targets would take before the men themselves began to move. Arkin *stalked*, and in the weeks and months at war, he sharpened and reveled in his talent for seeing death in life, the awful moment yet to come in the breathless frame of now.

———————

Arkin's career as a physician, ultimately honed during the COVID-19 pandemic, exposed in him (he liked to believe) the opposite skill. With death all around, he excelled, or (again) liked to believe he did, in seeing life and the possibility for life in his acutely ill patients. Arkin, like all his colleagues, had made choices about who should be intubated, admitted to the ICU or RCU, or to the PCU or CTSU when those other units were overflowing with patients, and who should be provided instead with comfort measures in the form of oxygen, morphine, Ativan, scopolamine. The others, those he thought could *live*, he tubed, proned, anticoagulated, titrated on and off pressors, up and down on their ventilators' FIO2 and PEEP settings, and more. Mostly, especially after vent selection was narrowed, and the new steroid protocols and antivirals and antibodies became available, they lived.

Arkin never confused the experience with war. He thought the politicians who relentlessly compared the fight against disease to war demonstrated a complete misunderstanding of both. At its most basic, the goal in war was to kill, while in medicine, it was to heal. But the virus, or the other pathogens of illness, or the mutations of cancer, were in fact *not* an enemy. They simply *were*, Arkin thought, more like the ranges of the Hindu Kush in Afghanistan, its passes and river valleys through which the actual enemy passed, the villages in which they hid. You didn't really kill viruses, which in any event weren't even alive, anymore than you killed mountains or drained rivers. You *could* destroy villages, of course, and this had happened in war, with much the same effect as killing your patients in order to deprive a disease of its host. The only point of connection was people as victim.

With COVID, the killer, in addition to straightforward respiratory failure, was often the patients' own immune systems overreacting to a novel viral challenge in a variety of ways, along with hyperactive blood clotting, all often complicated by a history of smoking or lack of exercise or poor diets and obesity and diabetes, or simply the biological decline of lives lived long. In Afghanistan, the killers were people like Arkin and Kelly, and the men they hunted, and who hunted them in return.

Sometimes Arkin wonders at this shift in his life, from the adolescent academic failure who'd found himself in sniper school and became expert in long-range killing—to college and med school grad who'd found his way somehow, mysterious even to himself, to healing. The only other thing war and medicine had in common, he thinks, is the bone-deep fatigue of unrelieved stress, sleep deprivation, and the fear of failure.

Arkin understands this about himself, that every time he walks into a patient's room, he walks the line between salvation and despair, not only for the patient but for himself. That's also why, he further understands, he leaves the hospital for out-of-the-way bars in a dying river town.

———

When the nurse brings his afternoon lactulose, Barnhardt is staring at the TV mounted on the wall opposite. Out in the hall, Arkin can hear the brief exchange, the confirmation of patient identity, the name of the med, the dose and purpose. Arkin cannot hear Barnhardt's words, just the throttled timbre of his voice. Since he had admitted him only that morning and has already written his orders, Arkin is not required to visit his new patient. He thinks he will not, that, in a sort of interlude he will pause here in the hall and confirm, what—stability?—and move on.

"Hello."

Arkin turns, and Kate is there, asking, "What are you doing?"

"Now?"

"What else? Tonight?"

In that moment the possibility, the consideration of *mistake* occurs to them both ... until some urge or impulse or possibly even need moves in Arkin and triggers, "I'm sorry. I was just thinking. I have a patient I don't want to see."

She smiles. "I'm trying to think of a patient I *do* want to see." She nods at the door. "He yours?" Arkin nods. "New?"

"Um, yeah. Yes, but not ... not important."

Today, she is in a sort of olive green, top and bottom, un-patterned and businesslike, under it a white long-sleeved stretch T. Her hair is pulled back again today, and there is a thin gold chain at her throat, a man's digital watch on her wrist. The photo of her on the hospital ID, hung on a lanyard around her neck, is direct, cool and, Arkin thinks, astonishingly beautiful. "So, yes. What are you doing tonight?"

Kate stares at him. A nurse comes out of Barnhardt's room, hesitates a moment at finding them there, the sort of silence between them unmistakable, then moves quickly on. Kate murmurs, "Now everybody will know."

After a moment, Arkin tells her, "I don't care about that." He has completely forgotten the man inside the room, for the moment. "I'm not sure what I care about."

She smiles, perhaps a little sadly—or perhaps not. "That's what I like about you."

———————

They leave her car in the hospital lot and drive south then cross the river at Beacon, traveling west another few miles to a little Italian restaurant Arkin has heard about. They drink a good Barolo, share a risotto with leeks; share a thick ribeye for two, *tagliata* they call it in Rome, the menu says. They have biscotti and coffee and, not wanting the meal to end, Centopercento grappa. The bill is $400, which pleases Arkin, who spends almost nothing on himself beyond rent and gas for the car. His clothes are from websites and the outlets on Route 9 south of the hospital.

"You always eat like this?" she asks.

"I never do. I could never afford it. I was a resident before I had more than a hundred dollars in the bank. I had a credit card in med school, but I had to deposit cash in the account if I wanted to use it."

She smiles at this, at the idea of a physician without money. "You?"

"My dad worked for IBM. Not a big tech guy—a shipping supervisor—but I had a credit card in high school. And a Toyota." The grappa stretches out the silence between them, easily. "Do you have school loans?"

"A little, from med school. Army paid for lots. Plus, I worked. I was lucky."

"That you were in the Army?"

Arkin smiles a thin smile, considering another round.

"What did you do? Were you a medic?"

He shakes his head. "Infantry," he says.

She waits, then pushes her glass, the rest of the brandy in it, across to him.

In return, he tells her, "Afghanistan."

"When did you decide you wanted to be a doctor?"

The waitress arrives before Arkin can answer, bringing the bottle of Centopercento. "Our treat," she says in celebration of apparent romance, the handsome couple, or perhaps it's the size of the bill—Arkin isn't sure but watches her pour the wine. It's faintly yellow with age, and the waitress is meticulous.

"I don't know when I decided. Maybe there, a little." Arkin never talks about this, possibly has never really thought to try; the words and phrases form awkwardly. "Someone said you die every day in combat. You just . . . assume you're going to. So if you live, you're someone different at the end of each day. You're someone new. You put enough of those days together . . ." He trails off, and the next silence is longer still.

Kate has taken her glass back, and they both sip. The brandy, warmed by her hand, is smooth and hot in her mouth.

"Maybe you *are* someone new. Plus, I thought medicine would be different."

"And is it?"

"Yes," Arkin says, draining his glass. "And no."

———

Later that night, after Kate has fallen asleep—once more they're in her bed, in her apartment—and after Arkin has listened to her breathing shallow, watched the steady rise and fall of her chest, seen the tiny pulse in her temple slow as sleep arrived, he cries, a little. He does not remember the last time he cried, even soundlessly like this. A few tears, as he turns his face away from her, drop onto the blue percale sheets she'd put on the bed, fresh that day. Arkin has noticed and is touched that she remade the bed for them, perhaps hoping for this next night together, a special date, the nice dinner.

Arkin doesn't remember the last time anyone might have thought about him in this way, or, for that matter, when he had sex two nights in a row with the same woman—when he went back to college, he guesses, although he doesn't remember specifically and doesn't care to remember. He'd worried, once, that med school and residency would change his feelings about women and sex, that seeing the inside of their bodies, the cervix, the vaginal walls and introitus, through the cold silvery frame of the speculum in his gynecology rotation, illuminated by the cold evidence-based light of science, would change him. But though something had changed in him, it hadn't been that. Or, perhaps more accurately, something hadn't *un*-changed in him, hadn't reawakened after his time at war. Perhaps that's why he was most relaxed around the women at work, nurses and doctors; with their ferocious matter-of-factness about bodies and all things sexual, he could be comfortably male, and opaque inside.

But this, now, was Kate. And while he couldn't say that it was the clean sheets, or the elegant dinner, or all the expensive wine he'd drunk, much less the palely delicate silk curtains she'd hung, incongruous with their hand-figured windflowers and poppies against the insistent yellow light from the fast-food places outside, whatever it was—something had made him cry and, this time, stay the night.

She had stretched against him, before sex, her breasts flattened against his chest, holding him tight, every part of her pressed against him, her thighs against his, her feet entwined with his, one hand in the small of his back, the other at his neck, pulling him close to her, closer still, her mouth near his ear and filling his head with a soft throaty laugh as she rolled onto her back and reached between them to guide him into her, the laugh itself gliding into a long smooth sigh, or whispered moan, like the echo or memory of a name not said. She had canted her head into the hollow of his neck and kissed him there, again and again, gently, softly, almost childlike against everything else that they were doing at that moment, which was adult and fucking, while that kissing was so tender and girl-like that, yes, thinking of it after, and the sign that it was of caring, not just wanting or needing, but caring, made him cry.

He feels her hand on his chest then; he thinks she is asleep still—he looks to her and her eyes are closed, her face relaxed and contented—but she fits her hand, the shape of it, to the shape of the muscles in his chest and then pats him once, twice, gentle, as if reassuring, protecting. Arkin feels the tears drying on his face and, as if she had asked or approved it, urged it even, falls into a warm and thought-ending sleep.

In the morning, Arkin attends the weekly meeting of the Enhanced Assessment and Treatment team. He is unsure why he was named to the committee. While streaming baseball games to his phone, along with managing the high-flow text burden of his work, he doesn't consider himself particularly tech savvy. His Facebook presence has long lapsed, and he has never had an Instagram account; he doesn't

Snapchat. He's adept with the EMR, or electronic medical record, but has known nothing else, having received all his training in med school and at hospitals that had long since abandoned the paper chart. It's generally assumed that older physicians had problems with that transition, but the people he works with in their forties, fifties, and sixties don't seem especially inept. Everybody hates it of course, as the EMR has vastly expanded the amount of data docs are exposed to without any meaningful elimination of unnecessary and irrelevant material. Coding suggestions and requests for clarifications, facilitated now by billers' real-time access to the chart, are never-ending. Coupled with the nonstop texts from nurses and pharmacists and administrators and ED colleagues, the overall burden of digital technology in health care is a principal driver of burnout, everyone agrees, a near-perfect example of the law of unintended consequences at work. No one believes technology will actually improve their performance. In fact, the main enjoyment most panel members seem to get from participation in this focus group, aside from breakfast catered in from the cafeteria, is the chance to gloat over the failure a few years earlier of IBM's Watson software, a previous effort at "digital D/POC support" for physicians, the abbreviation meaning diagnosis and plan of care. The acronym for the current *enhanced assessment and treatment* effort, EAT, amuses everyone and seems particularly fitting as team members once again scavenge the multigrain bagels and scallion cream cheese.

"Can we get started?" This from Eva Tern, the twenty-something IT coordinator, preternaturally unimpressed by the roomful of physicians. As always, she wears a black pencil skirt and white rayon blouse and her hair in a pixie cut, and she has her presentation loaded and up on the projector as people find their places around the conference room table. "I wanted to just review before Dr. Emory joins us. He'll be introducing Bill Flood, who's here from corporate."

This produces a bit of a stir—not the Walt Emory part, who, as the physician head of tech, is viewed as something of hanger-on, end-of-career-wise, having dropped out of active medical practice years earlier. Bill Flood, however, is COO of EnterMed, the multi-billion-dollar corporation of which their medical center is merely a part, one of its nine hospitals, plus several hundred outpatient providers, their associated offices, staff, labs, imaging locations, and so on—Arkin thinks he's heard *eleven thousand* employees but knows those numbers could be old, and low. Arkin also thinks he's heard Flood's a "good guy" but understands such labels can be apocryphal, like CEOs being "vision guys." What he does know is that neither he nor likely anyone else at the table has ever *really* met someone as high up the food chain as Flood, the prospect creating a bit of a pause in the bagel and coffee consumption.

And Eva herself, noting the atypical level of focus she's suddenly garnered, jumps right in. "To recap, we've looked at the various modules, from lab, imaging, nursing, and data input, through history and medication reconciliation . . ." with which team members begin drifting back to the hard work of plastic knives on cold cream cheese. "We've looked at the physical piece, how you can free-dictate your observations, with contextual integration via software," which Eva apparently thinks is a big deal as she always smiles contentedly when mentioning this feature. She probably also thinks the physicians in the room have actually been modifying the preloaded physical exam templates in the current system. But Arkin cannot count the number of times he's seen patients in acute heart failure, for instance, with oxygen saturations in the 80s and legs as big a tree trunks, documented as having no "wheeze, rales, or ronchi" via auto-populated forms that most of the docs forget to edit. He thinks Eva Tern's enthu-siasm about doctors' rigorous documentation of physical findings is touching.

Bill Flood, when he arrives, dressed in relaxed tweed sport coat and Polo tie, followed meekly by IT/MD Emory, is amiable, as adver-tised. "Hi, everyone. Really pleased to meet you all, and sorry to keep you from your work. I just wanted to say"—he hesitates, everyone waiting for the corporate shoe to drop—"that this is all about making life easier for you guys. The first *and* second generation EMRs just screwed everything up—we know that. You have no cross-platform access to previous records. The interface is a relic from the paper chart. It's like Citibank said we're gonna have this new online digital banking thing, and it's gonna look just like a savings account pass-book from 1950."

This actually gets a laugh from the docs, even those too young to have seen a school passbook. But everyone knows health care is a decade or two behind the Big Tech crowd, and everyone loves it when corporate execs trash their own previous efforts; they admire that Flood has mastered the humorous version of the form. "We understand that if we don't fix the physicians' interface, we may not have many physicians left to run it." He pauses for effect, then: "More than that, it doesn't *help*. We're in the helping profession here; we oughta be able to help ourselves. It should be an aid; it should lift you up, not hold you down."

Arkin respects the smooth transition here, from "my past mistake" to "our future success," out of some Big Ten post-loss coach-ing handbook.

"You'll have a prototype to play with soon, and I came by just to underscore how *eager* we are for your feedback at *every* milestone. You have my email; write me, directly. Now finish your breakfast and have a good day." Flood waves as he heads for the door, still trailing Dr. Emory behind him like a lab-coated dust bunny.

Eva Tern beams, backlit by the forgotten PowerPoint, as the others head for the units.

———————

Later, on South Eight, Arkin again reviews the paperwork from Keller Army Hospital in Barnhardt's otherwise unused chart binder. For a moment, he relishes the incongruity of it, these cheaply faxed copies of the patient's old-fashioned paperwork, after the meeting earlier this morning on the promise of a new EMR, of countrywide interoperability, of efficient data streams and workflow. He understands that he has avoided the real-world collision the chart represents: of Arkin's technology-laden professional present with his murkily analog late-adolescent past. Ever since Barnhardt mentioned the word *Salerno* in the Emergency Department the day before, he'd tried not to think about the inevitable next encounter. And mostly, he'd succeeded, though possibly that in part, too, was why he'd cried, he thinks now. Not love, but loss.

Salerno. Arkin has never been to the real Salerno, which he knows is a port city near Naples, and the start of the Amalfi drive leading to places he's also never seen: Ravello, Positano, Sorrento. He has looked at pictures of lovely seaside towns along the coast and has read about the wines and food of Campania. He clings vaguely to those images against the prospect of a plunge *back* into the past, of war in Afghanistan, of *Firebase* Salerno, and God knows what else this dying cirrhotic patient may have in mind for him. Arkin suspects, despite its many failures and overall clunkiness, that his immersion in even the current technology of medical charting and research retrieval has acted as a sort of barrier against the memory of his previous life at the other Salerno. He folds the old-fashioned paperwork in half lengthwise, and then in half again, and again, ever more narrow. It could become anything, he thinks, a toy glider, a doorjamb, a table shim. He shoves it into one of his lab coat pockets, rubs disinfectant foam onto his hands, and walks into the room.

The old man, Barnhardt, lies in bed, tray table jammed against his protuberant belly. He has left untouched the clear liquid breakfast, is weakly stirring some coffee that he plainly also will not drink, and barely glances at Arkin, who comes to a stop at the foot of the bed, his standard greeting forming, when Barnhardt himself, with a shakily incongruous grin, announces, "Well, Sergeant Arkin—pretty well fucked, aren't we?"

It's been a dozen years since anyone called Arkin *sergeant*, and he thinks to say, to reorder the small world of this hospital room, *Doctor* Arkin. Instead, the phrase *worst fears realized* forms itself across his otherwise arrested thinking. He goes and sits in the vinyl lounge chair by the window and stares northeast across the ragged terrain of the broken old city. That single word, *sergeant*, has jarred him into a sort of telescopic new perspective. A long way off, he can see a water tower with a faded "Raider Pride" painted in old-fashioned banner font, the letters an aged and hazy coral against the oxidized gray of the tower. He doubts anyone is proud now. That Barnhardt is *fucked* is obvious, and though it is less apparent why Arkin might be, he dreads that Barnhardt will explain.

"I was in Kabul," the patient says.

"Were you?"

"At the embassy," Barnhardt says, trying vaguely for a sip of coffee, struggling to locate the rim of the cup with his mouth. His hand trembles from the buildup of ammonia in his bloodstream—*asterixis*, the medical term, Arkin reminds himself—flapping tremor. He holds to this nugget of pathophysiology, a grounding memory from med school.

"I was. When you left FOB . . . What was it again?"

Arkin says nothing.

"Salerno. I saw the reports. I wrote a few of them myself."

Arkin turns away from the window, willing himself to look at Barnhardt, willing himself to a steadiness he does not feel, waiting for the eventual, inevitable: "Including about you."

Arkin manages to say and do nothing, to not respond, except to wish himself in a bar somewhere, the Riverside for instance, where he could drink to again obliterate the memory of events leading to exactly this conversation. Despite his disease, despite the disparity of their power in the hospital—Arkin with all of it, the patient with none—Barnhardt clearly feels himself the master of the moment. "I'm sorry if I just dumped that on you," he says with a smile and no regret. "Who was that asshole you sent to me this morning? Barry?"

Arkin mutters, tonelessly, "Dr. Perry?"

"Yeah. Pain guy. I'm not interested in that shit."

Arkin says nothing, can say nothing. And Barnhardt's savoring of the dismissal—condescending, yes, but really closer to jaded in a way—makes Arkin feel even smaller in his chair, the chart, his own stethoscope, his lab coat, all suddenly, incongruously, adult.

"I want a transplant," Barnhardt says. "Liver. Lungs for the emphysema. That's what I want. I've been reading about it."

Still, Arkin says nothing.

Barnhardt laughs briefly, trailing off into a spasmodic cough, gurgle, before he goes on. "That's why I'm here. I did a search. I was looking for someone young, possibly ex-military and manageable. I had access to . . . a variety of databases because of my work. And

I found you. I recognized your name—How many Abel Arkins are there? What a surprise. I might have guessed . . . a security guard. But no, a doctor. Perfect."

This final sarcasm, its negation of Arkin's dozen years of education and training, at last provokes. "You had doctors at West Point."

"There's a problem."

"What?"

"I drink. Still. Not at the moment, of course. But they say I can't have the liver. And without that, there's no point to the other part." Meaning, with a wave toward his chest, a transplant of his diseased lungs. But something like a smile, only not, plays around the corners of Barnhardt's eyes, heavy-lidded as they are. Not exactly a grimace, certainly not guilt or shame, more like a connoisseur's appreciation of the contrivances of the world, its rules, and of his own confidence, even now, in the face of them. "I'm not supposed to drink—I get it. But I do."

"But you need to be sober, clean and completely sober, for six months. Every transplant center requires it," Arkin says. "I can't help with that."

"You can lie," Barnhardt says. "Like I did for you."

The room seems to empty of sound. Even out on South Eight, a silence seems to take hold of the day's ordinary routines and noises: the shouting of the delirious; of the maintenance staff; of floor washers and waxers; the rumble of food carts on their worn rubber casters, or the large portable X-ray machine sliding to patient rooms, or dialysis machines, or ultrasound equipment, or the transporters' fresh-sheeted gurneys; or complaining family, or worried family, or disinterested or bored or frightened family, or of their children, who as a rule are not respectful of hospital quiet; and of the usual chatter among the nurses or patient care techs, or the lab techs, or the

IV team techs, all perhaps for just this one moment either gone off the unit, or on break in the staff room, or deep in thought over their workstations. Or simply sensing the avalanche of silence coming from 836 and accommodating it, as one accommodates a river or season or fall in temperature from day to night.

Can silence, like sound, be directionless? Arkin wonders. This one seems to be emanating from both inside him and from the hospital around him, and he forms a word for it, pan-silent, with the remainder of his cognitive reserve, that part not taking up with spinning out over the idea that this man, this patient, Barnhardt, lied for him.

It's Barnhardt who breaks into the mental loop. "I want you to meet someone."

"Who?"

"The doctor who did this to me."

Some questions, Arkin thinks to himself (inanely, he knows, even as the idea forms) are better left unasked.

Barnhardt seems not to care. "There're a lot of ways a person can suffer, aren't there, Sergeant Arkin?"

"Call me Doctor."

"But you know what I mean, don't you?"

Arkin does not answer.

"Of all people."

"Because I'm a doctor?"

"I suppose, and because of Salerno. And what happened there. This is a simple matter," he says, reaching tremulously for a few papers on his bedside table. "Here's the information," he says, handing over an old-fashioned snapshot-size photograph and a slip of paper. At last, Arkin can hear sounds out in the hall: two techs gowning and gloving before cleaning the bed and overflowing diaper of the clostridium difficile patient in the next room. Active C. diff diarrhea has an unmistakable odor, unlike anything else the human body can emit. Barnhardt sniffs it, wolflike.

"I didn't come here to threaten you." Barnhardt lets this hover for a moment, nothing *but* threat in the air, if not precisely in the tone. "I didn't come here to ruin your career. I came so you could do me a service."

Arkin had not thought until this moment that his *career* might be at risk. And even now, even with *ruin your career* echoing among the other returning sounds around him, he finds himself clinging to an almost desperate focus on Barnhardt's lips alone, moving, turgid yellow, swollen with retained fluid, limned with bile.

"Will you do it?" Barnhardt asks almost gently. And then, into Arkin's insistent and impregnable silence, "Go see her, discuss my case—it's not what you think—then tell me you're ready to help."

———

As a child, Arkin had a kind of dreamy and hopeful nature that even at the time he sensed was at odds with the fearful world awaiting him. As a child does, he sought to bring order and sense to that world with fantasy, child's play, but even then, early on, he felt it a hopeless task. At six, Arkin constructed an extensive saga of himself, sometimes as a marshal, other times a guide, riding the western plains and mountains on a handsome chestnut mare. He dressed the set of his story with rifle and canteen, saddle and saddle blanket, the horse herself with reins and bridle and brushed mane, all so detailed and specific that nightly Arkin would vary for aesthetic effect the color and shape of his saddle, whether horned or not, high or low cantled, latigo knotted or buckled, hours more on the contents of his saddlebags and blanket roll, on his sidearm and rifle. In this story of himself, he knew the ways of the wolves and bears and coyotes and cougar, and imagined himself safe against these and other wilderness threats.

But in every telling, he and the mare crested the same western rise and beyond it found either a valley and yet another ridge, or perhaps a wide flat plain—the next ridge sometimes lost in haze—but in any case simply more of the trail and the journey, with never a destination and never a companion. And it was this, the absence of others, that even as a child he noticed—the loneliness of his inner terrain, the horse, as the song went, his only companion.

Arkin's mother had attended Colorado College, where she majored in anthropology and had planned to write her thesis on the role of language in the formation of cognitive patterns. Instead, she had conceived Arkin at the end of her junior year in the bed of her course number 5016/Research In Anthropology professor, who then counseled her on the importance of continuing her education and, providentially, of an immediate termination of her pregnancy. Alma, Arkin's mom, did neither. Instead, she dropped out of "CC," as it was known, found work at the big Progressive Insurance campus just off Voyager Parkway, rising through a series of promotions to the position of marketing sales representative. She rarely visited Butte, where her own bitterly disappointed and disapproving parents lived, so that when she committed suicide during Arkin's senior year in high school, there was no other family to which he could or was inclined to turn. Instead, he lived in the apartment above Coach King's garage until he graduated, after which he moved to a place on South Academy and, after two years' community college, to Georgia and Fort Benning.

Even now, Arkin cannot quite parse the connection he feels between the unchanging and inward journeys of his childhood's western fantasy and his mother's determined and equally unchanging pursuit of gainshare bonuses and existing account metrics at Progressive, followed by her equally determined suicide with the Mossberg Super Bantam shotgun she'd owned since her own childhood. He thinks (or feels, as scientists feel the fierce momentum of hypothesis) the connection must be there. Perhaps he felt it the first time he picked up his M16 in basic training and thought, as new soldiers sometimes do in those difficult early weeks, of turning it on himself because of the unchanging and at times unbearable landscape of military indoctrination. Or in the southern rim of the Pamir Mountains north of Khost, where the peaks rolled on below and past his team's Chinook, as they'd floated past and above him and his chestnut mare idyll, dangers all around and, while on the move, immaterial. Here on the eighth floor, however, with the water tower and its faded banner in the distance, and Barnhardt swollen and inescapably present in the bed, he feels he may have crested the final rise.

Later, at the Riverside, Arkin considers that he hasn't really thought about death in a long time. And he doesn't think many of his colleagues do, either, although death is their domain and is considered, though no one speaks in such banal terms these days, the enemy. He wonders at the transition he made, unthinkingly he now realizes, from the Army—where death was the *goal*—to this state of presumptive enmity. He understands that it is Barnhardt, who knows of Arkin in both his worlds, soldier and physician, who has brought him to this moment.

As a physician, Arkin is fully aware that death is a relief for many patients and their families, and like almost all of his colleagues, he

has sometimes hastened its arrival through the more or less aggressive withdrawal of certain treatments, followed by the more or less
aggressive provision of palliative medication. But even in these cases,
death remains the enemy, the necessarily and inevitably victorious
enemy, to whom the physician has surrendered (and surrendered
the patient) sooner rather than later. More or less aggressively.

In the Army, death wasn't the enemy—it was the point, even if it
wasn't spoken of in those terms. It was the *job*, even though soldiers
almost always spoke in terms of mission, task, operational goals.
Even the most avid of Arkin's fellow soldiers would have described
themselves as warriors, not killers. But on the other hand, no one
would have talked about minimizing enemy casualties; unlike in
medicine, casualties *were* the point. And this was more true and
direct for Arkin than for most. His team's job was not aiming artil-
lery rounds at a range of miles, or mortars over thousands of yards,
but rifle bullets at individual targets, targets that Arkin himself had
selected for Kelly.

Before Arkin saw people actually shot, he'd had a different idea
about how it worked. He'd thought people fought back when shot,
as in the movies, or if mortally shot (perfectly shot, as it were), then
knocked off their feet. He now knows that in the movies, this effect
(it's actually called the "knock-back") is achieved by stuntmen wearing harnesses attached to wires and hydraulic pistons. In real life, in
war, humans drop like cut-string marionettes when shot. And this
had been a shock to Arkin. In training at Fort Benning, he'd fired at
hinged and motorized silhouettes that would pop up to surprise the
shooter but didn't fall when hit. Instead, they electronically registered the location of the bullet's impact—these were newly in use
when Arkin trained—but they didn't *drop*. So the first time Arkin had
seen a man shot, near Spin Buldak on the Pakistan border, he was

surprised at how he crumpled, how his legs appeared to simply give out beneath him as he fell in place, a heap, unmoving. This was the objective of the sniper's job, to make the enemy not move, forever. In theory, one could aim for the head, for the base of the skull, in fact, and (if successful) sever the brainstem from the spine and thus the entire efferent nerve complex, guaranteeing the end of movement. But at a distance, they always aimed for the "center of mass"—the chest—and this had the same effect, the end of movement, except in the event of a miss, and Kelly never missed. Nor did Arkin when his turn came.

He looks up when the next bourbon-rocks arrives. He realizes he has lost track of time, that two hours have passed. He wonders whether he is safe to drive home. He wonders whether Barnhardt knows what the villagers looked like that afternoon when Kelly, after three already perfect shots, did a speed reload with a fresh twenty-round magazine, rose up out of their camouflaged position and started downslope, in the open. Or when Arkin had leaped to his feet behind him, scrambling for his own rifle, instinctively following. Or how balletically Kelly would pause, the toe of his front boot barely kissing the ground as he steadied his M110 and fired again and again, more forms collapsing in heaps, one to each round Kelly fired, dizzyingly inerrant, each in less than a second. Incomprehensibly, Arkin's first thought was that Kelly was violating the protocols of target selection, which was Arkin's role, prerogative even. So it took some time—possibly *seconds*—before Arkin realized Kelly was shooting everyone, not selecting at all, and by then Arkin was up and moving, too, and like Kelly, screaming.

For Arkin, it is impossible even years later to decipher what had driven Kelly to this. There had never been a moment in their months together when Arkin had thought Kelly might be capable of such what, such . . . fear? Anger? Or possibly a dissociative state, Arkin thinks now, though he wouldn't have known the phrase then. But, to be precise, his first thought was, *He's seen something.* Followed by the shame of *Why didn't I see it? It's my job to see it,* and then immediately, *But I didn't because there was nothing to see. He's just shooting.* By then, those perhaps five seconds, or maybe it was ten, or more, although whatever it was to Arkin, immediately afterward it seemed like nothing, needing to believe that no time had elapsed, certainly no time in which he could have *joined* Kelly in the shooting—even though there were rounds missing from the clip in his own rifle, and even though they had run thirty meters downslope from their FP. It takes *time* to go thirty meters. But Arkin can remember nothing of either the time or the distance. Try though he might, and he tried for weeks and months after, he also and specifically can't remember what, if anything, he'd seen balanced on the front sight post of his own rifle, framed by the rear aperture. Because in that period of no-time, pausing when Kelly paused, and raising his rifle when Kelly raised his, and trained as he was, he must have seen *targets* because he had, it seems, *fired* nine rounds. But all he can remember of those thirty meters is the shrill resonance of his own wordless bellow reverberating inside the Kevlar hollow of his helmet. And it is possible he fired aimlessly, literally aimlessly, at nothing, even though there were fourteen bodies when it was over—and could so many have been hit by Kelly alone, even Kelly with his extraordinary expertise, with Arkin entirely *aimless*? What he does know, because he remembers it, is stopping, and watching Kelly continue on another step or two, and then pausing again, and aiming, and shooting a small boy hiding behind the folds of his mother's burqa, and then shooting the boy's mother. And he remembers then shouting Kelly's name, and something like *What the fuck?* or something equally and entirely insufficient to the moment, and then he also does remember, this quite clearly, how Kelly turned back toward him, the M110 also swinging around, and then up, and then Arkin firing.

Arkin leaves the Taconic at Route 117, drives northeast through a town actually called Pleasantville, past a Dunkin' Donuts, a library of red brick, a cinder block school, on to where South Bedford Road forked to the right. From there, it's a few hundred yards to King Street, and then a handful of minutes—time seems to be accelerating—until he reaches the address Barnhardt had given him. By now, time has so compressed that the decision to cancel his evening with Kate, to not *go home for some rest,* to come instead to Chappaqua, and then the actual drive, seems not to have been the work of an hour, or minutes, or even a breath or a heartbeat, but not to have happened at all. Arkin recalls having this feeling in combat, where the worst events were perceived only after they had occurred. Unlike high school baseball, the fast pitch of war-fighting did not slow down; it sped up until the only evidence that it had happened lay not in one's senses at all but in an instantaneous New World of destruction around you. Waiting to fight, on the other hand, was endless.

And the evidence of Arkin's new world, including of his complete capitulation to Barnhardt's resurrection of *Sergeant* Arkin, is here: he has arrived, and in the light of the full moon, the house is imposing, six thousand square feet, says the real estate website he'd looked up—to himself, he denies the word "scouted"—five bedrooms, a view of the lake from the paneled library, the living room, the kitchen, the stone terrace off the back of the house. Lights are on throughout, and Arkin finds himself noting the pools of shadow that he could use to approach, where contiguous, where not, where shafts of light might pick him out against the darkness. He has not thought of anything like this in years. Cover and concealment was something he first heard about in basic training but was immersed in at sniper school. He remembers *Field Manual 21-75*—in particular, the section on camouflage, with its list of items that could reveal you to your enemy, things such as your position, your shadow, the shine of your weapon or your wristwatch, the color of your skin. Arkin most especially liked the advice on shape, which the Army taught was: "outline or form. The shape of a helmet is easily recognized. A human body is also easily recognized. Use camouflage and concealment to breakup shapes and blend them with their surroundings. Be careful not to overdo it." Arkin liked the advice about not appearing to be what he was, but he also liked the manual's uncharacteristically colloquial, even nuanced, "Be careful not to overdo it." Could a person appear so little like what he really was, so blended with his surroundings, that he entirely disappeared? Would this be "overdoing" it, Arkin wondered? Or, tactically speaking, wasn't disappearing the point of sniper training, that the sniper disappears first, followed by his target?

When she opens the door, Arkin recognizes her immediately, although the picture Barnhardt gave him is a decade old. She has fine gray hair flowing back and to the left of her head in a salon-made sweep of expense. It curves over the ear and then around and down to frame a gold earring in the shape of a bird, a dove, Arkin thinks. She is wearing black pants—improbably, the phrase "high-waisted" comes to Arkin's mind—and a plain silk button-front blouse in ivory. She is barefoot, with just a hint of lipstick and eye makeup. Arkin registers that she has opened the door without hesitation, as if expecting someone, though he hasn't called. She glances quizzically at him, at the rumpled cheap shirt and tie, the J.Crew cords. Arkin wishes he had worn something other than running shoes.

"Yes?" Her voice is smooth, just a halftone above deep.

"Dr. Oliver?" Arkin manages, his mouth dry either from the long air-conditioned drive or from lack of forethought about this moment that time has delivered him into.

"Yes?"

"My name is . . ." He has to clear his throat, unfortunately, since simply identifying himself has now sounded somehow put on. "Dr. Arkin. I'm, uh, on the hospitalist staff at Upstate."

"Okay." Just a hint of amusement now, not inviting him in, not asking a next, easy sort of question to ease this botched introduction of his.

"We're colleagues," Arkin says brightly, sounding foolish even to himself. "We're all one big corporation now, right? There're what . . ."

"Nine hospitals, yes." She supplies the number indulgently, adding an amused, "We're one big family."

And Arkin, his introductory offerings exhausted, starts in on an explanation that rings hollow even to himself. "I'm seeing, I think, a former patient of yours."

Her brow lifts fractionally, still waiting.

"Robert Barnhardt? I believe you saw him quite a long time . . ." But he stops, as Oliver has taken a step back from the door, as if unbalanced by a gust of wind, though there is no wind.

"How . . ." she says, and then again, "How . . ." the pause so long that Arkin has stepped into the foyer and closed the door before she completes her sentence. "How is he?"

He wonders at the sudden turnaround, not so much from offense to defense as in space: he now filling the one she'd blocked then shrank from. For just an instant, he wonders at how much this feels like breaking cover and rising from concealment, and just that fast, the thought is gone and Arkin resumes the role of deferential junior, inquiring of his senior, "You're chief of medicine at DMC?"

"I've just retired. The first was my last day." Arkin nods encouragingly, and Oliver nods, too, almost in unison, twice, recovering with a strangled laugh. "That's a funny way to put it, 'The first was my last day.'" And then, "How long have you . . . been treating Bob?"

"Just a few days. He's not well, he's, um, cirrhotic, end-stage, infected. We took off like six liters; his breathing's better. But he's COPD, still hypoxic, and his sodium is still mid one twenties, that's with hypertonic saline, water restriction. So, not good." And then, "He was your patient?" Oliver just nods. "Well . . . I'm here because he"—at which point Arkin stalls, unsure how to describe his own broad uncertainty. "He suggested I come see you. He asked me to. And he's quite sick."

Oliver looks around, as if to sit, but there's no chair in the entrance hall, which is the size of Arkin's apartment, or Kate's, or the exercise center of a luxury hotel. There's gray silk wallpaper, a console table, marble floor tile, and on the wall behind her, a small Picasso etching. It's of three female nudes, which unaccountably Arkin recognizes as the *Three Graces*; the print is numbered and signed and, though part of a series, probably cost what he makes in a few months of work. Beyond, he can see a large living room, opposing sofas, a blazing fire although it is warm outside.

"I knew him in the Army. I was working for the government; I treated him when . . . he first . . . fell ill." Arkin smiles at the old formulation, but Oliver seems not to notice. Her hand flutters once, vaguely inward, again abandoning space. "Would you like something? A drink?"

———————

"Where did you study?" she asks over her shoulder as she leads him through the living room and into a walnut paneled library. There's an English mahogany writing table, its top of embossed brown leather; beside the table is a glass display case, shelves neat with collectible chess sets, ivory, vaguely Asian, Arkin thinks.

Without waiting for Arkin's answer, Oliver moves behind the desk to a dropdown panel behind which are wines, liquor bottles, ice bucket, glasses, tongs, openers, coasters, mixes. "Drink?" she asks again.

Arkin thinks about the clearance of earlier drinks from his system before, "Bourbon, please."

"Elijah Craig?" she asks.

Arkin nods, though his experience with hundred-dollar bourbons is limited. He notices the bottle shaking as she pours, a few drops spilling, a rotational tremor originating in the wrist, Arkin registers—possibly triggered by nervousness, which is apparent as she starts to sit at the desk then gestures instead to a leather sofa, too near another unnecessary fire, this one a gas insert.

"So how well do you know Bob?" she asks.

Arkin notes the new forced calm in her voice, the impression of confidence behind her use of the patient's first name but also the care with which she avoids Arkin's gaze, as well as the amount of bourbon gone from her glass when she lowers it to the coffee table between them.

"Not well. Admitted him yesterday, saw him this morning," he answered, determinedly keeping his own nervousness at bay.

"But you came to see me?" Very controlled, precise even. "That's interesting."

Well, this, it must be said, is true. Arkin hesitates over the realization that while on the drive down he ignored the background rumble of fear, he has in fact yielded to Barnhardt's threats. He fumbles out an explanation: "It seemed important to him. He called you . . ."

Oliver glances his way, a fleeting look of alarm there behind the whiskey's softening glaze.

Arkin recalls Barnhardt's description of her—*the doctor who did this to me*—and chooses a less punishing alternative: "Well, it seemed like a sort of last request."

Oliver says nothing, only finishes the rest of her bourbon, holding the empty glass in her lap, the ghost of whiskey.

"Like you would have something to tell me." This shred of inspiration gets him a different look, although more fatigued than alarmed.

Oliver goes for more bourbon, forgetting to offer Arkin a refill of his own, absorbed in the business of the bottle and pouring. "We must know some of the same people," she says a little too gamely, transparently. "Being colleagues. You know Dick Warden, our CEO?"

"No, I don't know that he's ever come to our hospital."

"Debbie Gross, CMO?"

"No. I met Bill Flood, yesterday, he's . . ." Arkin has momentarily forgotten Flood's title.

"COO, yes, I know him well." Oliver seems to have run out of delaying maneuvers, corporate connection shopping, even energy; she looks at her glass, unable for the moment to raise it to her lips. Finally, "I made a mistake." Then, "With Bob. Did you get a CT?"

"Just abdominal. Cirrhotic, ascites, of course."

"Well, yes. And that was my impression when he first started having symptoms, and, um . . ." She trails off, her gaze touring the study, its display of chess sets, the bar, a small terra-cotta sculpted horse on one of the bookshelves—legless, Arkin notes.

"You said you're what, an internist? In hospital practice?" Oliver asks.

"Yes."

"I was GI, originally, but . . . by the time I met Bob, I was already . . . an administrator. I was civilian codirector of the clinical support division of the Defense Health Agency. I wasn't military, but I worked for DOD."

Arkin watches as she seeks words, as if to a script, and finding something of a rhythm, if without much conviction.

"But I still practiced, saw some patients. I felt I needed to because . . . there weren't enough docs and it seemed right . . . and it kept me in the flow of things. I traveled a lot in that position. I was in Afghanistan, at Bagram."

Arkin puts down his glass, for perhaps the first time in a year not wanting an immediate refill.

"So . . . when Bob came in, I thought I'd see him. Not just because it was a GI issue but also because he was a . . . very significant figure." She looks out from beneath that sweep of hair, undisturbed even now, to see what Arkin might know of Barnhardt's significance. "A VIP," she says.

Arkin is unmoving; so still, in fact, that he feels a vague, unwelcome remnant of spotter training at Benning.

There is a pause, this part of Oliver's script even less comfortable, unrehearsed. "I got it wrong." Another delay, into which she inserts a nod, then, "I thought . . . he was a drunk. Which he was, but . . . that wasn't the cause of his liver fibrosis." She looks at Arkin, her hand a little steadier now, with two large bourbons-worth of stress management. She asks almost lazily, "How're his lungs?"

"Bad. COPD, he's a smoker, ex. Chest X-ray looked like pretty severe emphysema, maybe a little more basilar than usual."

"I thought it was the cigarettes too. Or maybe that it was his liver, hepatopulmonary syndrome, that's what I thought. Although the CT didn't show... dilations in the pulmonary vasculature. But I let that go. And I treated him conservatively—I mean, there wasn't much choice. Diuretics for the ascites, lactulose for the ammonia levels, oxygen for his hypoxemia. I tried to get him to stop drinking." She smiles a watery smile, the shape of her failure unaltered by the years since. "And of course, we basically had to rule him out for transplant. He wasn't sick enough then, at that point, and he was a drinker. Still is?" she asks of Arkin, who nods minutely. Oliver pauses, glances over at the bourbon bottle, but then her gaze comes back to Arkin, defocusing slightly as she gathers herself to report: "But I was wrong. It wasn't alcoholic liver disease at all. It was... uh... alpha antitrypsin deficiency. Which did not occur to me. We didn't have a pulmonologist, much less an alpha specialist. And I wasn't a liver specialist. But I was a gastroenterologist. I should have thought of it. He was the right age for late presentation. And if I had, we could have treated him, at least his lungs, and we could've transplanted him. But I didn't, and his FEV was less than thirty percent predicted when, a few years later... they finally diagnosed him at Reed. When someone else diagnosed him. Correctly."

"What about... did they start him on Prolastin?"

"Not indicated for FEV below thirty-five. Care at that point was basically... supportive. The Army felt." Her voice is muted, the words muffled. "Supportive," she repeats methodically.

"Oh," Arkin says quietly. "I understand." And he does, as all physicians understand the vertiginous prospect of a misdiagnosis leading to death.

"Of course, at that time, even then, no one could say anything about *me*, because Bob didn't exist. Not officially. He wasn't in the Defense Department; officially, he was working for a private company based in Lodi, California, at least at that time. Because what he was actually doing in Afghanistan was so secret that even his presence there wasn't openly acknowledged. And I could hardly be his doctor for three years if he wasn't there. So I could hardly be blamed for missing the diagnosis. Or for my egotism in insisting on treating him when I should have sent him elsewhere. In fact, instead of being sued or ... punished, I got a wonderful recommendation ... for my next job."

"It's not your fault."

"I thought his emphysema was garden variety COPD. And of course I could treat that too. Anyone can treat that." She has looked away by now, as if unwilling to be seen or to see Arkin seeing her. With dry self-deprecation, she repeats, "Anybody could." She puts the empty glass down on the sofa beside her. "I counseled him to quit smoking. At least I got that right."

Arkin doesn't bother to sympathize, which would be beside the point and anyway not what he's interested in now. "What *was* he doing in Afghanistan?"

Oliver hesitates before saying, "I can't talk about that." She seems to reflect on this additional shortcoming. "How's he doing? I mean, in terms of planning."

"A few months, maybe, at most."

"Why did you come, then? Really. I have nothing to offer."

Arkin realizes this is true, of course. Why *would* he come all this way? Nothing she could say could alter the plan of care.

"He asked me to."

"Did he tell you this? Already, before you came?"

"No. Nothing. His documentation was incomplete, he didn't bring any notes, anything from the Army docs. He . . . wanted me to see you. So I suppose he wanted *you* to tell me. And . . . he wanted *me* to certify him sober so he could get on the list for a liver. And lungs. He wants everything."

"Do you think he's a candidate?"

"No. I can't imagine. I mean, it's not my area, but he's really sick, he's probably colonized, he's old. I have an echo pending, but I'm sure his heart's an issue. So—no."

"But you're . . ." The pause is long enough that Arkin looks up to see if she's drifted off. But she finishes it. "Being pressured?"

Reflexively, a weak smile accompanies his reply. "No more than usual."

But Oliver appears to have heard something in his tone, for now she does focus on him, the grit of suspicion or doubt, with possibly an edge of worry, or perhaps all of these, in her look. In that moment, she seems an attractive middle-aged woman in whom the patina of elegance imparted by her money and clothes and haircut and fine whiskey has dropped away to reveal sudden, personal fear. That Arkin drove an hour to see her, a complete stranger, without calling in advance, at request of a new patient he'd never met before, is on its face ridiculous. Likely the implications, despite the Elijah Craig, have finally dawned on her.

Arkin wonders now whether his decision to drive down, made after several drinks of his own at the Riverside, was entirely, well, wise. He wonders whether the additional bourbon he's drunk here might be clouding his judgement now about disclosure, even as he admits, "Well. Pressure. Maybe, yes." Oliver waits, and the suspicion that was there moments before has morphed into a look, almost, of pity. "I was in Afghanistan, in the Army. He knew my name from that."

"I see." And possibly she may, although she closes her eyes for a moment—seeing within, Arkin wonders?—and then says, "People like Bob . . . we're not like them. People like us . . . we're not strong in that way. Or dangerous. He's a very dangerous man. And in his case, I guess you would say it's . . ." She hesitates, looking away, at her empty glass, anywhere but at Arkin, before concluding, "A moral issue. Be careful."

Arkin has nothing to say to this, the mention of *morality* so unexpected in this *professional* context, and unusual generally, as to end the conversation. He stares at her for a while longer, the gas fire a dull background hiss, until she says, "Well, thank you for coming." And then: "Good luck."

———

Later that night, in the rented apartment he calls home, with only a few hours before he has to be back at the hospital, Arkin thinks again of Kelly, the team they'd been, and the end they'd reached. Kate had asked him when he thought of becoming a doctor, and Arkin thinks it might have been, in some remote functioning corner of rationality, during those last moments when Kelly was killing people in Mata Khan and in the first moments after Arkin had fired and stopped him. Of course, not anything so comically specific as *I'm going to medical school*, but possibly something more desperately general as *no more*. He senses the many-sided moral algebra in that, the solution to which eludes him.

So, he cannot imagine what he would have done if he hadn't gone back to college and then medical school. The pace of study and training, and of residency and work since, have consumed him to an extent that, once begun, all other possibilities evaporated. His mind balks when he tries to consider how his life now connects with his life in the Army or with his mother's suicide. He idly asks himself what, as a physician, he might have thought or done, coming upon his mother's body, or later, Kelly's. The answer's clear enough—even at 2:00 a.m. and through a too-familiar haze of alcohol and exhaustion: *Nothing could have been done.* He would have known both were gone, as he could not believe, much less accept at seventeen and twenty-one. At thirty-three, fully clothed, still half drunk and sweating from it in the middle of the night, he sleeps at last.

FOUR

ARKIN SINKS INTO WORK in the morning. He has not called Kate, has not eaten. He has only shaved and dressed and driven to the hospital, where he ducks into the office to pick up his patient list. He successfully ignores Barnhardt's name printed on it, starts his rounds on the north side of the complex with the post-cardiac and respiratory care units, two heart failures, a sick sinus, three COPDers. He will devote himself to routine, he thinks, peremptory and businesslike in the face of the uncertainty that awaits him on the south side building, specifically on South Eight. And Arkin likes the PCU, the mostly long-serving nurses there, experienced and less demanding of the doctors and nurse practitioners than some of the newer nurses. Judy, a twenty-year veteran of the unit, greets him with a theatrical "Dr. Arkin has arrived. Good morning, Dr. Arkin."

"Good morning, Judy. How are you?"

"I have, I believe he's yours, Mr. Messina? I wonder if you'd like me to give him some atropine." She gestures to the telemetry monitors on the other side of the core, the nurses' station with its cluster of desks. Arkin sees that the patient in room 326 has a heart rate of 30.

"I would like you to call a cardiologist."

"One's in the ER, two are in the cath lab with acute MIs, and the NP is doing stress tests."

"I've never met this patient." To Judy, who merely smiles at him, this matters not at all; Arkin is the doctor in the room, and she waits for his response. "Is he symptomatic?"

"I would say yes. Short of breath. And a little . . . dizzy."

Arkin pauses, having in just that moment thought of Barnhardt, his shortness of breath, even in the face of 326's semi-emergency.

Judy prompts him. "We already have the cart in the room if you want to pace him instead."

———————

On the way around the circular hallway that forms the PCU, Judy asks, "And how are you liking our little hospital?"

"Not so little."

"And our little nurses?" Judy, enjoying herself, avoids his questioning glance.

"I think you've lost me."

"I doubt it," she says and turns into the patient's room, seamlessly announcing, "Mr. Messina, this is Dr. Arkin," ignoring what looks to be a hundred-year-old man in the bed by the door, who seems to have fallen asleep, Arkin notes, with a plastic urinal propped between his legs, breezing past him to another nurse and a tech at the window bed, clustered by the code cart, the patient there an obese man of about fifty.

"Good morning, Mr. Messina. The nurse tells me you're a little light-headed," Arkin begins. "Is that right?"

But Messina has moved beyond light-headed, is gasping for air, mildly cyanotic with a faintly bluish tinge to his lips. Eyelids drooping, he manages a faint nod.

The young nurse standing by the code cart, dressed in novice whites, in a show of painfully forced composure, announces too brightly, "Heart rate just twenty now." Everyone can hear the quaver in her voice, sound bouncing off panic.

"And you did . . . ?" asks Judy, but the younger nurse's eyes merely widen more brightly, her mouth a perfect "O" of fuckup. "Dr. Arkin, this is Molly Hammond, my preceptee. Molly, you might want to put the pads on him now," she says, gesturing to the unattached combo pads draped over the LifePak. To Arkin, low: "This is worse."

"And draw up point five of atropine," Arkin says as he moves to the patient, lifts the bed sheet to reveal thighs and calves, enormous and now faintly mottled blue and white from the failing blood supply. The patient, Messina, reaches vaguely for Arkin as he puts his stethoscope to the man's chest, where even through the layers of fat, he can hear the crackle of fluids in the lungs. He sees the young nurse's hands trembling as she shakily applies the first combo pad to the patient's right chest wall. Arkin takes the second pad from her, bodily heaves a groaning Messina up onto his side in order to apply the second to the left side of his back so that current can flow directly through the heart if they have to pace him. The patient must weigh three hundred pounds, Arkin thinks, as he glances at the LifePak, now registering the man's steady but very slow heart rhythm. "Sinus rhythm, first-degree block, yeah?"

"I think so," Judy says, glancing at it as she cracks the seal on the code cart, opens the top drawer, finds the atropine.

"Then let's give the atropine, get another point five ready, and switch us to pace."

Judy resets the LifePak as she moves to the patient to administer the atropine. Arkin looks to the tech, a woman of at least sixty with forty years on the job. Without prompting, she's got the Ambu Bag ready, hooked up to the oxygen outlet in the wall, and her hand rests on the bedside table—near the large blue code button on the wall above it, between the two patients' beds. Her chin lifts a quarter inch, inquiringly, and Arkin feels himself smile tightly. "Let's see what the atropine does."

The tech nods then glances in the direction of the new nurse, Molly, still frozen at the bedside even as Judy administers the atropine, following with a saline flush.

"Molly," Arkin says, "why don't you go get some of the other nurses. We need a lab tech, respiratory therapy. Could you call them?" Molly nods, mute. "We have a bag of dopamine or epi in the cart?"

Arkin's voice has grown softer, but Molly's is softer still, a near whisper: "I don't know."

Judy tells the girl, across the mound of the patient's belly, "Yes we do, Molly."

So Arkin, still to the new nurse, says, "That's good. Then why don't you find us another pump, with at least three channels?" Molly nods, relieved to have a straightforward assignment, a simple objective—outside the room—and goes. Arkin offhandedly asks Judy, who struggles under the weight of the patient's arm, holding it aloft so that the atropine can drain into his system, "What was that about little nurses?"

At which point Messina emits a little groan and stops breathing.

The old tech moves her hand to the code button, lets it hover there for just a fraction of second before Arkin nods, says, "Go ahead," and the code alarm sounds throughout the unit, and the public address system erupts hospital-wide with "Code blue, PCU, room 326, code blue."

The dream state is not a place Arkin often visits. Now, he thinks he must have been *very* dreamy as child, by which he means easily lost between the pages of whatever he happened to be reading or the words of whatever class he was in or TV show he was watching. But he thinks of these as merely the continuum of the child's imagination, not the *displacement* that adults might feel at being lifted, as if bodily, out of whatever was going on in the corporeal world around them. He thinks he may have begun to experience this sort of dream state on the rifle range at sniper school, inhabiting the air between his rifle's muzzle and the target, traveling along the arc of the round even before it was fired. He has read of Japanese archers who attain a state in which for them, it is said, the arrow *exists in the target* before it is released from the bow.

There is little similarity between the stillness of the archer, or of his former self on the rifle range, with the organized chaos of a dozen nurses and respiratory therapists and lab technicians pouring into room 326 of the PCU. And yet there is something of it within him, a stillness descending within the cloud of voices, a fold within the rush of time and movement. He sees: the sleeping man in the other bed awaken with a start as CNAs unlock his bed and sweep it and him out into the hallway; the lab tech setting out her tubes for the expected orders for blood draws; a nurse beginning a log of events, jotting down the code's start time; another nurse clamping the Ambu Bag to the patient's face as the respiratory therapist begins ventilating; the LifePak illuminating with its ECG trace.

"Hold atropine," he hears himself say, seeing the coarse and irregular waves of ventricular fibrillation. "Let's shock him, one hundred and twenty joules." His voice sounds a little high, a little above his normal register, and far away, like Judy's when she says, "Charging." And then, as the LifePak's tone whines upward toward full charge, "Clear," and the assembled dozen or so people back away from the bed as Judy touches the "shock" button on the LifePak and the electrical charge flashes back and forth in a millisecond between the two pads on the man's torso, traversing the heart as the body spasms and heaves and the ECG trace changes not at all, and Judy says, dryly redundant, "Shock delivered," followed by his own voice, pitched lower but just as distant as he says, "Switch to two hundred joules," and "Give one milligram epi," and someone answers, "Epi going in."

And in just this state of, if not mere reverie, not true dream, Arkin suddenly revises his sense of his sniper self, his error of self-esteem, for Arkin sees now that in Afghanistan, it was not so much that he knew who had to die—anymore that he knows now that this patient in room 326 is about to do so (for the moment Arkin has forgotten his name): it's that he knew whom he and Kelly were about to *kill*, which is anything but a subtle distinction when you are the one pointing out targets to the man next to you, who can put a high velocity NATO round through a can of tuna at eight hundred yards. Anymore than predicting the success of this resuscitation—and this thought propagates a wave of sudden near panic on the surface of his reflection—is a subtle art when you are the one in the room giving orders that will or won't revive someone. Arkin has never actually killed a patient, that he knows, although he also knows it likely that he has done so. Along the line, of the thousands he has treated, first as a resident and now as an attending, he has surely made the fatal error or missed the crucial fact, and either managed to deny the catastrophe-level doubt such a miss would create (as opposed to *routine* doubt, in which he marinates continuously) or more likely managed to block the self-scrutiny that would reveal it. He worries now about how many times this may have happened as he wrestles with the deeper understanding that he never *knew* his targets in wartime, only *documented* them as such after he and Kelly had killed them. It was *always* a guess. Possibly dozens of innocents died, and equal dozens of HVTs (high value targets, in the language of their mission logs) escaped. And possibly dozens—or hundreds?—of patients have done the same, escaped or not.

———————

And seven minutes into the code, Arkin is sure this patient will not survive. He has ordered three shocks with two minutes of chest compressions between. He has given two doses of epinephrine, now orders amiodarone, "Three hundred milligrams," which Judy dutifully repeats, adding "Pushing amio," as she injects it into the patient's saline lock. Nurses are taking turns doing the best they can with chest compressions, given the man's enormous bulk. One of the smaller ones has climbed up onto the bed, kneeling beside his body in order to push directly down on the chest. There has been no change in his rhythm on the LifePak beyond what appears to be a slow degeneration of the original coarse fibrillation into a finer waveform. The next step in the process will be asystole, or "flatline" as classic episodic TV would have it, although Arkin has never heard anyone use that term that he can recall. He struggles also to recall the "H's and T's," the acronym for the causes of cardiac arrest, but can remember only the first two, hypovolemia and hypoxia, neither of which applies in this case, he thinks. The man is hypervolemic if anything, still overloaded with fluid from his heart failure; and the respiratory therapist and the nurse managing the Ambu Bag clamped to the man's face are getting good "chest rise" with each squeeze of the bag by the RT, so at least for now, there's pure oxygen flowing to his lungs and presumably, with good chest compressions, to his brain. But what the third or fourth "H" is, much less any of the "T's," Arkin cannot recall just now. Instead, he feels the fine sweat, not only of panic but of impending humiliation, begin to form on his brow just as a nurse runs into the room to announce blood gas and lab results: "He has a pH of seven point one five and a potassium level of seven point two."

This is almost miraculous news, not least because the lab has never resulted chemistry so quickly, but also because it reminds Arkin of two more "H's," *hyperkalemia* (high potassium) and *hydrogen ion*, or elevated acid level. And equally miraculously, Arkin emerges from his dream state into the realization they can be treated the same way: "Bicarb . . ." and Arkin steadies his voice, in which he'd heard a momentary vibrato of nervousness (unacceptable) or possibly excitement (less so), forcing him to repeat, "Bicarb, give one amp, get a second amp ready." Arkin takes a breath, adds, "And calcium chloride, do we have that in the cart? Five hundred milligrams IV, to give after the first amp of bicarb." And just that quickly, as quickly as the cardiac arrest algorithm has come into focus, Arkin himself focuses more sharply still, can see more of the larger picture: how obesity and the resulting poor respiratory effort, along with pulmonary edema from the heart failure, plus bradycardia and poor perfusion of the kidneys, had caused the acidosis, along with a likely overdosing of potassium to offset aggressive diuresis—whatever—and as all that falls into place for him, and the 50 milliequivalents of bicarbonate have drained into the patient's vein, Judy announces, far too coolly, "We have a rhythm."

And just *that* quickly, the memory of Barnhardt, lying in a bed across the complex, and of Elizabeth Oliver, his long-ago physician draining her expensive bourbon in her expensive home, also comes flooding back into his mind with an attendant sudden queasiness and repeat sweat, this time of fear for himself. Arkin wonders at the sudden almost incomprehensible duality of this, the rush of good feeling at the authority and expertise he deployed in this perfectly run code, literally reversing the cardiac arrest in 326, restarting a heart that would otherwise never have beaten again, versus the dread he feels at the prospect of facing the patient on South Eight.

"Nice job." This from Jamal Franklin, today's rounding cardiologist, whom Arkin finds standing idly in the doorway.

"Thanks," Arkin says. "Your patient?" Jamal grins, nods. "How much beta blocker and potassium did you give him?"

Another grin, then, "Maybe too much? Thanks for your help," and moves on into the room, telling the nurses, "Take him to CCU. I'll write orders."

Standing outside Barnhardt's room, Arkin had decided on a detached and authoritative approach. Standing inside it, with Barnhardt glaring up at him, his determination—along with his satisfaction at the outcome with Mr. Messina (the name has come back to him) in the PCU—has evaporated.

"Where the fuck have you been?" Barnhardt's expression is an odd mix: the lips are pulled back into an angry grimace while the rest of the face remains puffed and yellow from the buildup of fluid, and jaundice.

He looks like a cartoon character, Arkin thinks, a little like the early unsmiling Popeye, the ochre sailor man, and the thought steadies Arkin somewhat. "How do you feel?"

"What did she say? You saw her. How was she, *Beth*?"

Arkin hesitates, having yet to decide what she was like, and only now recalls her first name, Beth. Dr. Beth Oliver. Instead, he glances down at the printout he holds. "Your numbers are stable, maybe a little worse," he says, *detached and authoritative* having devolved into blunt and humorless. He reels off the cheerless points: "Your LFTs, liver function tests, are going up. Your kidneys are about the same, maybe a little better, but chronic insufficiency. Your sodium is still low. Your ammonia level is unchanged. Your bilirubin is up a bit."

Barnhardt says nothing.

"And . . ." Arkin begins, the slight pause signaling the arrival of more bad news, "We have the results of your echocardiogram. It shows significant heart failure. The ability of the left side of your heart to pump blood to your body is diminished significantly. And . . . the *right* side of your heart is working far too hard to pump blood to your lungs, because of what we call pulmonary hypertension. We often see that with emphysema." Although he's simplified it, Arkin knows this is already too technical; he makes it simpler. "So this means your heart is now also a problem, a big problem, in addition to the liver and lungs. I know this is hard to hear." And for a moment, Arkin actually feels a twinge of sympathy toward the man in bed, even while recalling Oliver's description of him the previous night as dangerous and a moral question mark. "The point is, I don't know there's much more we can do for you here right now. I think you're ready for rehab though. I think you'll do better there."

Barnhardt remains silent, and his lips close, transforming him from Popeye to . . . Droopy? It appears as if he may cry, and Arkin wonders vaguely if tears form, whether they will be yellow from jaundice.

And Barnhardt mumbles, almost implores, "Could you sit down?"

And Arkin does, readying himself for bullying, threats, and not at all for what comes.

"When you were at Salerno, when that happened, with your . . . partner . . . How did you feel?"

"I don't think it's appropriate . . . to discuss what happened to me. This is not about me; this is about you. I met with your previous doctor, as you requested. She had nothing to offer in the way of suggestions going forward." Arkin's not sure himself what this means; it feels entirely vacuous, not just the heavily overused "going forward" but his avoidance of the issue of the patient's initial missed diagnosis.

It seems to have worked for a moment, though, as Barnhardt turns his head to stare out the window—the distant water tower with its "Raider Pride" still there. But Barnhardt's thoughts appear far removed from his lab results; eventually, he says, "It's all connected, you know, me and you. We're connected."

"I understand. We were both there."

"No, no—that's not it at all . . ." followed by, after a pause to catch his breath, "I took care of it. Your situation, I cleaned it up. I wrote the reports. That was me. That's why I knew your name. That's why I came here. So you could . . . clean things up for me."

Until this moment, the idea of an actual coverup at Salerno has never occurred to Arkin, not at the time and not in the dozen-plus years since he'd left it and Afghanistan. He feels his belly clench, a seismic lurch of the inner landscape, even as he maintains his clinician's steady pitch. "There was no coverup. This is not helpful. There was a hearing. What happened to Kelly . . ."

"I'm not talking about him. You're right. There was a review, you did nothing wrong there, you defended yourself. I'm talking about the others. The witnesses . . . the review did not . . . consider."

Arkin's mouth is suddenly desert dry, dune-like; he hates that he has to swallow twice before speaking. "I don't know what you're talking about."

Barnhardt manages a ghastly, lemony smile. "I was head of the Political Action Group. There's Special Activities Division, that's 'SAD.' And inside SAD is SOG, Special Operations Group. They work with Delta, Seals, Special Forces, that stuff, very dramatic. But also inside SAD is PAG. Political Action Group. That's what I did in Afghanistan. Working their elections, propaganda, influencing media, religious types. And friendly fire incidents involving civilians. Those we paid off. Soften the blow, earn their silence. That's what I did for your partner, shooting those people. And you."

"I didn't shoot . . . like that. I fired at . . . Kelly." Arkin's entire body is oddly loose, lax, as if he were trying to melt into the chair beneath him.

"There were ten bullets missing from your magazine. Your friend was shot once, in the chest. Where did the other nine go? Doctor?"

This is a question Arkin has been asking himself for years, if with decreasing frequency. The harder he works, the more he drinks, the more years pass, the less he asks, though he has never not asked at all nor thought he would.

Softly now: "In the air. While I ran. Trying . . ." And here Arkin stumbles, as he has stumbled over the years reconstructing the moment and his explanation of it. "Trying to distract him."

Barnhardt's smile is if anything more ghastly in commiseration. "Not what they said. The survivors. That's what I paid for. For their silence. For them to forget—*you*. Shooting. Them."

Whatever he'd felt before, running the code, a sense of airy remoteness, abstraction, whatever it was, during it and since, or that he often felt wandering down the halls of the hospital at the odd moment of despair—pretty much everything he'd felt for years except, and only recently, in Kate's arms—is nothing compared to the enveloping vastness he feels around him now. The door to the hall is a thousand feet away, nurses' voices out there as distant and content-less as the background track of the news on Barnhardt's room TV. He feels his breath shallow, rapid but exertionless, like a dog panting in the heat; he feels his vision beginning to narrow into a long gray tunnel that precedes a faint, imagines he really may slide off the chair onto the floor, his lab coat up around his shoulders like a toy doctor's costume.

Out of the deepening leaden fog, Barnhardt's voice snaps, "Wake up!" He waits a decent moment for Arkin to drag his gaze around to him, the bed, the room. "No one has to know, no one here. It's over. You know—done. Don't worry about the shit you swam through a dozen years ago. I took care of it. Worry about drowning now. That's how I feel. Worry about me."

"I explained," Arkin manages somehow. "There's too much going on with you, medically, to do what you want."

To which Barnhardt responds with a pause during which his chin sinks deeper into his chest as he appears to refocus, both within and toward Arkin. "I'm not asking you to *do* anything. I want you to *write* something. I want you to say, I want you to document, that I haven't had a drink in, what, a year. And that I should be put into a transplant program somewhere. I don't care where. That's all you have to do. You said my lungs are hurting—are damaging—my heart. So replacing the lungs would help, right?" Arkin doesn't answer. "And we know the liver is bad, because you spoke to that cunt . . ." Arkin's head lifts at the sudden vulgarity, the anger in Barnhardt's voice, which continues with, "That fucking cunt who fucked me!"

"I don't . . . I can't," is all Arkin can manage.

Barnhardt laughs, furious. "A *doctor* did this to me! You have to! I don't care if you think it will work or not! You people are wrong all the fucking time! All you have to say is I stopped drinking—for once, you'd be right about something!"

"But there're other records, from the Army, West Point . . ."

"Don't tell them! It's not hard! You just have to lie! And you save your career! How hard is that? How bad would it be for your friends here, and your profession, to know *what you did*?"

Neither man moves. Neither's expression changes: Barnhardt's yellow grin gaping angrily, bulging eyes and lips, Arkin's numbed impassivity.

Although it's not a thing uppermost in his mind, not a thing discussed in the halls of the units or their break rooms, health care workers do not lie, or rather, they do not lie to each other. There are any number of reasons for this beyond simple morality, chief among them that clinical decisions are based on data and reports provided by other clinicians, and intentionally inaccurate or falsified data can lead to unexpected bad outcomes, which will likely then be looked into, with the original falsification discovered. Arkin has been asked on occasion to perhaps *emphasize* a patient's need for, say, rehab versus home care, but he's never been asked to outright lie to other physicians. Then again, he's never been told he killed innocent civilian bystanders, never been told it was covered up, never been threatened with exposure. A panoply of potential loss flashes through his mind, his job, his license, the value of eleven years of college and residency and practice, Kate's good opinion of . . . and here, the parade of catastrophes stops. Kate is too new, her potential reaction and their future altogether too unknowable, his need for her too mysterious for him to think of anything but a single next step that will take him out of this room to somewhere else. He cannot think of anything other than escape, and he specifically cannot think he executed civilians at Mata Khan, an hour from Khost in Paktia Province of eastern Afghanistan.

The bargain he makes is entirely short term. He himself is functioning only in the short term, moment to moment. A minute into the future is beyond the featureless horizon of his paralysis. He barely manages a grotesque, "I need to think about what you've said." They will discuss again—*consideration* is what he commits to—he *understands* Barnhardt's anger and hurt. (Barnhardt actually laughs aloud at this.) *I need time to reflect*—Barnhardt smothers a giggle—*on my own situation*. He sounds like a management consultant. In return, Barnhardt, appearing to believe that time is on his side (except for his potential demise, which is not discussed), agrees to this, what, caesura? Agrees to short-term rehab, which will, in any case, lessen, his exposure to dangerous hospital pathogens, the possibility of a drug-resistant pneumonia for example, while Arkin . . . considers.

But Arkin considers nothing as he wanders down to the nurses' station, sits, and begins entering his discharge orders into the computer. In these, he will continue antibiotics, oral sodium chloride, spironolactone and furosemide in the guideline-consistent 5 to 2 ratio. He will continue lactulose for the elevated ammonia and incipient (or demonstrated?) encephalopathy and cardio-selective beta blocker for the heart failure. Barnhardt is already receiving these medications, they're all in the electronic record, so Arkin has only to check the box marked "continue" on the discharge med reconciliation and orders. Continue DVT prophylaxis, frequent ambulation, incentive spirometry, breathing treatments, CPAP at hours of sleep, and more—the medical equivalents of have a nice day. But Arkin holds to the security and certainty of "continue" with near-prayerful gratitude. Continue fluid restriction. The case manager has anticipated the discharge and arranged for a bed in a subacute rehab facility across the river, with a twenty-one-day stay preapproved. Arkin hesitates, hesitates some more, then free-texts a noncommittal and unrevealing "Continue sobriety" and hits enter. The orders submitted, and Arkin's electronic signature confirmed, Barnhardt becomes an outpatient and, on Arkin's newly narrowed horizon, out of sight.

Arkin thinks again of walking out of the hospital and up Route 9 to the Metro North station, imagines the rumble of dilapidated rail bed penetrating the worn fake rattan of the old MTA cars. Instead, he pours himself a black coffee in the group office; he doesn't remember consciously deciding on coffee, or more particularly on a coffee *break*, but coffee seems as reasonable as any other move he might make now. He thinks it will steady his nerves.

Or possibly, it's not nervousness Arkin feels. He has been nervous before, of course. He was nervous before baseball games; he was nervous before his occasional dates in high school. Later, he was especially nervous before his jumps at Airborne school; he remembers the etched and ashen faces of fellow trainees as they loaded aboard the C-130 at Lawson Field for their first jump, their "nerves" (he persists, for now, in avoiding the word "fear") accentuated by the awkwardness and overall helplessness imparted by seventy-plus pounds of equipment they carried, the noise of the turboprops, the shouting of instructors. He remembers his shock at the sight of the Hercules's open door in flight, the ground impossibly otherworldly and yet immediate and fast-moving below them, and his further shock at "green light" as his fellow trainees shuffled to the door and then *walked out of the airplane* and into the thin air and heavy prop blast. He remembers being so shocked at this final impossibility that he felt nothing at all as he lockstepped toward the door and then lurched into space, the opening parachute jerking him upright before he knew what had happened, the receding whine of the plane's turboprops replaced by the sound of his own animal hyperventilation.

But he doesn't think he was ever actually frightened before—or since—Afghanistan. Because there, the concern was not so much for what he was about to do (pitch, date, jump—in other words, *action*) as it was for the possibility of *extinction*. Of course, he feared pain, feared being wounded, feared the sight of his wounded comrades' blood and bone—but what took that fear to a whole other level was the potential for personal extinction.

And strangely, he realizes, that is what he fears now.

———————

By the time he shows up at her door, Kate has not seen or heard from Arkin in forty-eight hours. In her experience, not hearing from a man for two days after sleeping with him is a bad sign for the relationship, to which his reappearance now, drunk, is but a different but additional omen. But Arkin's state, she immediately sees, is more than simple drunkenness. For one, he cannot seem to sit still, moving first from the chair by the window to the bed, then to a kitchen stool, watching as she makes coffee. Whatever he drank, however much he drank, seems not to have calmed him. His hands shake; he flinches at traffic sounds. In fact, despite the odor of alcohol, she begins to think he's not drunk at all, but instead (merely?) in some state of shock.

Casually, as she pours coffee, she says, "Where'd you go tonight?" He mumbles, spills some sugar into his cup. "I thought of going to the Riverside, look for you. When you didn't call."

Arkin avoids her gaze as he sips, manages a muffled, "I'm sorry."

Kate shrugs, drinks some of her own coffee. She leans against the counter, studying him.

Slowly, as if disbelieving his own report: "I went to . . . Fridays. TGI. Fridays. On Route 9."

"Ah." She can't think of another response.

"I'd never been inside one before." There's a brief pause as he reflects. "I've never had . . . Jack Daniels . . . chicken strips."

"It's not . . . tasty?" *No,* he shakes his head. "Would you like something to eat?" Again, he shakes his head. After a moment, she asks, "Are you all right?"

Softly, "No." He takes another sip of the coffee; she notices his hand is steadier this time. "I don't know what I'm doing."

FIVE

ARKIN HAS NEVER OWNED a gun. On paper, he inherited the family Mossberg but had never reclaimed it from the police after his mother killed herself with it. In the Army, everyone carried the government's weapons, in his case an M4A1 rifle. Arkin has only rarely thought about this in the years since, of his assigned weapon, the solid factuality of it in his hand, or slung over his shoulder, night and day for months on end. In his first few weeks in Afghanistan, he'd attached a grenade launcher, but he'd never used it, never liked the extra weight of it, and returned it to the arms room. But as for the rifle itself, for many months after leaving Afghanistan, Arkin would catch himself looking around for it before leaving his apartment, or a classroom, the limb-ness of it, its phantom absence.

Not that Arkin liked guns especially. He liked knowing about them, and being comfortable with them, and he especially liked shooting them well, even phenomenally well. Shockingly well? In retrospect, he may have "liked" his own rifle because it performed so reliably well for him, but he didn't like it as a thing apart from its performance, and he didn't like guns in general or even other guns he'd carried. He'd carried an M9 pistol, for example, and while he'd qualified expert with it, his preternatural skill with the rifle never translated to handguns, and he didn't feel the oneness with it he felt with his M4. It would not have occurred to him to think of the M9 as a limb.

He thinks of this now as he crosses the Neversink River at Port Jervis, and then the Delaware River, and on into Pennsylvania. It's not that he's in Pennsylvania to buy a gun—although the range he's located online does sell guns and also rents them. He wonders now whether other people who've lived with guns continuously at their side, as he had done, feel not just the weapon's absence afterward, but instead, a weakness. He was not accustomed to thinking of a gun as an object of power. Obviously, it gave the shooter power; that was inescapable. But now he wonders whether the power his rifle gave to kill at a distance prefigured his power as a doctor to—here his line of thinking stalls. To what? He can think of no useful analogy. As a doctor, he is a figure of authority to his patients and their families, but a figure of power? Of power over life and death? Hardly; even the use of that phrase would elicit a smirk from colleagues who reflexively feel themselves power*less* in the face of patients' deaths, which are often inevitable, even predictable. Authority, yes—after all, they're the ones who write the *orders*. But powerless also at the hands of administrators, insurers, conservators, QC evaluators, coders and billers, and on and on. Doctors are mostly merely tolerated by the nurses—and inevitably, this recalls for him Kate's early departure for the hospital that morning, leaving him in bed for the first of two days off. He has a memory of her expression, possibly of concern but also of doubt and perhaps some weariness as well. He can't blame her. He can't remember ever doing such a thing, showing up at a woman's apartment not just so late, or even unannounced and drunk, but so lost.

He remembers falling spectacularly and stupidly silent, sitting there at the kitchen table, unable to tell her the cause, the connection with Barnhardt both too complicated and too mysterious to Arkin himself to be shared. He thinks of the simple transactions by which Barnhardt appears to have lived his life. Pay impoverished villagers to forget wartime atrocities; threaten his physician with ruin to obtain falsified medical records. Arkin's inability to say no, or to say yes, or to walk out of the room, or to call for witnesses, or to tell Kate, or his director, or the risk management team, or to actually *do* anything about the threat Barnhardt has leveled at him is what has propelled him onto Interstate 84 and this flight to a gun range. He fears he is poised at some fulcrum between lying to others and self-deceit, between past and present, between the life he has constructed and—the word comes back to him—extinction. He begins to feel that the multiple unexplained extinctions in his past—the suicide of his mother, the absence since birth of his father, the killing of Kelly, the incessant deaths of patients—are preludes to personal disappearance.

He saves himself further reflection in this vein by taking the next exit. At the bottom of the ramp, there's a left onto the Lake Wallenpaupack Road, following the map on his phone, and on into the Poconos of southeastern Pennsylvania. Arkin has been to rural Pennsylvania only once before. Over spring break, while in his first year of medical school in Greenville, he'd driven north with the idea of seeing Washington, DC. He didn't know anyone in Washington and could just as easily have gone to Philadelphia or south to Florida. Still just two years out of the Army, he wanted to see the Capitol and the White House, possibly the Pentagon, center of the Army command structure that had so directed his life. Instead, on the way there, he was sidetracked by famous names along the way: Wilderness, Spotsylvania, Fredericksburg, Chancellorsville. By the accident of his northward route, he visited them in reverse historical order, beginning with Spotsylvania Court House, where he looked at the remnants of the Confederate earthworks known as the Mule Shoe, where Union forces experienced nine thousand casualties in a single day, May 9, 1864. From there, he'd driven about ten miles to the northwest, to the site of the Wilderness Battlefield, where only five days earlier, the Union had lost eighteen thousand killed or injured. A year before that, in spring of 1863 (and four miles to the east in his old Chevy Nova), another eighteen thousand Union dead at Chancellorsville. And finally, six months before that, in December 1862, the Union had lost twelve thousand killed or wounded at Fredericksburg. An additional six-mile drive to the east, Arkin had stopped at the Cancun Mexican Margarita Bar and Grill, enjoyed the Mexican Pizza. In Fredericksburg, after lunch (We bring Cancun to Fredericksburg!) Arkin had walked around the battlefield, stared at monuments to the Fifth Corps, the Irish Brigade, the Seventh Michigan, and to Richard Kirkland, a Confederate Army sergeant. Arkin read how, on the morning of December 14, 1862, Kirkland looked out from behind the stone wall at Marye's Heights and saw that many of the eight thousand Union soldiers shot the day before were still lying on the battlefield, alive. He gathered canteens, blankets, and clothing and went to help, walking out onto the battlefield not once but many times. Soldiers on both sides watched for hours as he worked, but no one fired a shot. Kirkland later fought at Chancellorsville, and at Gettysburg, and was killed at Chickamauga.

Driving away, Arkin had reflected on the dead and wounded—over one hundred thousand—recorded within this single Virginia county, the battlefields within ten miles of one another, so many years before. While at Chancellorsville, he'd read a brochure that mentioned that there'd been 384 battles during the Civil War, the first at Fort Sumter, the last at Appomattox Court House. There were no dead at Fort Sumter, and only about five hundred killed at Appomattox before the remaining thirty thousand soldiers of Lee's army surrendered. In between, almost a million soldiers, nearly one in every ten eligible men in the whole country, had died.

So Arkin had decided to go on to Gettysburg, the site of the worst battle of that war, during that earlier visit. At the time, Arkin was twenty-five years old, and the largest fight he'd experienced, in Afghanistan, had involved the entire Second Battalion of the Eighty-Seventh, around seven hundred men. At Gettysburg, one hundred seventy-five thousand men fought, about a third of whom were killed or wounded. Arkin could not imagine such a collision, such casualties, particularly as he drove through the placid countryside, taking back roads to avoid the traffic of modern America. He'd passed signs for the sites of still more battles: Manassas, Winchester, Fort Collier, New Market. He passed also the Tysons Galleria and the Fair Oaks Mall, where (signs told him) there was a new Apple Store, a J.Crew, a Pottery Barn, Michael Kors, and Williams Sonoma. His mother had liked to shop at the Williams Sonoma in Colorado Springs—the Promenade Shops at Briargate, their mall was called. She would look at copper pans and muffin tins while her son stared at the windows of Victoria's Secret, eight stores away. The country's flagrant abundance, the ebullient sameness of its commerce, both as a child and later, on the way to Gettysburg, stunned him.

Arkin found it hard to imagine what the field hospitals must have been like at Gettysburg. He thought about it at the battlefield itself, as he walked north on the Emmitsburg Road, looking east toward Cemetery Ridge. There, Pickett led and ended his famous charge, which lasted less than an hour and left six thousand dead and wounded on the gentle incline of the hillside. There was chloroform, Arkin had read, so most of the wounded felt minimal pain as their broken limbs were amputated. But their doctors knew little of infection, much less how to prevent it, so many of those men later died of sepsis. Arkin knows, because he saw it firsthand, that Americans injured in Afghanistan almost always survived their wounds, 97 percent of them did, he and his fellow soldiers were told. It was there that Arkin had first heard of the "golden hour," meaning the time after injury in which wounds had to be managed and bleeding controlled in order for the injured to survive. But later, a medic had told him what really mattered was the "platinum ten minutes," that an hour was too long, that survival hinged on those first few moments after being wounded. Arkin had thought about that, too, as he walked through the National Cemetery at Gettysburg, how the wounded there had lain on the battlefield for hours on that sunny day in July 1863 and then died. Of course, those few who survived their wounds mostly lived well enough, unlike many of those he saw injured in Afghanistan, whose traumatic brain injuries and spinal cord paralyses and extensive amputations were far more extreme than anything a Civil War soldier could have survived. Most soldiers today lived in fear of such injuries, of the lives they would lead after, with their trajectories forever altered at age nineteen or twenty; the old men were twenty-five.

Now, almost ten years later, he wonders whether those facts and fears might have started him thinking of medical school even earlier than Mata Khan, before the attainment of critical mass in that moment, the heat of which drove him from the trajectory his own life had followed until that day. Arkin was not unmindful that teaming with Kelly had awakened in him a certain fierce tranquility around their success in long distance (even clinical) elimination (the clinical word) of their enemy. Arkin is also not unmindful now—although such terms were unavailable to him at the time—that this was possibly a reaction formation prompted by his mother's suicide, as though the inevitability of enemy combatants' deaths at their hands somehow obscured the mysterious inevitability of his mother's by her own. That experiencing some depersonalization of the one category of death might denature the grief ignited by the other.

Death is death, Arkin might have thought to himself, having learned that death could indeed be inevitable at a thousand yards, the same distance as Arkin's high school from his mom's home office, where she shot and killed herself. *Why* she did so was, and remained, more problematic. But when Kelly died, even this line of thinking was exposed for the ludicrous proposition, the wobbly defense, it had always been. He didn't *love* the Tajik warriors he and Kelly killed; he didn't love Kelly, for that matter, but in the moment Kelly died, whatever distance he had placed between the death of his mother— the sole object of a fatherless boy's love—and his own plodding journey to that village near Firebase Salerno collapsed, and with it, it seems, his entire fictionalization of death. He understands that the *elimination* of disease is not the same as the *elimination* of a human enemy but grasps the irony of the transposition, the possibly desperate substitution. So Arkin never again fired his rifle. And in the ten years since, had never considered *arming* himself until now, surrounded by the rolling hills of Pennsylvania, about three hours north and east of Gettysburg.

He drives past Cake and Scones Bakery (Good Coffee Sold Here!) and the Keystone Propane store, arriving at a four-way stop empty of buildings. He follows a dirt road trailing a meandering creek (Creek Road), turning a couple miles later onto Deep Hollow Road and then into the drive marked "Wall-Pack Bench Rest Club," and beneath it "Birthplace of 1,000 yard Shooting." Arkin pulls into the customer parking area, by an arrowed sign reading "Firearm Rentals," and then—with no memory of leaving his car or going into the shop—finds himself staring at dozens of weapons displayed behind locked glass cases, a few familiar, many not, pistols, rifles, shotguns.

"Can I help you?" This from a burly middle-aged man in jeans, a polo shirt marked "Wall-Pack Instructor." He wears a name tag, "Paul Shepherd, Instructor/Coach," and an NRA baseball cap with a caption, "Stand and Fight." "What can I do for you?" the man asks, his voice an aggressive, smoke-coarsened rumble.

"I understand I can rent..." here Arkin's lack of planning reveals itself. "A rifle?" Shepherd does not conceal his skepticism and perhaps his suspicion—Arkin looks more like a reporter than a prospective NRA member. "I haven't done this in a while."

"You shoot as a kid?"

"Army," Arkin manages.

Paul inclines his head, Arkin's answer serving merely to invite greater skepticism and more questions. "What'd you shoot in the Army?"

Arkin pauses, gathers himself around the old list: "M16. Then an M24, M110. Then a M4A1."

And with that succession of succinct designations, the fact that Arkin knows them, the atmosphere changes. Everyone in the Army trains on the M16, had since Vietnam, but Instructor/Coach Shepherd appears to know that snipers fire the 24 or 110 and that only "special ops" units carry the M4A1. On the other hand (and in truth, Shepherd still appears somewhat dubious), Arkin appreciates that in his chinos and button collar oxford shirt, he doesn't look much like anyone's idea of *special ops*. His Honda Civic out in the parking lot doesn't scream Airborne eagle. Accordingly, Shepherd offers only a noncommittal, "Okay."

Arkin scans the displayed weapons, putting, he hopes, a neutral face on the building regret that he's come all this way and no small degree of embarrassment at the way he's handling the moment.

Shepherd prods him with a too-polite, "What would you like to shoot today?" Arkin's eye settles on one rifle that looks familiar. "That one? That's a Heckler & Koch." Shepherd's voice takes on a bit of singsong quality, authoritative and with the sort of homey feeling one has about only the most familiar of subjects. "MR762A1, based on the HK417. You mighta seen some of them . . . Where were you in the Army?"

Arkin regrets mentioning the military at all now. "Benning," he says, leaving out the years and assignments that followed. Shepherd is unimpressed. "I think some Marines in . . . jump school . . . carried them. Some Navy guys." It's likely that Shepherd, unless he'd gone to Army jump school himself, is unaware that Marines train there, too, along with Navy Seals. But he relents, takes down the HK, offers it to Arkin.

Improbably, Arkin thinks—as he first holds the rifle—how much hands and touch matter in medicine. He has learned to feel for the pulsation of the abdominal aorta as a sign of potential dissection and rupture. He can hear the thrum of valvular stenosis in his patients' heartbeats, can palpate an enlarged liver in cirrhosis or spleen in lymphoma. With the rifle, now, he feels the sheen of gun oil, the fine heft of its ten and a half pounds, its balance point just ahead of the trigger guard. He doesn't remember ever having fired the HK417, much less its civilian variant, but it seems like sense memory when he finds the selector under his right thumb, flicks it to safe, then ejects the magazine, racks the charging handle and locks it with the bolt catch, checks the empty chamber. All this happens not even automatically but almost autonomously, as though the rifle itself were guiding the process, Arkin its instrument. He wonders idly as he continues his inspection of the weapon—its front flip-up and rear diopter sights—whether any medical equipment has ever felt quite this familiar to him, this natural. Even his stethoscope, which he uses dozens of times a day year in and out, doesn't *fall to hand* (the phrase comes to mind) quite so readily, so comfortably. Arkin slaps the magazine back into its receiver, thumbs the bolt catch, feels the action spring slide the bolt back into place.

"Can I try it?" Arkin asks this unthinkingly, since of course it's why he's traveled all this way, to ask this question, to have it answered. He lifts the weapon to his shoulder, takes in the sight picture, flicks the safety off, dry fires.

"Sure," Shepherd says, his tone completely altered by the behavior of this now clearly non-novice, non-reporter. "We charge two and a quarter per round, sixteen bucks for seven shots, that covers the weapon rental—"

"That's fine." Arkin cuts him off. "That's fine," he says again, softly, as he puts the weapon back on safe, hands it to Shepherd. "Set me up," he says, turns, and heads for the range.

As he exhales and squeezes the trigger, as the first round leaves the weapon, as the bolt racks backward and forward, as the first shell casing is ejected, as the first wave of sound reaches his ears, as the first blast of superheated gas exits the muzzle, as the bullet spins three thousand times per second, as it accelerates toward two thousand miles per hour, as the recoil pad bucks into his shoulder, as the buttstock rasps against his cheek, for the first time in a decade, Arkin feels complete. It is not just that he hits the target—all six inches of it—at four hundred yards. He expected to do that, expected his half-target-width adjustment for wind would be correct, that his aiming point eighteen inches high, with the rifle zeroed at one hundred yards, would allow for the expected fall of the bullet in the half second it took to reach the target.

And it's not just that the alignment of the rifle barrel with his body has perfectly transmitted the weapon's recoil in such a way that the sight has returned exactly to his aiming point, despite the twenty foot-pounds of impact against his shoulder after the half ounce of gunpowder in the NATO round detonated. It's not just that he hasn't flinched or that his finger has followed through smoothly and precisely after the initial squeeze on the trigger, long after the first bullet hit the target, the next cartridge fed into the chamber, the bolt head pivoted and locked into the receiver, the rifle ready to fire again a tenth of a second later. It's more than that.

It's the exact correctness of the entire picture: of the feel of his body against the range mat, the instant silence after the report, the sound of birdcalls filtering past his ear protection, the acrid lingering smell of propellent, the mild breeze from the south ruffling his hair, pressing lightly against his left temple, reminding him of those first days in sniper school at the Burroughs and Galloway Ranges at Fort Benning, soft breezes hot off the Chattahoochee River and coastal plain of Alabama beyond.

He can sense Shepherd behind him, spotting the impact in the X ring of the target, this without a scope, the first round out of the rifle, hears the sharp, surprised inhalation—the X ring is three inches across—and Arkin doubts Shepherd has ever seen a shot like it at such a range, cold, on an unfamiliar rented rifle. Because it could have been chance, but mostly because Arkin is feeling an unusual sensation, which he cannot recall feeling in *years* but which he is able now to identify as one of complete *relaxation* (and possibly, more foreign still, of complete *confidence*), he fires another round, and then another, and then a fourth, all into the X ring, the last two actually obliterating the center of the X itself, but discernibly separate rounds nonetheless, striking within an eighth of an inch of one another, inside a three-inch ring, twelve hundred feet away.

"Wow," Shepherd whispers, to which Arkin reports to himself: *That's nothing.*

And that phrase, spoken only within him, within a surrounding silence disturbed only by the echo of the last shot fired, suddenly encapsulates everything Arkin thinks he knows about himself. Whether it's Barnhardt's threat to destroy him, or Oliver's confession of having destroyed Barnhardt, or Kelly's (and his own?) destruction of the Afghan village outside Firebase Salerno, *That's nothing* seems to have been the emotional chord played out in his head, as when Kate's patient had died, as with the twenty-some patients he sees daily, the hundreds each month, the thousands in his career, their cries and spells and pains and dispiriting prognoses, all met with a silent *That's nothing* inside Arkin, who now wonders, *Where did that come from?* Because he cannot remember not feeling this way, although he thinks (now, at this instant, with the last gunshot *still* echoing) that there must have been such a time. And as he thinks, there comes to him an image from his childhood, of a grand old narrowleaf cottonwood, fifty feet tall, that he'd often climbed as a boy of five and six, so light at that age that it could support his weight almost to its top. From which he could see, from the spot the cottonwood grew in Cheyenne Canyon Park, almost all of Colorado Springs spread out below him, the boy Arkin laughing and screaming with excitement and pride at the height he'd climbed, and the sights he saw, down to his mother who sat below with the picnic she'd brought for their lunch. And he could see his mother laughing, too, at one of his Little League games at El Pomar and yelling for him as he rounded the bases on his way home during a game, the other parents, dads mostly, laughing and clapping for him, and her.

With that, Arkin fires a fifth round, across the near quarter mile to the target, as unerring and luminously precise as the ones before it, passing through the now-empty space of the X ring, the hole blown open by the four rounds before, but he and Shepherd can both see the puff of backstop dirt behind the target, signaling its passage though that space. And Arkin thinks again of his mother, this time not of her laughing but again now of his silent *That's nothing*, knowing that it was born when she died, when the incomprehensibility of her death took over the inner life of the boy who'd climbed the tree, slugged the home run, brought home stories, fished in the summer, played ball into the autumn. That here with this rifle, as in other places and times with another weapon, he most perfectly controls and excludes everything that has gone before and that may come after this particular focus, this particular bullet's flight, this particular impact.

He wonders when he stopped thinking about that day, about his mother's death, about the woman herself, Alma. He knows that in Spanish, "alma" means "soul." He wondered whether his mother ever thought about that, when contemplating killing herself, for however long that contemplation lasted—months? days? seconds?—that she was giving up, surrendering up, her soul. He had many questions along these lines. Had she thought she was giving him up, to whatever vicissitudes might await a seventeen-year-old boy alone in the world, or had she thought he was old enough not to need her any longer? Arkin has treated suicidal patients and knows most of them thought their loved ones would be better off with them dead. Arkin cannot imagine, even now, why Alma might have felt that way about him. But it's true she had sought out a perfectly un-soulful way through life, abandoned as *she* was by Arkin's father and her own family. She gave up school, gave up the love of art she may have had, gave up on relationships with men, gave up on everything but Arkin, whom she accompanied as long as she could before exiting life. He wondered if she herself thought, *That's nothing,* all those years, and whether it was this, even at the end, that allowed her to pick up the Mossberg and wedge it (because it must have barely fit) beneath her chin and pull the trigger.

SIX

KATE SITS IN THE break room, her lunch a Cobb salad from the cafeteria, the other nurses jammed in around her eating delivered anchovy and pepperoni pizza, the traditional unit pie. They laugh and tell stories about their patients, about the nurse manager, and about their children and husbands and boyfriends, the shows they're watching on Netflix and Amazon. They'd like to hear anything she's willing to say about . . . but she doesn't even know what to call him. Probably not her boyfriend—better "her guy," or better yet, "her new guy," neatly deflecting the commitment questions. Nurses are among the most practical people on the planet, Kate has always believed, their frank experience of the frankest parts of humanity—birth, blood, terror, shit, piss—inclining them toward a blunt acceptance of the facts of life. "I've blown a hundred guys hoping each one would be *the* one," one nurse friend had told her. "Big no-fucking deal," and laughed.

But Kate's experience of her *new guy* eludes the normal categories. She has never dated a doctor before and finds it inter-esting—given the totality with which the physician-nurse boundary defines hospital life—how rarely she thinks of Arkin as a doctor. She knows the other nurses think of him as "one of the good ones," but this, though a compliment, is not especially definitive. *Good* doctors can be good for any number of reasons, at least in the as-always-frank view of nurses. It may mean that—whether out of competence or simple attention—they don't kill patients. That on occasion some doctors do in fact kill patients angers nurses, not unreasonably, voiding their normal nonchalance about death. That patients die, after all, is a given: they're old and sick, most of them, and many of them "have permission," meaning variously that they or their families have agreed to DNR orders, or comfort measures, or simple if unspoken palliation in the face of overwhelmingly poor outlook. Sometimes, it means patients themselves have declined aggressive care (not uncommon), or most care (less common), or have actually stopped eating and drinking (uncommon). Depending on their moment-to-moment condition, such patients may be said, by the nurses, to be "circling," as in circling the drain, or "heading to the light," as in heavenly.

Nurses generally like these developments since they, more than anyone else in health care, experience the suffering of patients directly and intimately. They spend many of their twelve-hour shifts struggling to manage what is often unmanageable in the way of cancer pain, or the mad winds of advanced dementia, or shortness of breath, or uncontrolled vomiting and diarrhea, or hypotension in septic shock, and so on. They have little patience for doctors who are unable to face the inevitability of their patients' deaths or, more often, the ignorance or denialism or religiosity or "fight to the end" mentality of family members. But they also have no patience for doctors who make lazy mistakes. Kate's colleagues are still ablaze over one physician's failure some months earlier to replace potassium, or even check potassium levels, in a patient with clostridium difficile diarrhea, admitted with near-critical low levels of it, who then proceeded to shit out the rest of her meager stores and go into cardiac arrest a few hours later. The doctor involved is a member of Arkin's same group and is treated with near universal disdain by the nurses for what they view as a truly careless mistake. They have all made mistakes, of all kinds, but they think this physician just didn't *care* enough to avoid this most obvious of errors.

None of the nurses think of Arkin this way. Now that he and Kate are dating, the nurses speak of him with a sort of insouciant approval, neither too demonstrative (in case Kate dumps him) or too affectionate (in case he dumps her). But they like him, she knows. They like that he sometimes seeks out their opinions about patients. They like that he answers questions about his orders, even sometimes explains himself before they have a chance to ask. They like that he sits at a computer poring over old records, lab reports, vital signs, even the nurses' own assessments, which almost no one reads. In short, he seems to care, and he is diligent. It does not occur to them that he's diligent because he's terrified of missing something, a fear which Kate has begun to sense in him. It would not occur to them that his outward confidence masks anything inward, probably because Arkin doesn't do any of the things that some other doctors do that irritate them. He doesn't make bad jokes about patients. He doesn't send the nurses pornographic text messages. He doesn't eat the food in their break room unless invited. He doesn't favor younger nurses over older ones. When nurses flirted with him (before Kate came on the scene), he didn't dissolve with pleasure. Some of the nurses might wish he'd paid them more attention at the time, but all the nurses like that he pays attention to their patients. Probably, they suspect he drinks too much, just as many of them do, and sense in him the same combination of fatigue and fatalism and sadness they feel themselves, which finds its way to the conscious sedation of alcohol.

But Kate wonders *why* Arkin cares about patients. *Caring,* in general, is not something nurses talk about much, possibly because on one level, the experience and work of nursing is a simple thing: most nurses are women, and women care about things like sick people. Kate knows her women friends at work might argue that this was an old-fashioned way of thinking about the sexes while at the same time laughing at the idea that there was anything really new about the way men feel about such things. Though it's also not something they talk about, Kate thinks most of them feel that the "workplace revolution" is all about how women have changed, not the men around them, basically—and this is evident among her nurse friends—by not giving a shit what the men around the hospital think of them. Of course, there're male nurses who care, but Kate thinks they care mostly because it's part of the job. Male nurses rarely cry about their patients; in fact, Kate can't remember ever seeing one of them do so. Women nurses do cry, though usually quietly, in the med room or the supply room, and briefly, with a hug from an alert friend—a woman friend—and then go back to work.

Kate wonders if Arkin cries about patients but doesn't think so. She remembers crying in front of him, a little, the day the patient in 868 died, the day she first met him. Sylvia Warren, that was the patient's name. Kate knows female nurses connect with their patients in a way male nurses don't. Male nurses don't see themselves in the wizened old men—the elderly guys struggling for air, or to walk, or urinate, or find a word—in the way female nurses do. The girls see themselves precisely and viscerally in the fat old ladies with sagging bellies and pendulous breasts and prolapsed uteruses. Kate, at thirty, is poised at the apogee of womanhood's arc (or perhaps a little beyond?) from first period to last, from the first budding of her chest at Tanner Stage Two to the intertrigo of under-breast yeast infections in old age. Most of her friends have had children already and are even more keenly aware of intimate and inalterable changes. This is part of each woman's life, and just as they have supplanted an older generation on the intoxicating curve of sexual power, so too are they now being supplanted by younger, perfect girls. All women know this. Some fight, but all know.

Kate wonders what it means that neither she nor Arkin have had children, that they have found each other with this nonentry on their sexual resume—*and* that they have never discussed it. The obvious explanation would be something in their childhoods. She knows Arkin's mother committed suicide, knows that much; he has never mentioned a father. Kate thinks of her own growing up as entirely conventional, parents attentive and loving and sober, though both gone early, in late middle age. So Arkin and she, childless orphans, cast adrift on a sea of . . . here she stops, laughing at herself, *of bourbon,* she thinks—with which Arkin rounds the corner, lets slip a lopsided smile, fugitive, but for her. For a second, she feels the planets align, gravity spinning the two of them around, binary for just that moment, and then he asks: "You have the man in 27?" To which, in a voice softer than she'd intended, feeling the change in space between them, she answers, "I do." The magic words, she thinks, with a brief smile of her own, as she pushes past him.

––––––––

The man in 27 is ninety-two. He is: tremulous, a scattered few wandering long white hairs emerging from a liver spotted scalp, his arms tendinous and veined, ecchymotic with venipuncture sites and bloodied with skin tears. Empty, milky blue eyes stare away from them, up at the perplexing acoustic tile overhead. He has advanced dementia, has been aspirating the diet of pureed food and thickened liquids he's fed at his nursing home. He was admitted on Arkin's day off with a fever and tachycardia and hypoxemia and was treated for health care–associated pneumonia because of his residence in a nursing home. Kate watches Arkin, how he places the bell of his stethoscope on the patient's chest, almost gently, closes his eyes to concentrate on the sounds of the heart, just an inch beneath the emaciated chest wall, devoid of muscle at this stage. After a while, Arkin straightens, says, "He has a muffled S2."

"Ah," Kate says.

"And a murmur, crescendo murmur. Stenosed."

"Oh, well then," Kate says, smiling at him. The old man in the bed is oblivious, of course. "How was your day off?"

"It was interesting." And then, "What are you doing later?" And after another moment, "Want to go for a ride?" Kate gives a brief nod of assent, curious, waiting, but Arkin returns to work, nodding at their patient. "So this guy, family been in?"

"Night shift said his daughter came in about eight. Stayed five minutes and left."

"Five," Arkin repeats. He gazes down at the old man, who licks his lips, closes his eyes as if savoring . . . something . . . then farts loudly—a long, soft, bubbling, emissive proof of life, gut-wise. Kate sighs. Arkin gazes at the old man for another moment then asks of the empty air above him, "I don't suppose he has advanced directives. Living will?"

"No."

"And his daughter?"

"Wants everything done."

Turning to her, he asks, "What should we do?"

"What do you mean?"

"He's chronically aspirating. Even if he doesn't eat, he aspirates his own saliva. May even be aspirating thrush out of his mouth and throat and has a fungal pneumonia. He has aortic insufficiency. Should I get CT surgery to come see him for a new valve?"

Kate can hear the irony, thinks she hasn't seen this side of Arkin before. "Daughter said something about a PEG tube. I got that in report."

Now it's Arkin's turn to sigh. "I'll tell her no, if she asks again."

"Can you just do that?"

"Yes. It's futile; it won't extend his life or improve it. And no one would put one in anyway."

"Could she sue you? Or GI?"

"Yeah. Sure."

"You ever been sued?"

"No. You?"

"No. But I'm just a nurse."

Arkin turns to look at her, meets her cool gaze, gray eyes. "Huh. 'Just a nurse.'"

Kate feels a momentary chill, a breath of sadness mixed with affection. Into the silence between them, she whispers, "Hi, Doc."

Arkin nods once, then, matching her tone, "Hello, Kate."

The old man punctuates their exchange with a prolonged cadence of vowels and consonants, completely nonsensical. "He defervesced?"

"Yep. Nothing for twenty-four hours."

"QTC is under four and a quarter. We'll skip an antifungal. Let's get him on Levaquin, get him out of here."

"Back to his nursing home?"

Arkin nods, adds, "I'll call the daughter, tell her how dangerous the hospital is." He pauses, touches the old man's wrist, sees the raised veins, an old chickenpox scar from childhood, fading remnants of callous on the fingers. "And how useless."

―――――――――

As Arkin drives east on Route 84, Kate looks at the passing topography of southeastern New York, the foothills of a low and old mountain range called the Taconics, she recalls. High atop a hill to their right are the imposing buildings of the Fishkill Correctional Facility, with its seventeen hundred prisoners. To the left, across the highway, is its maximum security counterpart, Downstate Correctional, double-ringed with barbwire-topped fences.

"God, this is cheerful."

"Just wait."

"I know. So great you're taking me to a nursing home. Did you ever work in one?"

"No. You?"

"Just in school, my first term of clinicals. I almost quit. I think a lot of new nurses have to start in nursing homes now."

"You didn't?"

She shakes her head. "Not in those days. Went right to ICU at Westchester. Then I worked in the city. Then I went to Santa Barbara. Dream job."

"I've never been. Wine country, right?"

"Not really. Close." Then, "Why are you doing this? For what's his name?"

"Barnhardt." Arkin's stare is fixed on the road ahead. "He wants something from me. I thought . . . I'd like for you to be there."

Kate prompts, perfectly neutral. "Okay."

"Why'd you go into nursing?"

Arkin must have a reason for such an awkward change of subject, Kate thinks, before accommodating it. "Well, I needed to make a living." Arkin offers her a ludicrously encouraging glance. "And . . . everything else seemed so . . . dull, I guess. Working in an office. Maybe doing IT I had a scholarship to SUNY for that, but it just, I just thought before I knew it I'd be fat, forty . . ."

"Fertile."

"We're not talking about gallbladder disease. I was in high school when my dad died. He had a heart attack. They did CPR on the kitchen floor. I followed the ambulance. There was more CPR in the emergency room. I saw this nurse, maybe five feet tall. My father was a big man. She climbed up on the gurney, knelt over him, did compressions." Arkin glances at her, in the grip of memory even now. "I'm sure he was dead. He was down ten minutes before the paramedics got there. I'm sure they knew. But that nurse, her . . . determination. Her . . . anger. I'd never seen anything like it. She didn't care how she looked. She didn't care what anybody thought about her. I wanted to feel like that." She looks over at him now. "Go ahead. Come on."

Arkin considers this for a long moment. "I wanted . . . it wasn't anything very dramatic. I wanted . . . to atone." Kate is startled at the word. "You know how my mom died. You know I was in the Army. People died." Kate notes the ambiguous agency of "People died" but says nothing. "I wanted to accomplish something . . . better, I think. *Do* something." He grins ruefully before adding an ironic, "Help."

"You do," Kate says. "You're so good at this."

Arkin shakes his head. "I just work. I just do a job. I show up." With a glance at Kate, he says, "You're the ones who really make the difference. You make them feel better. You hold their hands, you listen to them, you take away their pain."

"You order the medications." Arkin shrugs. Kate studies him a moment, the hills of the lower Hudson Valley passing by in the window behind him, a season passing by. "You ever think of doing some other kind of medicine?" This gets a glance. "Maybe go somewhere, somewhere interesting where people don't have doctors, medical care."

"There was some group," he recalls vaguely. "They went for like two weeks to Thailand or Cambodia. There was something happening—I couldn't go." He glances at her again. "You mean like that?"

"No. Something more. Doctors Without Borders maybe. Go for a year, more, whatever."

"Well," he says and actually looks at her, long enough that Kate begins to worry about the road ahead. Finally, he looks back to it and says her name: "Kate."

"Abel," she says, amused. It's the first time he's heard her use his first name, that he can recall.

"No one calls me that," he says, "unless I'm in trouble."

"Hmm," she says, followed by a derisive little snort and an assertive pat on his shoulder.

"Like I said, it's the nurses who make the difference."

In the end, they don't see Barnhardt. Or rather, they see him, but Barnhardt—who appears to be sleeping when they find him in the lounge of the nursing home, three days out from discharge—cannot be awakened, is unresponsive even to the so-called "noxious" stimuli which Kate tries, a sternal rub, as Arkin calls for the latest lab results. Which an obliging and worried LPN provides even though she's never met Arkin and he's not on staff; but he clearly is a doctor and what the doctor says goes, particularly when it's your patient who's unconscious without your having noticed.

Arkin even rides along in the ambulance, Kate following behind in his car. In the ambulance, he orders hypertonic saline and again, though he has no official role here and the paramedics don't work for the hospital, his instruction is followed. So by the time they reach the hospital, Barnhardt has already groggily come to, sodium level probably already rising toward 120 milliequivalents, though this is only Arkin's guess.

He climbs out of the ambulance first, somewhat to the surprise of the ER nurses and techs, who know him only from inside the emergency room rather than the loading area outside, handing them the blue, lavender, and red top vacutainer tubes, which he has also had drawn in the ambulance. He tells them, in passing, about the "fifty ccs of three percent hypertonic saline" Barnhardt's already received then disappears into the physician's office in the ER to do the admission orders.

Which is where Kate finds him after she parks the car. He glances up at her as she comes into the room, even as he continues dictating the H&P. "Plan, number one, hyponatremia. Patient has received hypertonic saline in the ambulance, and we will check lytes every four hours seeking a maximum increase of not more than ten milliequivalents in a twenty-four-hour period. Number two, end-stage hepatic failure secondary to cirrhosis . . ." He pauses the dictating software, staring bleakly at the monitor, the lab values there.

"So I guess it's not date night after all," Kate says.

"No, I'm just doing this because . . ." and there he stops, unsure of *because*. He considers, offers at last: "Because I know him."

"Oh." There's a silence between them, Arkin seated and staring at the monitor, Kate standing, stranded. "I don't have a way home," she says eventually.

"I'll just finish this," Arkin tells her before adding, "I'm not staying."

"I was in Afghanistan during the war. I was twenty. Twenty-one." They're back at the Riverside Bar, where Kate had joined him that first time, that night of the day they met. Outside, the mountains rising in the west have taken on the slightly dingier cast of their late summer fade. Inside the bar, Arkin is again drinking bourbon with beer back, Kate again a margarita. To Kate, it feels as though there have been no intervening days, that Arkin's story—as stories in bars often do—has simply resumed after a pause, a breath of uncertain length, with no change of the unfolding through line. She also feels she has spent possibly too much time listening to men telling her stories in bars. She hopes—believes, she insists to herself—that Arkin's story, however delayed, is true, which would set it apart from most of those others. It is certainly . . . different.

"I was a sniper, part of a sniper team. A very good sniper team." This seems to matter to him, although it is said with little inflection, presented as information rather than commentary. Kate notes to herself that no man has ever said *this* to her before, in a bar or otherwise. Arkin clarifies, though it brings him no closer to any sort of bar chat norm, "I was the spotter."

Unsure of the appropriate response, down an utterly unfamiliar conversational pathway, Kate offers, "You didn't shoot?"

Very deliberately, he tells her, "I was the spotter on our team. I . . . identified targets. But I was . . . trained. I was a good shot. Very good."

"Don't hear that around the hospital much," she says.

Arkin, recalling his trip to the range in Pennsylvania, observes, "There're about eight hundred thousand MDs in the United States. I would be the best one, with a rifle."

Kate finds this hard to square with his smile, which is gentle, almost wistful. "That makes me feel . . ." she says before pausing to wonder exactly how it does make her feel. She takes a sip of margarita. "Safe?" she says.

Arkin registers this, the faint resonant chord of uncertainty in her voice, along with the attempt at humor. He downs the rest of his bourbon, gestures to the bartender. "My shooter was better. His name was Ralph Kelly." He watches the bartender refill his shot glass. "Over a period of, I guess five months, we identified—I identified, and he shot—twenty-three Taliban fighters. Killed them."

"That's . . ." Astonished, Kate takes a while to settle on what *that* might be. Finally, she says softly, "Awful." Which earns her a look, flat and uninformative. "I mean, it must have been awful . . . for you."

"I was a kid. I was completely . . . a blank, even before it started. So it was just what we were doing. Kelly was older. And he knew more. He was more . . . at ease with it. Matter of fact. The only time I fired my weapon was when we were under attack. And that was suppressive fire, like covering a withdrawal."

He stops. His second bourbon is gone. Kate hasn't noticed him drinking and hasn't made much progress on her margarita. The noise of the bar, the setting of the sun, the flow of the river that never stops flowing, all seem to have dropped away.

"One day, in a village called Mata Khan, about an hour by helicopter from Khost, we were supposed to identify and kill a Taliban leader, an organizer. We were watching from a hill just above the village. I had not . . . I could not identify the target, any target. There was a little market area, villagers, trading, I guess, a few stalls. Kelly had this way of . . . whistling, low, under his breath, you couldn't hear him, I mean, *they* couldn't. And he stopped. Just stopped. I only realized a few weeks later; it was so quiet. It was this song, "My Darling Clementine." But he stopped, and I heard him—except that he never talked, we never talked, when we were in position—but he said, out loud, "Okay. I got it." And I started to ask him what it was he got, but he'd . . . stood up. Just stood right up—anybody who was looking could see him. Could see when he . . . started shooting—the people down in the market."

Kate is quiet, the lyric of the song Arkin named now playing inconsequentially in her own head, *"Ruby lips above the water."*

Arkin continues. "He just stood up, right there, on the hillside, in his camo veil, and started firing. They weren't targets. They were just people, regular people. And Kelly . . . never, ever . . . missed. So I stood up and . . . went after him." Kate reaches out, touches the back of his hand. "Barnhardt knows all this. That's why he came to us, to me. He knows this."

"I don't understand."

"I was shouting at him. At Kelly. But he wouldn't stop. He shot this little boy. And his mother."

Kate waits, the lyrics of the old song now replaced by an inner certainty, and dread, of what she's about to hear.

"More. He never missed. So I shot him." His words are so soft that the buzz of the bar, previously distanced by Arkin's backward travel in time, seems now to be rising around them, so that she can barely make out the next words. "And I never miss."

Kate, at possibly the most complete loss she's ever experienced, manages initially only a vaguely breathless "Oh."

Arkin looks suddenly older, slumped over his empty beer mug and shot glass, lost somewhere on the way downhill into that desert canyon.

"Did you . . . get in trouble?"

"No. It was . . ." There's quite a pause as Arkin searches for the word. "Managed." Another pause. "By Barnhardt. He says people were paid off in the village. The survivors. He says we did a lot of that. Barnhardt says he covered up . . . everything that happened." There is another pause, a considerable rift, as if an internal barrier had to be crossed, before he adds in a near whisper, "I can't . . . *stand* . . . that I was part of it."

The import of those words is lost on Kate; she takes it to be a sort of general statement, maybe about the war itself, but anyway something beyond further discussion, for now.

Arkin looks around the bar as if for a sign. Of which there are plenty, beer logos mostly, but also warnings about age and pregnancy and driving. His eye drifts from one to the next, never settling, barely focusing. "I think shooting my friend . . . may have been the only thing I ever really . . . *did*." His gaze travels briefly to her then away. "Did you ever have that feeling? That all we do is watch? I just . . . wandered through school and the Army, until . . ." He hesitates, the unwanted sunbaked image of Kelly's death drifting up for him again. "Until *that* happened. Eventually I got out. Then I feel like I wandered through the rest of college and medical school. I had no real reason, I did not have a . . ." He barely hesitates before finishing, "Mission," a word that, in his voice, is as indeterminate of action and void of direction as anything Kate can imagine.

"You're a wonderful doctor," she says, a remark that surprises them both. It occurs to Kate that she thinks about him in terms of things he says to patients and the way he looks at her and touches her; she thinks about what he does, not why he does it. Still, with ten seconds to reflect, the comment seems far too formal for where they are and what he's told her and how much they've drunk. "You're a great piece of ass too. But you're a wonderful doctor."

"I don't even know what that means," he whispers.

"It's enough that I know," she says and covers his hand with hers.

SEVEN

ARKIN SITS OPPOSITE IT paragon Eva Tern, a big iMac in front of him, mirrored on the eighty-inch LG screen on the wall behind her. Tern again wears a black pencil skirt, a white rayon blouse (today faintly patterned with tiny gray blossoms), and a fixed shining smile of anticipatory satisfaction. On the screens, both the Retina display in front of him and the big quantum dot one behind her, is a neutral blue desktop with a single icon of radiant gold concentric circles, a cryptic Greek alpha in its center. Until now, no one outside the development team in San Jose and a few of the local IT guys have seen the actual new EAT interface. The consulting doctors' group has mostly taken surveys, engaged in discussion about physician documentation and workflow, offered opinions about what would or wouldn't be "helpful," as Bill Flood had put it, but have not seen the end product of their work. Arkin has signed up for this early test drive, mostly to get it out of the way; he has signed the requisite NDAs and disclaimers; he has had three cups of coffee and worries that if the *drive* is prolonged, he may need a rest area.

Tern appears never to have had any worries at all. On the contrary, at every encounter, she has the sunny project manager's mix of code-writing chops and process algorithm expertise and has shown a near indomitable dedication to marking off check blocks on the project flowchart, misplaced within days by everyone on the doctors' panel but neatly tabbed in her own ever-present five-inch log sheet binder, a cutely eponymous flying E.T. decal on its spine. "Go ahead," she says, as confident and casually amused as if this reveal were no more weighty than the opening of a Zoom window.

Arkin clicks on the alpha icon, which fractalizes outward, filling the screen, rapidly coalescing into a human form, outstretched arms, nude, male, further revealing itself in a few more seconds as Leonardo's Vitruvian Man, a moderately *cool* and (Arkin acknowledges to himself) somewhat un-techy departure from the usual EMR design ethos.

Tern grins as though DaVinci was her very own first choice for the Content Strategy Group. The image is luminous, its Renaissance silverpoint lines shimmering as they migrate around the rim of the color wheel. "Swipe your ID," says Tern, enjoying Arkin's momentary . . . absorption?

But he does wave his ID at the keyboard, and the screen fills with a rotating 3D model of the medical center, its multiple units gradually populating with text, which Arkin soon realizes are the patients on his personal census, scattered throughout the campus. "Do I—" he begins, moving the trackball to select a name.

"Nope, wait," Tern says. "Click on the little helicopter."

Along the upper border of the screen, Arkin now sees a series of icons, the first of which is another DaVinci contribution, his design for a helicopter, circa 1450. From somewhere in the distant recesses of stored undergraduate memories, Arkin dredges up the name *Aerial Screw*.

"What?" says Tern, and Arkin realizes he must've said this aloud.

"That's what DaVinci called it." Tern is predictably nonplussed, but Arkin clicks on it anyway. The main screen spins briefly into a reproduction of Copernicus's heliocentric model of the universe—Arkin marvels now at the use of Renaissance genius inventors in something so mundane as an EMR model—but not for long, as the planets in the Copernican model rapidly spin off into a column of patients' names and photographs. These are arranged, well, Arkin can't quite see how they're arranged, certainly not alphabetically, not by unit, or age, or . . .

"By Intricant," Tern says, a newer tinge, this one of smugness, in her voice and smile, at their made-up word. "Our own little term of art. Meant to represent complexity, acuity, complications, risk factors, a whole range of data groups designed to identify, well, your most *challenging* patients. In order. You can change criteria, you can sort anyway you want, but the idea here, with Intricant, is to help the physician manage the day's workload in an entirely different way, one that's more efficient, less stressful, more *in tune* with the physician's actual work mode."

"I don't think I understand."

"So," she explains, unfazed and peering at the first patient in the column, "this first name, Richard Grunman, yes? He's in the CCU, he has six active problems, with overall acuity determined by a mix of DRG, MCC, CCs, and the current ICD-10-CM codes." Arkin has spun through only half the meanings of these abbreviations, but Eva Tern isn't waiting for him. "But that's not all. The system, the *design*, is way smarter than that. You could have someone with all the medical problems in the world, but they're stable, their labs are good, their vital signs, they're just waiting on a nursing home bed for discharge; they're not *challenging* at all. So we take that all into account. Labs are incorporated, nursing assessments, consultants' billing and diagnoses, planned procedures, the *schedule* for those procedures, vital signs, everything. And all that, put together with the known problem list and acuity descriptors, basically, is saying, 'According to Intricant standing, this is the first patient you should see today. And this is the next, and the next, and so on.' So think about what that's done: How much time do you spend in the morning checking labs, reading overnight notes, looking at vitals, figuring out whose white count is going up, who's still got a fever, blood pressure falling, who needs clearance for the OR? But the new system is intelligent; it's done all that for you, saved all that time."

Arkin, despite his natural reluctance to be impressed by Gen-Z technologists, is somewhat impressed.

"But that's not all," she goes on, building what she thinks, and what may in fact be, momentum. "It saves you from the *later* stresses of your workday. It's arranged that you see your patients in an order that makes sense, but it *continually monitors* developments during the day and constantly updates your schedule in response. So you may have planned to see the patient in CT Stepdown at, maybe, around noon, but if the nine o'clock vitals are bad, or if nursing has documented a change in condition, or a consultant has been called, new labs ordered, the nurse manager alerted, or any of dozens of other continuously monitored variables and parameters, then that patient is automatically moved up your list of priorities. That does two things—well, three really. First, you're prompted to see the patient *before* he deteriorates further; you've saved, in that example, a lag of a couple hours, in which lots of bad things can happen. Two, obviously, that creates better outcomes, good for you, good for the hospital, and of course, good for the patient." Eva—Arkin notes that already this morning she's slipped off his last-name-only

list—smiles at this bit of shared if tired medico-legal sophistica-
tion. "Third,"—and this, he senses, is her capper—"all those texts
you hate?" She gestures at the iMac. "Done. No more. Every one of
those Intricant parameters that *the system* included in *its* evalua-
tions and conclusions, is automatically marked 'physician notified'
in the nurse's software, the lab's, the tech's, and so forth. What they
see is that you've already been told and they don't have to call you,
they don't have to text, and *you* don't need to be interrupted in your
workflow." She smiles, triumphant.

"Then how do I know?"

"You don't have to know. *It knows.*" This time, she waves at the
eighty-inch screen behind her, as if the big authority of the system
requires the big display of its prowess. "It's already adjusted your
schedule, said 'You need to see this patient *now*,' and when you
call up that chart, there's a simple summary of everything that
changed since the initial, or last, priority update." And indeed, on
the Stepdown patient she's selected, a chyron-like crawl across
the bottom of the screen (like a CNN breaking news banner, Arkin
thinks), reveals an amber update of the last hour's developments,
temperature, medication, the surgeon's time of documentation, and
more. "That's just the beginning. For example . . ." she selects and
expands the summary crawl, filling the screen with it. "Notice how
certain variables here have been highlighted to focus your attention,
catch your eye. The system has limited the number of highlighted
parameters so as not to confuse or overburden the clinician. And
it can change the number of highlighted parameters, add new text
fonts, colors, even provide audible cues, depending on PCPI, which
is also monitored in real time."

"What does that mean?" Arkin is as well-versed as most in medical jargon, abbreviations, acronyms, but "PCPI" is new to him.

"PCPI is Physician Cognitive Performance Index. Basically, to simplify, the system monitors the user's, well, reaction status, how long it takes you to focus on a piece of flagged onscreen data, how long you remain on that data point before moving on to the next one, how often you return to the earlier data point, and so on. It's using the desktop camera, the built-in camera, to track your eye movements, time them, log them, assess them. That's how it knows that you've seen the alerts it's posted. Essentially, it's . . . seeing how *sharp* you are, how rapidly you're absorbing—and really, processing—information. If you're tired, slowing down, *impaired* in any way,"—this with a companionable laugh that Arkin doesn't share—"it compensates. Helps you . . . *function*."

"That's . . ." Arkin searches for what *that* actually is (his own mental function rather slow this morning), shuffling through a deck of fear, doubt, guilt, shock, and more, until, surprised himself at the word that comes to mind, he whispers, "Intelligent."

Tern smiles, and Arkin realizes he's delivered her the ultimate in bingo moments for AI project managers.

"Exactly," she says, "and more to come."

Arkin ambles, wanders almost, down the admin wing hallway outside Eva Tern's office, reflecting on the vagaries of health care privacy. As a physician, he is routinely, semiannually, educated about the laws and corporate practices governing patient privacy, and then, along with virtually all his colleagues, violates them with some regularity. In their daily rounds and meetings, doctors, nurses, case managers, pharmacists, laboratory and nursing directors, respiratory and physical therapists, all of them, discuss patients' families, substance use history, legal and financial straits, not to mention diagnoses, progress, foibles, and prognoses. They do this whether or not all those present are involved in the care of the particular patient being discussed and in possible, even likely, violation of HIPAA and other applicable laws and regulations. Arkin can think of no more than a handful of instances in which anyone suggested that a case be discussed in a smaller setting, or after rounds, only with those directly involved in patient care, whatever. Much more rare, however, are instances in which a *physician's* privacy is invaded. Though Arkin himself has never been the subject of one, there are peer reviews, discussions in which concerns about a physician's handling of a particular case or cases may be discussed with him or her by clinical supervisors. But these are held behind closed doors, with summary paperwork committed to legally protected HR files. No one outside the process knows it occurred, much less what it concluded; except in defined circumstances, it's protected even from discovery in court. This, like much else about any individual physician's professional conduct and performance, is largely sacrosanct.

And so, the realization that their new EMR can follow what Arkin reads, or doesn't read, of medical data and alerts, how *fast* he reads them, how often he *rereads* them, leaves Arkin somewhat—he searches for the word—disoriented. Once again, he is put uncomfortably in mind of the strange mix of fear and self-doubt that haunts his every decision, overlain by the enormous power behind every one of his orders. At a single keyboard stroke, he can deploy any of a thousand medications, initiate procedures, diagnostic and laboratory testing, nursing interventions, spend tens of thousands of dollars. And with the same stroke of the keyboard, he can misinterpret crucial clues, create untold harm, kill. Instinctively, Arkin has always understood that if he stopped to think about this (or thinks about it without the tranquilizing effect of alcohol), he might never write another order. He has never learned the trick, which he believes some of his colleagues have mastered, of *simply not caring.* Humans make mistakes, doctors are human, ergo, doctors make mistakes, and this requires not much more reflection than that they also require oxygen. Arkin remembers from his residency a renowned and brilliant chief of service who, on being told that a patient he'd admitted the previous day had coded and died overnight due to mitral valve problem he'd missed, responded, "Huh." *Huh,* and then continued with rounds. *We miss things, there're more variables than any one mind can encompass, we're only human, mistakes happen.* But Arkin has never mastered these defenses. The only thing Arkin has ever truly mastered, he still fears, is rifle marksmanship, and the last time he exercised *that* mastery, it was in the destruction of Staff Sergeant Ralph Kelly amid the mountains and mistakes and irresistible variables of war.

Arkin conducts a family meeting with Arthur Senex in room 418 of the RCU, or respiratory care unit, and with his wife and daughter. The patient is seventy-eight years old, with the overinflated barrel chest but otherwise anorectic appearance of advanced COPD. He sits propped up in bed, leaning forward in a position known as "tripoding," hands on his knees, head stiffly erect, to ease the work of breathing. And it's hard work—the "accessory" muscles of the chest and neck heave and recoil with each breath—despite three days of continuous noninvasive pressure-controlled ventilation via one of the unit's BiPAP machines, along with the high-dose IV steroids, nebulizers, and antibiotics that Arkin has ordered. On the chair to the patient's left is his wife, restless hands clasped in her lap, equally thin, equally gray, like Senex himself an ongoing smoker.

Across the room is their middle-aged daughter; Arkin thinks her name is Polly. Next to her is Mandy Moran, the unit case manager who's suggested this meeting and who, after thirty years of hospital work, is an old hand at these "goals of care" get-togethers. She looks perhaps slightly over-cheery with her round middle-aging face haloed by bright red hair, but Arkin knows she can steady the most emotional of family members. He assumes it no accident she's chosen a spot next to the patient's daughter.

"So first," Arkin begins, with the standard opening employed in family meetings, "why don't you tell me what *you* understand about where we are"—he turns to Senex—"and what's going on with you. And then I'll try to answer any questions you have, and we'll go from there."

Senex looks to his wife to speak, knowing the BiPAP mask will make it difficult to be heard, and that he'd be too short of breath without it to form useful sentences.

"Well," his wife starts, voice high, soft but determined, "we know about the bronchitis . . ."

"Chronic bronchitis," Arkin clarifies.

"With some emphysema, right?" Arkin nods. "So COPD. And that's . . . been a long time." She turns to her husband. "Right, Artie?"

"But it's not . . ." This from the patient himself, behind the mask, muffled. He beckons his wife closer, and he manages: "Getting any better."

She repeats for him, "It's not getting any better."

"Usually, it gets better," the daughter says. "We're a little disappointed." This is said with an edge of grievance, drawing an understanding look from the case manager but no nod of agreement.

Arkin understands the good-bad cop dynamic he and the case manager will engage in here.

"You're right, usually it does," he says, "until it doesn't. This is your dad's fourth exacerbation in the last twelve months. And his measurements of disease progression are pretty significant." This is his opening, cautious, understatement: the patient's FEV1 or forced expiratory volume in one second is perhaps 10 percent of predicted for a man his age; he's moving hardly any air, as the pulmonologists say. "Quite significant," Arkin clarifies. "And as I'm sure you know," — makes this as determinedly nonjudgmental as possible—"COPD is progressive. There's no cure. The only thing to do, and it can slow it, is stopping smoking, and your dad hasn't been able to do that."

Senex blinks at him from behind his mask, not disputing this. His wife reaches for his hand; both his and hers are nicotine stained.

Arkin continues, directing most of this at the daughter: "So the exacerbations become more frequent even with maximal therapy at home, which Mr. Senex has been on, and they become more resistant to treatment, even here in the hospital, when they happen."

The daughter's mouth is clamped tightly shut, opening only for, "We know that."

"The only other treatment at this stage, in this situation, is intubation, to go on a ventilator . . ." Here, Arkin shifts his focus to the patient himself. "And Arthur, you've declined that. You've said you don't want that."

The patient nods once, surprisingly assertive at last, on this one point. But Polly is not much swayed by his feelings on the subject. "But, Doctor, isn't that what you *have* to do? Isn't that what *you* would do?"

Arkin pauses, and though he resists the idea that he's paused for effect, he knows they've reached the first inflection point of meetings such as this and he must at least appear to consider the question before responding. "Well, first, this is the patient's decision, and something to be discussed with family, which is part of the reason we're here." Another pause—for effect, it's true—then: "But the outcome with disease this advanced is not good. There's a chance, a really good chance, that he might never come off the machine if we intubated. He'd probably end up with a tracheostomy. You know what that is . . ." He points to his throat, where the trach incision is made; the daughter nods minutely. "And even if he came off the vent, it wouldn't alter the course of the disease." He waits, but Polly seems less angry, ready for the next step; Mandy Moran looks from her to Arkin, facilitating: "So no, I agree with your dad. I wouldn't recommend it. I wouldn't do it myself."

Polly is almost plaintive now. "So where do we go from here?"

Arkin looks at her, finds himself trying and failing to tally the number of times patients' children argued for more aggressive care than the patient himself wanted—more than half, he thinks, probably much more. Conventional wisdom among his colleagues is that this stems from unmet childhood needs, and there's an alternative view that at least some children may derive satisfaction from Dad's prolonged suffering (it's less often Mom in this alternate view). Arkin is agnostic on this debate, generally lumping all such encounters into the "can't let go for whatever reason" category. He knows, too, that there's a third and almost certainly larger category of "lacks the courage to make a decision." About this, Arkin, like most of his colleagues, is more understanding. Death and dying are the province of doctors, the more enlightened of whom understand this is to some degree their doing, the product of the business of medicine, which depends in part on assuming *ownership* of subjects that formerly belonged to all. Death, which used to be a part of everyone's experience, is now mediated by people like Arkin, and Mandy, and Senex's nurses; and those outside the circle of initiates are ever less able to talk and think and feel clearly about this most essential aspect of their *own* lives.

Not that it matters. Arkin *still* has to help these people toward *some* next step. "Well, I would suggest there're two ways to think about this." He's chosen "suggest" rather than the more authority-laden "recommend," and "ways to think" rather than the pressurized "choices." He begins gently enough: "The first is to continue basically what we're doing. We're already at maximal treatment levels, so there will be more exacerbations, and he will probably need to be on BiPAP more often, continuing at night but probably most of the time now, to help him breathe. As long as he's okay with that"—he nods to the patient—"that's one way." And then, after a moment: "Another way is to think more in terms of comfort. As we discussed, we know this disease is incurable, and progressive, and at some point, you might say, 'I just want to be comfortable now, even if that means maybe shortening my life a bit,' not coming back to the hospital, not going on a ventilator, as we already said. If you don't want to, not even being on the BiPAP, which a lot of people don't like very much."

Senex obligingly agrees with a nod.

"So what would that mean?" Polly's voice is quieter now, her eyes beginning to fill.

"Well, first, we don't stop treating. We would continue inhalers, oxygen, again BiPAP if your dad wanted. I think continuing low-dose steroids is reasonable at this point," as is Arkin's own tone, paving the way for the last hurdle. "I think it would be really smart to involve hospice, because they have a lot expertise in making sure that you're comfortable, helping you stay at home . . ." He adds the real payoff: "That you're not *short of breath*." This to Senex, who closes his eyes—possibly in anticipatory relief, or perhaps supplication, it isn't clear. Arkin turns back to the daughter. "We actually often find that people do *better* when we focus more on comfort and less on every, um, acute episode along the way."

"So he would just die?" Polly's eyes now fill completely, overflow.

Matching her tone, Arkin lowers his voice to a near whisper. "I think the question is *how*. How much pain, or anxiety, do we have along the way? How many times do we go to the hospital? *Do* we go to the hospital? Do we end our lives in the ICU? Or are we at home, in our own place?"

Polly manages a nod as case management pats her hand; the patient and his wife are silent, unmoving, possibly, comparatively, unemotional.

"And again, this is your decision. No one's telling you what to do; you're not committing to anything. But I think you might really benefit from talking to hospice."

This does, strangely, seem to empower the patient's wife, who finds her voice once more, stronger this time. "Well, I think we should talk to them. We should talk about that."

Mandy is patting the daughter's hand like a bongo by now; the woman manages a tearful nod, says nothing more.

Arkin creates his progress note for the encounter, now dictates the A-for-Assessment and P-for-Plan portions of the SOAP format. As usual, he combines the two in narrative form, rolling out of him into the speech-to-text translator with the toneless ease of endless practice: "This is a seventy-eight-year-old Caucasian male with history of severe advanced COPD, on three drug inhaler regimen as an outpatient, chronic hypoxemic respiratory failure with round-the-clock oxygen, right side heart failure secondary pulmonary hypertension, and protein deficient malnutrition. He is day three after admission for acute exacerbation of COPD, with acute on chronic respiratory distress. This is his fourth admission in the past twelve months. His ABG on arrival revealed a pH of . . ." Arkin takes a breath, glances at the lab panel on the computer screen. "Seven point one eight, PCO2 of seventy-four percent, and PO2 of thirty-four percent. He declined intubation and is a DNR. He was started on Solu-Medrol, Duonebs, and azithromycin, along with continuous BiPAP. His PCO2 this morning is somewhat improved at sixty-four percent; pH is seven point two three. He continues to require BiPAP to maintain acceptable O2 levels in the low eighties, likely a new baseline." Arkin pauses, hand still on the mic button, head down, concentrating on . . . well, too much to merit "concentration" as a descriptor. Too many drawn and gasping faces of COPD patients who continue to smoke, overweight diabetics overeating candy and cookies, edematous CHFers who skip their diuretics to avoid bathroom trips, and . . . more to come of all these, he knows, and—he realizes more keenly every day—dreads. For the first time since he began practicing, he has occasional flashes of resentment, even outright anger, when called to admit these patients, or when rounding on them, as he has just done with MRN 7814768, Arthur Senex. At the front of his mind is a guardrail of compassion for his patients' desperation, fear, and sense of failure in the grip of their own bad habits, inability to exercise, change, learn. In the back of his mind, however, is resentment at the tens of thousands of dollars spent, his own years of training expended, notes written, educational interventions attempted, and family meetings taken with so little effect. This feeling of resentment disgusts him, but still: FEV1s drop in the emphysematic, ejection fractions fall in heart failure, and HbA1Cs rise in the diabetics, with only the rare patient who might actually improve some marker or sign of disease in the face of general futility. He is also aware that this feeling of resentment comes in high on the list of burnout signs, along with insomnia, isolation, low self-esteem, loss of empathy, and substance use.

(He consoles himself with the idea that no one yet has questioned him about his drinking and that he's never felt an actual *need* to drink in the morning to steady his nerves—no, not *really*. This yields a CAGE alcohol assessment score of 2 [he does sometimes feel guilty, and does think he *should* cut down], which has only a 91 percent sensitivity and 77 percent specificity for the identification of alcoholism, essentially diagnostic. Possibly he added the numbers wrong.)

He resumes work, dictating: "His BODE index suggests eighty percent mortality within the next twelve months, and his Ottawa score is eleven, placing him at high risk for death or severe acute event in the next thirty days. Given this, and after discussing with the patient, his wife, and daughter, hospice will be consulted to see him prior to discharge. I will discontinue Solu-Medrol, convert to prednisone twice daily to start, and continue his other usual medications. For his dyspnea, we will start MS Contin, fifteen milligrams PO twice daily, and titrate for comfort, with immediate release morphine five milligrams every four hours as needed for breakthrough dyspnea; we will consider benzodiazepines for anxiety. Further decisions in this area will await guidance from the palliative care provider. Estimated length of stay is another twenty-four to forty-eight hours pending hospice referral and arrangements, which should be made prior to discharge." Arkin notes the brief lag on the monitor as the system translates the remainder of his dictation to text in the body of his note. He puts down the mic and looks up from the computer.

Like other units in this part of the hospital, the Respiratory Care Unit is circular in design. An elderly woman walks gingerly past the nursing station where Arkin sits. Her husband walks slowly at her side, pushing her oxygen tank caddy. The man nods to the physician at his computer, behind the counter, in his long white coat—Arkin—perhaps thinking how tired the doctor looks. Perhaps the old man also thinks what a hard few years it's been for doctors and nurses, what with the pandemic, and the aging of the population generally. His wife rests her hand on his forearm, steadying herself; the old man smiles at her, behind his bifocals, under a thinning halo of white hair. With a few inaudible words of encouragement, he helps her reverse course and begin the return to her hospital room.

Arkin closes his eyes, in part against the sight of those two, and because he feels tears may form if he continues watching. He already wants the day to be over, when his director, Assam Massood, rounds the corner with a broad smile and a cheery, "Dr. Arkin, how is your day?"

————————

Massood has brought him to the group's office and settled them at the long conference table, built to accommodate the team of eighteen hospitalist doctors and nurse practitioners. Arkin takes the use of the conference room as a good sign, that privacy isn't required. But Massood frowns, with the familiar worried reluctance of uncomfortable administrators everywhere. "So we have a bit of a situation."

"Yes?"

"So, yes," Massood says, almost in a singsong, deployed in hopes of avoiding offense. "We have a request from a patient."

Arkin knows what he's going to say before the name is pronounced.

"Mr. Barnhardt. He asked case management for your credentials and CV. He wanted to see your recommendations."

"Oh."

"Yes. And they came to me, because this is new, first time." Massood can't bring himself to look at Arkin, such is his embarrassment. "So I had them print up your hospital page, that's all. And give it to him. It's public information, education, residency, certification. And anything else"—he dismisses the possibility with a wave of his hand—"he has to look up himself, go to the state board, whatever."

"I'm happy to step away from this case," Arkin says, feeling a sudden wave of relief at even the thought of it.

"No, no," Massood is emphatic. "He just says he is interested"—here he hesitates—"in your past."

Arkin closes his eyes, suppresses all but the slightest exhalation, as the nature of Barnhardt's tactic becomes clear.

"So I just wanted to know . . . if there's some other situation or problem. That perhaps we need to help you with."

"No, I think . . ." but this before Arkin has thought at all. He stops, attempts to organize thoughts which are vague, racing, refusing to be organized. Eventually he arrives at: "I think he's just . . . one of those people . . . who used to be in charge of things." This so far, though evasive, has the advantage of being true. "And now he finds himself . . ."

"Powerless?" Massood offers helpfully.

"Yes."

"And this is just his way of asserting something, yes?"

"Yes," Arkin says, relieved that Massood is doing the work for him, eager to put the issue and conversation behind them. Arkin idly surfaces the notion that this is often the central goal of all administrators.

"So there's nothing else . . . of concern here?"

"No."

"He's not drug seeking, trying to, what, leverage this . . . request?"

"No." Arkin thinks to himself, *If only,* followed immediately by affection for Massood, his willingness to assume this all too common explanation of patients' worst behaviors toward their doctors, and his *un*willingness to think ill of Arkin himself.

———————

Arkin, fueled by unease on both his own and his boss's behalf, walks into Barnhardt's room to find Elizabeth Oliver sitting in a chair near the foot of the patient's bed. Her gaze shifts to Arkin only briefly, from Barnhardt, who remains jaundiced, bloated, asleep.

"How is he?"

Arkin is brought up short. He was ready to confront Barnhardt, face the music, accept consequences—he is cycling cliches—but his resolve evaporates at the surprise presence of Barnhardt's former physician. Amid a dozen questions, he wonders at the propriety of discussing the case with her, at the constraints of HIPAA—but also, now, at the subdued aura of exhausted and guilty interest that seems to emanate from her, his patient's first, formal, failed provider. Eventually, even ubiquitous HIPAA seems beside the point. "His sodium is a little better. I've started him on tolvaptan and went down on the diuretics. His ammonia level is down slightly. LFTs are still in the thousands."

Oliver closes her eyes, and for that moment, Arkin thinks of her and Barnhardt as paired sleepers, twinned in repose, although he can see the tight line of her mouth, the inner clenching at this news, while Barnhardt is, neurologically speaking, near flaccid. In time, she manages a long, ragged sigh, then: "What's the plan for him?"

This—as with the previous patient in the RCU—is, of course, a question Arkin often asks of himself. It's one to which physicians contrive different answers at different times, governed mostly by the immediacy of specific acute medical problems, poised against the uncertain timelines of progressive disease. Often, he and others temporize, as he does now. "I consulted our palliative care team when he was here last week." This gets him a more focused look from Downstate's retired chief of medicine. "He wasn't ready, they said. He sent them away."

"And now he can't decide."

"No. But he should wake up. I think he may have seized from the low sodium while he was at rehab; his prolactin was fifty. Like I said, his numbers are better."

"I'm glad . . ." and then she stops, leaving Arkin to wonder what might have gladdened her in this report. She finishes softly. "I guess. I'm glad I don't do this anymore." After another moment: "I haven't been inside a hospital since I retired."

Arkin could choose to say nothing. He feels himself at one of those conversational crossroads—*bifurcations*, he thinks, in medical parlance—where silence on his part will lead to further silence on hers, and an end to this possibly inappropriate, and certainly odd, case conference. But her "glad I don't do this anymore" gives him pause. It echoes his own hangover-enhanced but otherwise typical flood tide of morning doubt, amplified and underscored by his earlier encounter with the new EMR interface. Followed by his meeting with Massood, which clarified Barnhardt's willingness to threaten Arkin openly and, presumably, to make good on his threat. And so, while also taking in the near-dead-in-bed Barnhardt, he voices his own question of the day: "Why are you here?"

Oliver looks at him for a time while Barnhardt snores, congested and ammoniacal. Arkin thinks she may get up and walk out at the bluntness of his question. And also at, well, the temerity of it, a thirty-something recent resident bracing an erstwhile chief of service, wealthy, no doubt still well-connected in the suburban New York medical elite. Instead, Oliver herself asks the even less-often heard question: "Have you ever killed anyone?"

Arkin is suddenly, completely, mute. Barnhardt, who knows at least one answer to this question, snores on.

"I mean, have you ever made a mistake that killed someone? Because you will."

Still Arkin is silent. Only a few hours earlier, in the Riverside Bar, he'd told Kate about Mata Khan, about Kelly, about the shooting of villagers ... though not, crucially, about the mystery of his own involvement (*if any,* he reminds himself, as always) in *those* deaths, those *mistakes.*

"I've made lots of mistakes," Arkin settles on at last, a lame recapitulation of all that has troubled him for days, months, all his life.

Oliver studies him for a moment then bestirs herself: "I don't know why I came." She stands, glances at Barnhardt, tells Arkin, "He's not a good man. I know it's wrong, or unprofessional, to say ... that he deserves this. But he did bad things. People around the facility, over there, hated him." She takes a breath, somewhere between gasp and sigh. "They were afraid of him. Maybe if I hadn't been afraid, I would've thought more clearly. More about his ... illness, less about him. But I didn't ... think clearly."

"Did he do something to you?"

"No, but . . ." at which she trails off, staring again at the man in the bed. When she resumes, it's with a clearly alternative, less loaded version of the past. "People, even the Army guys, the officers, would stop talking when he walked in the room. People felt threatened and that he could make good on threats."

This seems all too possible to Arkin. "Anything in particular?"

Again, Oliver hesitates, choosing the words. "Primarily, well, he was involved in relations with local tribesman, with the Afghans. And with their medical facilities. And with NGOs, Doctors Without Borders. Others. And he could be very difficult with them, with anything that he viewed as interference, or support for adversaries." She glances sideways at Arkin, possibly aware this is about as informative as, say, a CIA press briefing. Looking back to Barnhardt, she notes the difficult to ignore bubble of saliva that has dribbled from his yellowed and pendulous lower lip, running down his chin. "He was very determined. Even cruel." Her sigh, when it comes, is long, too long for a normal tidal volume.

Arkin thinks, inconsequentially, that she must have been holding her breath this whole time.

"But I had to treat him. And I did it badly."

"I see."

"Do you?" Oliver says.

"He threatened me," Arkin says. "With something that happened in the Army. If I didn't . . ." and here he hesitates, wondering just where this will take him, this conjoining of past and present, hers and his. "If I didn't go see you the other night."

Oliver stares at him, processing that information, the implied ellipsis.

"Plus, there's the whole transplant issue. My writing something to document sobriety."

"You mentioned that."

"Yes." Arkin considers that he's talking with the physician most would think responsible for Barnhardt's condition, who could in theory have halted or at least slowed the progress of his disease. And this in turn, and at the time, might have allowed for at least the possibility of transplantation. Along with gratitude that it wasn't *his* mistake, he feels a wave of sympathy for her: "I can't imagine he was ever a candidate." This earns him a look so complex he can't decipher it. On the surface there's a flash of thanks, of relief, followed instantly by disbelief and pain. *Self*-canceling is the phrase that occurs to him, improbably. "He certainly isn't now."

"He's going to die?"

"Yes."

"And you've told him."

"Yes."

"And he's still threatening you?"

"Yes."

Oliver nods, slowly, and then again. "Look at him," she says. Arkin can hear the disgust and bitterness in her voice, although to him Barnhardt's simultaneously shriveled and bloated self signifies little more than the power of his disease. "I'm sorry you're in this spot," Oliver says. "People like him, even like this . . . they always have the advantage over the rest of us. They'll do anything."

"And we won't?"

"No."

Arkin shakes his head, glad Barnhardt is unconscious. The question of what he might or might not do, or did, and under what circumstances, is simply too complicated at the moment. And he wonders at the chain of events, none of which he controlled, that has brought him to this moment, which he also does not control.

He does not try to awaken Barnhardt. He does not bother to examine him, listen to his heart or lungs, palpate his abdomen. He does not look at the vital signs on the bedside monitor. He hears the blood pressure cuff inflate on its automatic hourly schedule but does not wait for the readout. Instead, he turns and walks from the room.

EIGHT

BARNHARDT'S FIRST THOUGHT IS of thirst. Possibly this is the result of water restriction and diuretics given intravenously while he was unconscious, perhaps made worse by the mouth breathing and the dehydrating effects of the bone-dry oxygen flowing through his nasal cannula. But he feels also a deeper thirst, he thinks centered at the top of his neck, and spreading up into his head, over his ears and circling in a band across his forehead, shouting not only for water (possibly mixed with scotch) but also air and relief from the weight of his grotesquely swollen body pressing down on the hospital bed, and life. He recalls dimly and with revulsion that somewhere within that three-day fog of low sodium and high ammonia levels, he awoke, only partially, but enough to be aware of the petulant voice within, the angry petulance familiar to him since childhood, shouting *not yet*. And so here he is, not just awake but alive, still.

The room is empty. It is gray and quiet. Possibly it is afternoon. Possibly it is that moment in the day when work is mostly done and anticipatory pauses occur in workflow. Barnhardt takes a breath. A harmonic wheeze, a chord, thrums in his chest. He notices it changes pitch when he breathes out. It is a major chord when he breaths in, minor when he breaths out.

He feels the weight of his own abdomen. It presses down and flattens out in all directions. Along his sides, it lies almost flat along the bed. He can feel fluid shifting in those parts. He can almost see, can certainly feel, the waves of fluid inside him lap from side to side as he squirms weakly against the weight of his own torso. The most distant part of his huge abdomen presses down on his bladder and colon. He should urgently have to piss, but the catheter in his penis drains the tannic urine out of him continuously, so there is no actual need. The catheter hurts, but he can't see his penis, so the pain seems somehow remote. He hasn't seen his penis in years; he pisses by approximation. He can feel that his scrotum is also swollen with fluid and is glad he can't see this either. He thinks, he feels, that someone has suspended the enlarged scrotum in something like a trapeze, made of a towel, so it won't be compressed too exquisitely by the twin hillsides of his also swollen thighs.

His abdomen presses up against his lungs, his diaphragm, and this would be worse except that the head of his bed has been raised. There is proportionally less pressure on his lungs than there is on his bladder and colon and scrotum, and he's grateful for this. It's bad enough as it is, breathing. He knows the diaphragm has to move down, toward his belly, in order to inflate the lungs, and his diaphragm has not much room to move. It's like he can't get a full breath. Barnhardt cannot quite remember what it's like to take a deep breath.

He wonders what it would be like to not breathe at all. He tries holding his breath to see what it would be like, but begins gasping almost immediately, and stops. He wants more air but will have to settle for what his enlarged belly will permit him.

The truth appears to be that he wants to go on living. He guesses that is why he awoke from what he thinks must have been a coma. *I was comatose,* he announces to himself, silently, *but I fought back.* This amuses Barnhardt, who has always ridiculed the idea of "fighting," say, cancer, or illness in general. You can't fight yourself, and cancer is your own cells, doing something they shouldn't, but they're still your own, still you. Barnhardt can't fight his own liver, or his sploshy abdomen. He also couldn't fight the critically low sodium level that sucked him down into unconsciousness. But others could be hired to do such things, and did, so Barnhardt lives on.

He tentatively stretches his arms upward, toward the drop ceiling of his hospital room. Behind that ceiling run wires, conduit, water pipe, fire sprinklers. He wiggles his fingers, weakly, at the unseen infrastructure. His fingers are pudgy, and the pads of his palms are orangeade in color, from the seepage of waste products around his mostly non-functioning liver. Barnhardt notices the enlarged knuckle on the middle finger of his right hand that he broke punching a mean girl in fourth grade. He hit her in the side of her face and broke her glasses. His parents must've been angry about it, but all he really remembers is the look of shock in her eyes, that a boy had hit her, a bigger boy, and the little cut beside her eyebrow the jagged frame edge made. He's pretty sure that he gave up hitting girls after that, for whatever reason.

Barnhardt wonders what any woman would think of him now, bloated and helpless. It's the last part that matters, he believes, as he's been obese for years and never had any problem finding women to be with. He is content that "to be with" is euphemistic at best, that all he wanted, once in a while, was to fuck someone. He recollects that being obese required changes in his sexual practice, specifically the use of rear entry intercourse. Which was fine with him, the impersonality of it. And also probably for the women involved, as well, not having to look at him. What would they think now? He almost giggles at the self-evident answer.

Barnhardt has concluded that Arkin is in a relationship with one of the nurses, the one named Maddox. He knows this because he saw them talking in his doorway once. Not touching, not kissing, just talking, but Barnhardt can scent such things. Scent, not sense, and Barnhardt enjoys the—what is it?—homophone? Or is it homograph? Barnhardt tires, as this recalls early and aggressive grammar lessons from his mother. Anyway, words that sound the same and mean the same. And Barnhardt *can*... scent it. And thinks it a good thing because it will be harder for Arkin to run away. In Barnhardt's mind, running away is a smart form of defense. If you can drop everything, every commitment, and run, then once you're out of sight, you're perfectly safe. Barnhardt considers almost all commitments conditional, the condition being "if it works for me."

In addition to serving that principle, he was employed by the United States government almost all his adult life and throughout was guided by his belief in the infallibility of markets. He believed his work was the monitoring of and adaptation to cultural and political market forces, and that whatever benefit his understanding of their invisible hand might bestow on him would also be good for the country. He believed regulation impaired the operation of markets, and of humans like himself, who formed an übermarket of influence and action. Even now, he feels himself, recollects himself, as the *master* of those who would have regulated him. If it hadn't been for (and here, Barnhardt stalls, hunting an appropriate descriptor for Beth Oliver, *doctor* feeling wrong in so many ways)—for *her,* that woman—he believes he would still be out there, market master and man of action. He has the sudden if somewhat sleep-impaired conviction that the sling under his balls and the tube in his cock are *her* work, the direct result of *her* practice. *Doctor* is inadequate, as is bitch, idiot, scum, and ... whore. Although, *whore*, for Barnhardt, moves a bit closer, denoting engagement without commitment, and the pretense of expertise. Or, possibly, *cunt*. Barnhardt likes this word precisely because it is not just frowned upon but forbidden in polite society, into which Barnhardt had never been welcomed nor aspired to anyway. *Cunt* because its very use suggests access to the most private and protected part of her, establishes dominion, degrades loving connection, elevates femaleness above personhood or profession or intelligence or any other *part* by which she might wish to define herself. Which is agreeable to Barnhardt, in depth.

Because, of course, she has killed him. At least his liver, lungs, and, if Arkin is to be believed, his heart now too. Of the liver and lungs, though, he is sure. He has confirmed it with other physicians, in follow-up, as doctors like to say. Although precluded by secrecy agreements from suing, he has even discussed it with medical malpractice attorneys and has been assured of its open and shutness, her misdiagnosis. Or better: missed diagnosis. Her original error is killing these parts of him, even now.

Naturally, Barnhardt is aware that he himself has misstepped, the word he prefers, missteps that have resulted in many deaths, too many to count really, even if he were inclined to count them, which he is serenely not. There is probably some *regulatory* context in which he might be compelled to enumerate or explain—but his mastery of regulatory contexts has freed him from such obligations, and he sees no equivalence between what he has done out in the marketplace and what Oliver did to his own private body.

Barnhardt is glad to see it is the nurse Maddox who answers his call bell. He offers what he thinks of as a smile, although he is aware that with the jaundice and the swelling and the bleeding gums, it may not be as appealing as, well, all that.

"Do you need something, Mr. Barnhardt?"

"That's a big question." His voice is throttled by shortness of breath, hardly befitting his ever more distant memories of (what he likes to think of as) seductions past. Instead, he pivots. "You're Arkin's friend."

"I'm a nurse. I work with Dr. Arkin."

"I saw you two together, in the doorway."

This seems to trouble her not at all. She stands watching him, hipshot, arms crossed across her chest. Barnhardt has to admit to himself that she's impressive. Tall, fit, her sexuality and air of competence and self-assurance and her experience of the worst life has to offer all mixing easily into a comfortable wall of relaxed readiness and poise. As in balanced, Barnhardt thinks randomly. Also, quite—here, he searches for the word—beautiful? Pretty? He wonders if there is a word that combines "beautiful" and "strong" at once. Handsome? He thinks not. If he were inclined to lean on a woman, this would be the sort he'd choose, if she'd let him.

"What's he like? To you?"

She doesn't answer, just stares, speculative, cooling somewhat further.

"It doesn't hurt to talk," Barnhardt says, with an air of pious hurt, an obvious and self-mocking twist on disarmament.

"Dr. Arkin is one of our favorites. He's really good; you're in good hands."

"Has he told you how I know him? How I picked him?" Barnhardt has decided on a direct tack, what they would call "blunt force" in Directorate planning sessions.

"I didn't know you had picked him."

Barnhardt senses in this a first, obvious sort of lie. "Oh yes, of course. Did he tell you why?" Maddox says nothing. "Let me." Still Maddox is silent. "I knew him, of him, during the war, in Afghanistan."

Slowly, unaware of it herself, Maddox's hands slip to her sides, rendering her at last, if slightly, awkward.

"Why don't you sit down?"

And after a moment, Maddox does sit, across the room, the chair no closer, metaphorically speaking, than Earth to Mars.

Barnhardt favors her with a look of contentment. "I was employed by a company called Western Analytics, which was a subsidiary of something called Dorn Technology, which was an actual business set up and operated by the Political Action Group, in the CIA. That's part of the Special Activities Center in the Directorate of Operations. Have you ever heard of any of this?"

"No," Maddox says, shifting in her chair.

Barnhardt can see muscles ripple in her legs as she does, which distracts him, if momentarily.

"Well, don't tell anyone," he says with another lupine grin. "We ... I ... cleaned up things." He watches her, is satisfied at the first slight movement of her gaze away from him. "Of course, there're always mistakes and problems everywhere—I'm sure you have them in hospitals—but in war, it's constant. And we solve them the same way in war as everywhere else, with *money*." He pauses, lets his labored breathing slow a bit. "I used to observe ... what you would call agitation ... of families, or aggrieved"—and here, he was disdainful—"*politicians* ... as I counted out the dollars. Or ... named a higher sum, and then ... higher, and how, sooner or later, usually sooner, the tears dried ... and the anger receded. Righteous, yes, but receding." He allows himself a magnanimous sigh at the elementality of it. "It is . . . the most American thing we could share with our . . . clients. We respect money, and we taught them, or at least persuaded them, to respect it too." He glances away, down, at the sheet covering his belly, smooths it somewhat delicately, even prissily.

It's a gesture, Maddox thinks, out of some old silent comedy, persnickety. Stan Laurel.

"I always loved that. Watching that . . . change, in their eyes. Watching their angry mouths . . . soften." He takes a breath. "When I paid them." He sees in Maddox's eyes, her gray eyes, a flash of gold, tawny, like a big angry cat, then gone. He's interested at how this thrills him, even in his reduced state. "I suppose you know I paid out some money for your friend. *Doctor* Arkin. Did he tell you?" Maddox says nothing. "Did he tell you about the man he shot?" Barnhardt feels his point disappearing into some deep gray pond on the other side of the room, but he also feels the force of words returning to him now, even his breathing somehow stronger. "But that didn't cost us anything, Arkin killing his friend." And then he almost whispers, the sound of it hanging in the air, mote-like: "It was the children that cost us."

A pause, before: "I don't believe you."

Barnhardt specifies, almost gently, "Four children. Plus the adults."

"I don't believe he would do such a thing."

"Hard to say."

"Not for me."

"Hard to say," Barnhardt insists, speculative, fatherly. "Twelve people were shot, plus his teammate. Thirteen. Eleven fatally, two wounded. Kelly fired his weapon sixteen times. Arkin ten. His teammate—his name was Ralph Kelly . . ." Barnhardt sees a brief flash of recognition in Maddox's eyes, thinks, *She knows,* and continues. "He was firing an M110, which is a 7.62 millimeter round, NATO round, a twenty-round magazine, and Arkin had an M4, which fires a 5.56. And we found one of those in Kelly, in his spine. On the way to his spine, it went through the left atrium. Love the terminology. And then into his back, somewhere around T5, I think you would call it? Which I suppose would've paralyzed him, where it hit. But I understand he would've been dead already. When he hit the ground, as they say." Here Barnhardt manages a rueful smile. "And that bullet was from Arkin's rifle. Dr. Arkin. But you must've heard this already."

Maddox says nothing, still.

Barnhardt takes her silence as a victory to be acknowledged with a deprecatory little wave of an edematous hand. The saline lock in his right wrist is filled with blood, and Maddox notes inconsequentially that it should be flushed, but Barnhardt draws her attention back with: "But that's the only bullet we recovered. That's the only body we were able to examine; the villagers insisted the bodies of the others belonged to them. So we had twenty-five shots fired, in addition to the one that killed Kelly. Twenty-four shots, twelve people hit, ten of them killed, plus his friend. And Kelly fired, what did I say, fifteen? And Arkin fired ten, one of which hit his partner, the rest of which . . ." he pauses with an air of elegant, even delicate, uncertainty. "Went elsewhere."

Maddox cannot help thinking of Arkin the night they first drank together at the Riverside. Of course, Maddox herself likes to drink, occasionally with abandon, but Arkin drinks like no one else she knows, almost doggedly. She thinks she remembers a quote from somewhere, that alcohol is the disappearing ink of memory, but she can't remember where, and wonders if this is why Arkin drinks the way he does.

Barnhardt interrupts her train of thought, asks, "How much longer do you think I'll be here?"

"I don't know. That's up to the doctors. You need to be evaluated by physical therapy too."

"And for, ah, transplant, yes?" Barnhardt almost manages a laugh at how beatifically he dispenses the cliche: "A 'life-saving procedure.'"

Her expression is unrevealing, and if there are storms within her, no wave shows as she stands and repeats, "That's up to the doctors."

NINE

KATE WATCHES THE EAST Pennsylvania landscape flow by; a sign on Interstate 84 reads "Stokes State Forest," which is actually across the border in New Jersey, and which she remembers from childhood visits. She and her family would climb to the top of Sunrise Mountain there, her parents both laboring under the burden of their pack-a-day Marlboro habits, as well as the weight of their takeout picnic sandwiches and cold drinks and ground cloth. Kate remembers the Brownie knapsack she'd carried on those hikes, from an early age, crammed with insect repellant and sunblock and her father's old Polaroid SX-70. She remembers, too, the sight of the serious hikers along the Appalachian Trail, which ran along the ridge of which Sunrise was a part. She can still feel her preadolescent wonder at their scruffiness, the boys' beards, the girls' short-shorts and muddy boots, lank hair, the huge backpacks. There was a pavilion with tables and benches where she and her family would spread their lunch and watch the hikers pass, most with the tired, sparkless smile of receding ambition.

She might share this with Arkin, but he's sunk in silence behind the wheel of the Honda. She thinks to tell him about her younger sister, Martha, who carried a kite up the mountain on those same trips. Martha is married and living in Ocala with her realtor husband and two overweight children; she and Kate exchange Christmas cards and speak every few months, little left in Martha of the girl who'd joyously flown her butterfly kite into the thin air above Sunrise Mountain. Even so, Kate is sometimes jealous of Martha and, at other times, worried when she isn't. Looking at Arkin, Kate thinks of her last serious boyfriend, a city planner in Santa Barbara named Rich Klein, who'd wanted to marry her, start a family, buy a starter home. Kate had thought about it, some, but eventually the prospect of an Ikea-furnished, factory-built three-bedroom, the unending sameness of Southern California weather and traffic, and Rich's almost mordant Los Angeles Angels fandom, had cooled her to the idea and eased her departure home when her mother fell ill. She didn't, and doesn't now, know how she feels about having children. She and Arkin have never discussed it, which is clearly odd given their ages and stage in life, despite having known each other for only a short while. People put out those feelers on first dates, and neither she nor Arkin has.

"What does he want from you?" she asks, unaware she was about to speak. "The cirrhosis patient, Barnhardt?"

Arkin glances at her, neutral, possibly appraising. "He says he wants to get on the transplant list. He wants me to document six months of sobriety."

"He hasn't been?"

Arkin shakes his head no, stares at the unfolding road ahead, the rise and fall of Pennsylvania's ancient mountains. "But I don't know what he really wants."

"He talked about you. About the war. And your friend. I didn't say I already knew. But I was glad—I am glad—you told me first."

Arkin glances at her, warily, Kate thinks, before looking back to the highway. After a time: "What I liked in med school, residency, was certainty. 'Does the patient have COPD, documented history?' 'Yes.' 'Do they have more than one previous exacerbation requiring hospitalization? Yes or no.' 'Yes.' 'Do they have contraindication to azithromycin? Yes or no?' 'No.' 'Give Zithro, one thousand milligrams PO or IV, times three days.' Done. I liked it, clarity. Only it's not clear. Hospital stay shortened, on average, by nine hours, in one study? That's not evidence; that's nothing."

This is perhaps the most Arkin's ever said in one stretch, about his practice, since they met. He seems completely absorbed. "With a dozen confounders. Did the patient have pneumonia? Was it diagnosed via X-ray or CT? If X-ray, was it bacterial, was there a procalcitonin, or was it viral? Did the Zithro help because of bacterial infection, or because it's an anti-inflammatory? Maybe. Nobody knows. We give it because . . . how else could we go on?"

The phrase surprises Kate. *Go on?* she thinks. *Go on?* More than perhaps anyone she knows, Arkin seems to have nothing other than *going on* to explain how he has come to be working in their hospital, living in his sterile condo, in the stasis of the mid–Hudson River valley, without children, unmarried, un-divorced, unloved so far as she can see (although she is not clear on this subject herself), even largely unmotivated to hear him tell it.

Which he seems to confirm with: "We don't *know* anything. We give drugs; we don't know if they really work. We inject steroids into lumbar spines, prescribe rest for concussions, exercise for TBI, Solu-Medrol for bronchospasm when prednisone works just as well, on and on. *Nothing is certain.*"

Kate is actually alarmed. Doctors act like they know what they're doing. Like there's a reason, that even if *you* don't know the reason, *they* do—and it has to be that way, not just for the patients and their families, but for the nurses and the administrators and the unit managers who carry out their orders, the authority around which the entire system is built. Order, Kate thinks, there's no order without that certainty. She offers gently, with a careful smile, "Doctors don't talk this way."

The doctor in question manages a fractional smile of his own then glances at the Honda's speedometer—ninety miles an hour. He takes a deep breath, lets it out, and lifts his foot from the accelerator.

Kate watches Arkin take a three-foot-long locked plastic case from the trunk of his car. In large white letters along the side is "Plano," above that "Made in USA." Next to it is a medium-size backpack, which Arkin also takes. With Kate following, he carries his gear around a low shed-like building with its fading "Wall-Pack Shooting Club" sign. There are a variety of decals in its windows: "Hard Ridin', Straight Shootin'" and "Shoot Like a Girl," and "Critter Gitter." There's a poster of a bull's-eye, with the caption "This is my peace symbol." There's another showing a line of weapons, arranged large to small, titled "My family." Behind the building is window where Arkin goes to check in with an overweight middle-aged man wearing a polo shirt, the name "Paul" embroidered in yellow script. There's also a covered wooden platform about twenty-five feet long, and beyond that a gently up-sloping field stretching out half a mile or more, with a variety of targets arrayed in front of bulldozed berms of dirt. Kate counts ten of these berms at approximately hundred-yard intervals, she guesses. Some of the targets are vaguely human-shaped silhouettes, some are simple metal squares or rectangles; they are a variety of colors, and at each distance, there're perhaps ten targets, most suspended from heavy-gauge cables or sometimes from free-standing steel frames. Finished checking in, Arkin picks a spot at the end of the platform, sits, opens the case he's brought. Inside, as Kate knew there would be, is a rifle.

"I didn't know you had a gun."

"I bought it a few days ago."

"Oh."

"You ever have a gun?"

"No. My dad had one, but he got rid of it when I was born."

"Smart."

Kate watches as he takes items from the backpack, ammunition boxes, rifle magazines. "It's not loaded?"

"No. It's against the law to transport a loaded rifle in this state. You always keep the ammo and rifle separate."

"Okay."

Arkin looks up to her at last, asks, "Do you want to load it?"

"Sure," Kate says lightly, although she is less than sure about all this. Possibly she is curious but also concerned in a casual but, she thinks, situationally appropriate way. The word *nuance* occurs to her, although she knows the moment is more charged than nuanced. "What kind of rifle is it?"

"This is an H&K, Hechler & Koch, MR762A1. It fires .308 Winchester ammunition." He holds up a rifle cartridge for her to see. "Ammunition is . . ." Here he stops, excavating layers of *what ammunition is* before settling on: "Complicated. Lot of different types, charges, measurements. This whole thing is called the cartridge. The tip of it, that's the bullet, the part that goes to the target when you fire. This is a .30-caliber rifle, which means the bullet is about point three inches across. That's basically the same as the NATO round, 7.62 millimeters. This brass part below is the cartridge case, that's where the gunpowder is. And this is the magazine." He hands her one of the curved twenty-round magazines. "You push each cartridge into the top of the magazine, like this," and demonstrates with one cartridge before handing her the box of ammunition. "Go ahead."

And Kate does, pushing in one cartridge after another, the weight of the whole growing in her hand, to perhaps half a pound; it feels cool, dense, utilitarian. She holds it up for Arkin to inspect.

"Good."

"I've never done this before."

Arkin's smile is oblique, muted, a sense of delicate momentousness passing between them. "So," he begins, "a few things to know before we load the weapon. First of all, a few rules: Never point it at anyone, obviously. Treat like it's loaded all the time, even if you're sure it's not. After you take it out of the case, point it downrange, at the targets only, even before you load it. Never put your finger on the trigger, don't even put it inside the trigger guard, until you're aiming at a target, in a safe direction, on a safe range, ready to shoot. Okay?" She nods. "You can take it out now, rest it on your legs, headed that way." He points toward the targets, and Kate lifts the rifle from its case, feeling the weight of it for the first time.

Arkin takes her through the steps of clearing the rifle, checking the safety, using the charging handle to rack the bolt three times then retracting it to check the empty chamber. He points out its various parts: the buttstock, the barrel assembly, the pistol grip, upper and lower receiver, the magazine catch and release button.

Kate thinks she has never seen Arkin in this light and can't help noting the inerrant certainty in his handling of the rifle, his directions about its use. She also can't help comparing this to his earlier, yes, complaints, about the *un*certainty of medical practice. He is not so much animated now, with the rifle, as settled, she thinks.

"You want to try?" he asks.

You mean shoot? she thinks to herself, ridiculously. Of course, that's what he means, the weapon is right there, in her hands. The normal gray of Arkin's eyes is lightened under the overhang of the shed, she notices, somehow more open, available. She thinks he has never seemed so unguarded, as though his offer of the rifle to her has revealed unsuspected generosity. Or possibly innocence, Kate thinks, and manages a nod.

"All right. So first, put on these, and these." He holds the rifle for her as Kate puts on a set of earmuffs and shooting goggles, then dons his own. "Then lie down. Up on your side a little bit." He hands the rifle to her, she feels an unexpected warmth to it, from his hands, she imagines. "Left hand up here on the stock, right hand along the trigger guard, but keep your fingers outside."

But Kate has a hard time shifting focus from the sensation of the rifle in her hands. She can feel the moistening of her palms on it, detects a faint scent of gun oil, even feels a vibration, possibly from a minute nervous tension in her arms.

"There're a lot of ways to think about shooting." She looks up to Arkin at last, close by, his voice steady, placid. "One way is, the rifle is really accurate. The scope is accurate. The ammunition is accurate. The least accurate part is the person holding the rifle. It's all about the shooter, it's all about you. The rifle will *always* do what you tell it to do." It seems to Kate that Arkin's voice has grown even softer as he repeats, *"Always."*

About now, Arkin realizes he has never had any sort of contact (the word springs to mind) with a woman and a rifle together at the same time. There is a faint blush of freckles across Kate's nose and cheeks, the one that he can see, the other blocked from view by the rifle, its cheekpiece pressing against her face. Kate wears a white cotton tank top, revealing the flexing of her upper arm muscles as she adjusts her grip on the weapon, a light odor of sweat and soap and of Kate herself. The furrow of her spine sweeps down from her shoulders to the waist of her blue jeans, a slight gap revealing the top hem of black underwear, then the rise of her buttocks, legs spread comfortably, feet pointing out. Arkin can see the veins in her bare ankles above her running shoes. Her chest is flat against the nylon of the shooting mat. Arkin cannot quite parse the mix of the sexual that her body presents, stretched out so unselfconsciously, known and familiar to him, with the weapon she holds, also pressed to herself, which looks natural enough next to her, and which can so remarkably kill at a distance. It fires a bullet that travels almost three times the speed of sound, so that at a thousand yards, the bullet strikes almost two seconds before the sound of it reaches its target, though this is briefer than a kiss or sigh or touch, thoughts of which also crowd in on Arkin as he looks at Kate.

Although he has often wondered about women's sense of their sexual presence, their knowledge of its effect on others, he doubts Kate's attention is divided now. She seems entirely focused on the new experience of the weapon, on his words, on the targets downrange; she seems unaware or anyway uncaring about any effect her body might be having on him at the moment. Or perhaps she is aware, but the awareness is so continuous, so much a given in her life as a woman, that most of the time it is merely background data, repressible when she wishes. His reverie on this, on the mystery of sexuality and the power Kate holds over him simply by *being*, is interrupted by her "What's next?" If it weren't that it would distract her, Arkin would laugh at himself.

"So, you can pull the caps off the scope, front and back." He has already boresighted the rifle at home, now talks her through the purpose and technique of zeroing in the rifle and its scope. Halfway through his explanation of minutes of angle, he senses Kate's attention may be flagging—Was that an eye roll when he mentioned *adjustments on target* at various distances?—and Arkin pauses to consider his tone of voice, the possibility that he's slipped unconsciously into doctor mode. In his mind, this consists of too much information using a too-technical vocabulary, overlaid with the confident assumption of the listener's interest. Arkin's aware that this could also be "bad boyfriend" mode and that smart guys stopped talking down to their girlfriends about the time Arkin started shaving.

"Is this boring?" Arkin asks, and a tightening of the muscles around Kate's mouth suggests the possibility of her laughing if he continues in this vein. "You wanna just shoot?" and Kate nods, letting the smile out now. "Okay." He turns to look at the man in the window, Paul, and asks, "Range is hot?"

"All yours," says the man, gesturing to the rest of the firing line, empty of other shooters.

"Okay," Arkin says to her. "Look through the scope, the target right there in front of you." Kate listens as he takes her through the next steps. "We're gonna put the magazine in then release the charging handle." Kate hears the snick of the bolt closing. "That puts a round in the chamber. And I'm gonna take off the safety."

Kate hears the safety click to off and wonders at the new feeling of the weapon in her hands, against her face. It's not exactly that the rifle has come to life; it doesn't feel alive much less, she thinks, awake. Better, she thinks is *potential*, a potentiality, that it can do something now that it couldn't do a moment before. *Armed* is a word that she has heard used; *it* is armed and of herself, more remotely, *she* is armed. Arkin has paused, she suspects, to let this sensation settle itself in her.

"Now, you can see the crosshairs in the reticle of the scope. Center them on the target bull's-eye. You do that?" Kate nods minutely. "And just let your breathing relax, don't hold it, just breathe. And just focus on the crosshairs, the reticle. You can put your finger on the trigger. Okay?" Kate does. "And when you're ready, you can just slowly start to squeeze the trigger, nice steady pressure. Don't think about that, just the target."

When the rifle fires, it comes as a complete surprise to Kate. She feels the jolt of it against her shoulder, the vibration of that jolt down through her body, the sound of the explosion remote but still jarring and intimate even through the earmuffs. She notices a distinct odor, and the word "cordite" comes to mind, although she has no idea what that smells like. This is the odor of, she flashes on it, *fireworks*, which she remembers from her childhood, with a taste of it in her mouth as well. She hasn't moved. The rifle feels somehow warmer in her hands and against her face, although she attributes the new sweat on her palms and cheek to ... excitement? To the suddenness of the shot and the noise and the jolt in her body and the instant silence except for some mild ringing in her ears and astonishingly ... to the small black hole that has appeared on the twenty-one-by-twenty-one-inch target a hundred yards from her, which she can see through the scope, a hole about five inches to the right of the black central bull's-eye. A hole that appeared almost before the sound and sensation of the rifle firing had registered with her, that appeared as if out of nowhere, inexplicably connected to that final sensation of the trigger slowly moving under her finger, until at the last moment the tension or resistance of the trigger eased and then suddenly released and the hole appeared and *only then* she registered the sound and jump of the weapon and the smell and taste of it. It feels like that new black spot on the target had come somehow and unimaginably *from her*, directly, almost without a role for the rifle or the scope, which never left her hands, or for the bullet itself for that matter, which was invisible. There was only sudden juddering sensation, and then that black spot three hundred feet away.

"Good job," comes Arkin's voice, and she glances up to see him looking at her, a guarded smile there, understanding. "Do it again."

And Kate does. She fires five more times, hitting the black bull's-eye twice, feeling the special glow at the white void of the bullet hole in the black part of the target. Again and again, she feels that strange connection between herself and the distant target, her marking or affecting or changing or marring of it, instantaneous and irresistible. Improbably, Einstein's phrase "spooky action at a distance" returns to her from some college physics course, a phrase she barely understood then but understands better now in the context of NATO ammunition and the squeeze of the trigger, and that taste in her mouth, and the feeling it arouses in her, to which she cannot put a name.

"Feels good, doesn't it?" Arkin asks.

Kate lifts her head from the weapon, nods, and smiles a bit uncertainly. "Here, you do it," and she offers Arkin the rifle. He reaches in, moves the selector to safe, removes the magazine, racks the charging handle and retracts the bolt, ejecting the cartridge in the chamber. Only then does he take the rifle from her, inspects the chamber, allows her to slide out of the way as he takes her place on the mat. She notices that he's fallen silent now, even more silent than usual. And also that Paul, the manager, has emerged from the range shed. He's brought with him a large scope on a tripod.

"What are you thinking?" he asks Arkin.

"Thousand."

"Okay if I spot?"

"Sure," Arkin says, and Kate watches as he settles into position. "How many MOA per click?"

"I'll just hold high to start." Kate has no idea what this means but can tell Paul is impressed. "Pretty calm."

"Yep."

"All right." Arkin puts the magazine back into the rifle, releases the bolt, switches the safety off.

"What are you shooting at?" Kate asks.

"Last row of targets. Thousand yards."

Kate looks far down the range, can barely make out the gray painted steel forms there. "How do you know if you hit it?"

"He'll tell me," with a nod toward Paul. "And the targets are metal. If you listen, you'll be able to hear the sound of the bullet hitting them, like a gong. Takes a few seconds, though. For the bullet to get there and the sound to get back."

"Okay," Kate says and then watches as Arkin seems to settle even more deeply into the mat, even the little movements diminishing until he is entirely still. She watches as he breathes, in then out, two cycles, three, and then, on the last out breath, the rifle fires.

Two seconds later, Paul says, "Shit," and a second after that, Kate does hear it, a faint *ping* from a thousand yards away. "Four inches high, two inches left." Arkin still hasn't moved. "Jesus," Paul says, and then again, "Shit." And Arkin fires, and then again, "Damn," and again the distant *ping* of bullet on steel, and Paul almost whispers, "One up, one left."

"Nice rifle," Arkin says. "I'll start playing with the scope now."

"Why bother?" Paul says, shaking his head, and Arkin glances over and up at Kate, with a brief nod, and a slight inward smile. He starts moving the knobs on the scope, and Paul turns to Kate and says, "I'm Paul, by the way. Sorry about my language."

"Kate," she says as they shake hands.

Paul grins, shakes his head again, and asks, "This monster your boyfriend?"

To which Kate just smiles, feels Arkin smiling, too, a little, then settling again, and then the rifle goes off.

———————

Between them, they fire four more magazines at different distances, Kate becoming more and more comfortable. *Doing really well*, Arkin says. He, in turn, never misses the bull's-eye on any target, at any range. From time to time, Kate catches Paul watching from the shed window, and she understands that he watches because it's something unusual, this level of accuracy. Kate finds herself unaccountably proud, even possessive, of Arkin's performance. Of course, she has no frame of reference, but something about the tone in his voice when Paul referred to Arkin as a *monster* is more than suggestive, she thinks. She thinks possibly Arkin has scared him.

When they've finished shooting, and the rifle is packed away in its case and leaning against a stand behind the firing line, they drink Cokes and sit on a bench. Other shooters have arrived and begin setting up on the firing line.

"So," Kate asks, "you like your rifle?"

"It's good," he says, nodding, sipping at his soft drink.

"Do you like to watch other people shoot?"

"Sometimes. I don't like . . ." and hesitates before concluding: "Cowboys." This with a sideways look at Kate, to see if she understands, or to see whether he's embarrassed himself.

"It should be more . . . businesslike?"

Arkin laughs a little, wryly. "That word is . . . difficult."

"Because of the war?"

"Yes." And then, although his tone unchanged: "Barnhardt . . . I've told you about all that happened there. With him. And me."

"Yes."

"Well . . . he got sick when he was there too. And he saw medical people in an Army hospital. One doctor in particular. A civilian, contractor, administrator. Who missed the diagnosis." He turns to her, asks, "You know what AAT deficiency is?"

"Sort of."

"Well, that's what he had. And it's treatable when caught. But he had a fairly late onset of symptoms, which probably made it easy to miss. And it was. And that's why he's sick now."

"I see."

And after a moment: "I met the doctor who saw him there. At his . . . request. She lives nearby."

"Okay?"

Arkin nods. "And she came to the hospital yesterday, I guess . . . to apologize. I'm not sure, but he was out of it. Which may be a good thing."

"Why?"

"He's angry; he blames her."

"He's a jerk."

"True." And then, more softly: "But he's right. It is her fault." Arkin looks at her for a minute before adding, "And we all make mistakes."

Kate thinks about this for a time, then, "When he talked about you, and your friend . . . it was obvious he thought, he said, that you'd hurt other people."

The silences between them are growing longer, Arkin helpless to shorten them. "I know."

"Did that happen?"

"I don't know."

Kate glances at the rifle in its case, safely packed away. "Is that why we're here?" Arkin says nothing. "Because the person I know, the person I see here, even with that rifle in his hand, especially . . . is not a person who could shoot innocent people."

Arkin looks at the Pennsylvanian hillside all around, the covering oak and white pine and maple. "It's not the same," he says.

"But how do you feel?" Kate asks.

Arkin thinks about this a while, studying his hands, intent, shut in. "I feel the same," he says.

In a moment, Paul's voice comes, calling to the new arrivals. "Is the line ready?" And then, in rapid succession: "Ready on the right, ready on the left, commence firing."

Arkin slips his ear protection back on, Kate does the same, effectively ending their conversation as the pop of gunfire erupts along the line. Kate reaches out, takes his hand in hers. She receives an answering squeeze, the two of them side by side, linked, as the shooting increases.

TEN

ARKIN RETURNS TO WORK after the day off resolved to focus on his patients and his practice. He considers now that Barnhardt's threats, and whatever it is that Barnhardt wants from him by way of those threats, are hollow. What, after all, will it benefit Barnhardt to damage Arkin? It won't make him well, and it won't get him a transplant. No doctor replacing Arkin—for he surely would be replaced—would have any incentive, much less inclination, to falsify records in pursuit of a procedure that no transplant hepatologist would consider, and no pulmonologist or cardiologist would endorse. Although Arkin imagines that most people under threat go through periods of denial, after a day away from the hospital he thinks his new appraisal of risk is reasonable, incisive, right.

His burst of optimism and confidence evaporates with his first patient, a seventy-year-old woman on another of the hospital's medical surgical units, South Seven. At first glance, the woman in room 740 appears well enough; she is sitting up in bed, reading on her iPad, with several glossy magazines spread around her. Admitted the previous day with mild shortness of breath, she was started on standard care for presumptive community-acquired pneumonia, consisting of ceftriaxone, an intravenous antibiotic, and azithromycin. When Arkin comes into the room, however, the tech there appears to already be having trouble obtaining vital signs. Specifically, the patient's pulse oximetry, the usual bedside measure of blood oxygenation, is registering just 72 percent on the tech's mobile equipment. Normal is 95 percent or better, and the finding is even more concerning as the patient is already receiving oxygen through the cannula in her nose. The tech, a young woman new on the job, has already tried the oxygen sensor on a different finger, is now attempting to position it on the patient's ear.

"What's the matter?" the patient asks, whether in alarm or irritation is unclear. What Arkin notices is that even those three words leave her more short of breath.

"Hello," he says from the doorway, "I'm Dr. Arkin," to which the patient can only wave a greeting. As with his hospice-bound COPD patient of a few days earlier, this patient, Roberta Cole, is working, breathing through pursed lips, the muscles in her neck taut, chest heaving. All this suggests the oxygen readings are not an error, and Arkin thinks she must be fit and healthy at baseline to be in so little obvious distress while working so hard to breathe. "You exercise?" he asks her as he casually reaches for an N95 mask and gloves.

Cole nods, but manages only, "Not today," with a grim smile, as Arkin arrives at her side, his mask now in place.

He reaches to the wall, increases the patient's oxygen flow to six liters per minute. "Go find the nurse, would you?" he asks the tech and then slips the tips of his stethoscope into his ears. "Can you lean forward?" he asks the patient. Moving the bell of the stethoscope around her back, he hears what the nurses refer to as "junk," and not just in one lung field, but everywhere. These are the classic rhonchi, or low-pitched wheezing, caused by mucous secretions in the airways, and while they are louder when the patient exhales, he can hear them, too, when she breathes in. "Can you cough?"

The patient does, and while ronchi sometimes clear with the cough, these barely do so. "Well?" she asks.

"So," Arkin says as he straightens, "usually with pneumonia, bacterial pneumonia, we'll hear abnormal sounds in just one part of the chest, maybe two. But with you, I'm hearing it everywhere. That's a little consistent with other infections."

"Is that why you put on the mask?"

Arkin nods, finds himself smiling reassuringly, although how much the patient might appreciate this is unclear, with the mask in place. He moves to the doorway, meets the patient's nurse there, an older and experienced woman named Margaret Hawley. "Hi, Margaret. Please call rapid response for this patient. I'm also gonna want to swab her for flu and COVID and start airborne precautions, okay?"

Without a word, Hawley nods, spins on her heel, and heads off to the nursing station. As she goes, he hears her speaking into her Vocera, a voice communication device: "Rapid response, room 740, rapid response, room 740."

Arkin has spent much of the fifteen minutes since initiating the rapid response on his cell phone in the entranceway to the patient's room. Even in that brief span, the patient's respiratory status has deteriorated. She's no longer reading on her iPad and is unable to form words. Her O_2 saturation is now in the mid–60 percent range even on high-flow oxygen. Her respiratory rate has increased to over thirty breaths per minute, and her blood gas shows an arterial

oxygen level of just 40 percent, far below normal. A bedside portable chest X-ray shows widespread peripheral opacities, including
in the bilateral lower lobes and mid-lung regions. Her bedside anti-
gen test is positive for COVID, and the entire team in the room is
gowned, gloved, masked, and shielded. Fortunately, 740 is a negative pressure room, meaning that airborne virus should not spread
into the hospital at large.

The hospital has not had many serious COVID cases for months,
not since the introduction of vaccines, the new monoclonal antibodies, and widespread adoption of various control measures, some
of which remain in effect even now. The hospital's airway response
team, maintained throughout the earlier long emergency period,
has been disbanded. Arkin has spoken with the intensive care unit
specialist, or intensivist, twice, briefly. She is juggling two critical
cases in "the unit" and is unable to leave them to assist. No anesthesiologist is available for possible intubation.

Arkin can only imagine how the team of nurses, respiratory therapists, and radiology and lab techs must feel about being called to
this room and this patient. They'd thought they were done with the
big COVID emergencies. They'd all had friends and coworkers sicken
and die. They'd all lived through the monthslong stress of possible
infection at any moment, at any patient contact. Their movements
now, almost from muscle memory, reflect the practiced ease of the
earlier emergency, but also, to Arkin's eye, anger and frustration.

Arkin is dealing with his own anger: that the patient hadn't
been tested on admission, a cardinal error; that the admitting physician had failed to ask about her travel, which included a recent
trip to Central America, where there are periodic ongoing COVID
outbreaks; and had failed also, finally, to document that the patient
had a history of refusing COVID vaccination in the past and was thus

at increased risk of presenting exactly as she has even now—acutely ill, contagious, and at risk of rapid decline and sudden death. Unlike many in-hospital emergencies, this one could easily have been foreseen and avoided, and Arkin is angry that managing someone else's major error has fallen to him.

And, he's also nervous. It's been at least a year since he intubated anyone, and he's spent the last ten minutes—while also awaiting lab results and the X-ray tech—trying to justify not doing it now, not intubating the patient himself. Many COVID patients did not require intubation, survived without it, but this patient is rapidly failing, is almost surely already suffering from ARDS, acute respiratory distress syndrome. Although measured hypoxemia—low oxygen levels on their monitoring equipment—can be misleading where COVID is concerned, the patient is clearly not getting enough oxygen to her organs. Even with high-flow supplementation, her heart rate is 140, increasing her already COVID-elevated risk of heart attack. She clearly needs to be on a ventilator then—and she has already agreed to the procedure: "If I really need it." But Arkin spends more minutes debating whether he can have her transported to ICU where—after waiting for the intensivist or an anesthesiologist to become available, however long that might take—she can be intubated by someone with daily experience, expert. Arguing against this, in addition to a potentially harmful delay, is the prospect of transporting a potential source of infection onto an elevator and through a half mile of hospital corridors. Arkin feels himself spiraling down a well of anxiety and self-doubt and fear of fucking up. Ultimately decisive is that he also subscribes to a profession-wide aversion to looking gutless.

"Okay, let's tube her, rapid sequence. Start her on non-rebreather. Got the vent ready? HEPA filter? Have an LMA and bougie ready in case of difficulty, Yankauer, of course." He says this to the nearby respiratory therapist. To one of the nurses: "I'll need a shield, booties, new gloves. Glidescope, seven point oh tube with stylet; check the balloon. We'll start with propofol, two milligram per kilogram, and once she's sedated rocuronium, one point two milligram per kilogram, suppress coughing. Let's have Levophed ready in case she drops her pressures. Any questions?" There are none, and Arkin is relieved again to see how smoothly the team operates as he struggles into his new PPE then goes to the patient.

"All right, Ms. Cole, you're gonna have a really nice nap here in a second," thinking even as he says this how inadequate it is for describing the days of sedation that are likely ahead for this woman, from which she may never awaken. But she nods, appears reasonably calm—certainly calmer than Arkin himself feels. He keeps repeating to himself the steps of medication and intubation, his backup plan should the procedure prove difficult. With the gown and gloves and mask and shield in place, he feels himself sweating through his shirt, feels the soaked waistband beneath his belt, worries that his face shield will fog with his own too-rapid exhalations. He is aware that this patient is already oxygenating poorly, even with aggressive preoxygenation now in progress. He knows she will stop breathing approximately thirty seconds after the IV propofol and rocuronium *go in*, as the nurses say, and that if he is unable to intubate correctly and within a matter of seconds, she may suffer an anoxic brain injury, along with the increasing possibility of demand cardiac ischemia and heart attack. As these forebodings cycle through his own brain, he becomes aware that the team of nurses and techs and RTs in the room are all now waiting for him, done with their preparations, ready for the order to start. He takes a breath, and another, and squeezes the patient's shoulder.

As it happens, the intubation is flawless. They never have to use the bag mask, avoiding spreading COVID aerosols through the room, and the patient is intubated and on the vent only seconds from the time the propofol takes effect. End-tidal carbon dioxide levels are consistent with proper placement of the ET tube. The patient has been started on low-tidal volume and PEEP and is ready to be transported to the ICU. Arkin thinks of the points he'll have earned with the intensivist when the patient arrives, tubed, on the right vent settings, vitals signs under control, properly sedated. Better, however, is the respiratory therapist's offer of "Nice job, Doc." The RTs are considered the toughest audience in the building.

"Great work, everyone," is Arkin's answer as the patient is wheeled away, the decontamination crew out in the hallway preparing to disinfect the room. He begins to take off his protective equipment but finds that he is shaking, possibly from fatigue but more likely from stress hormones leaving his system. Possibly contributing, too, (he thinks, ever more slowly) is the stress of his situation with Barnhardt, the pent-up fear of threatened exposure and humiliation. He is momentarily nauseated, breaks out in a cold sweat for the second time this morning, and, with his vision blurring, sinks to the floor. He's glad none of the nurses or other staff are there to see his near faint. He's glad especially that Kate is one floor up and on the other side of the building. He is aware that she's worried about him, that their day at the range was confusing. He feels she may be wondering what she's gotten herself into, who he really is, this doctor-sniper-drinker—*cipher*, he thinks. He realizes that all through the morning's events in room 740, he exchanged perhaps twenty words, no more, with his seventy-year-old patient who may not live through the week. He tries out the inner interrogative: *What kind of doctor does that make me? What kind of person?* He has no answer, only waits for the dizziness to pass and the sweat to cool before he struggles to his feet, and resumes his day.

Kate has completed her morning "med pass," administering 10:00 a.m. medications to all six of her patients. Prior to this, she checked all their morning labs and confirmed new medication orders from the physicians and nurse practitioners. She has completed her assessment of each patient and the extensive corresponding documentation required of her, of their physical and emotional status, skin integrity, intake, fluid balance, and more. She knows which patients are in pain, or short of breath, or not eating. She knows which need dressing changes and who will need assistance to the bathroom or bed pan or urinal. She knows which urinary catheters should be discontinued and whose saline locks will be changed. She knows who'll be going for imaging and, in one case, surgery. She knows who's planned for discharge.

Kate knows from the older staff that burdens on nurses have grown exponentially in recent years, in large part from the advent of electronic charting, with its dozens and dozens of data entries to be made, assessments to be done, tasks to be confirmed. As a younger nurse, Kate is perhaps less overwhelmed by this, in part because she's comfortable with the technology but mostly because it's all she's ever known. Nurses speak of "drowning" on busy days, days filled with discharges and admissions, heavy medication schedules, needy patients, emergencies. Falling behind leads to cascading missed tasks, computer-generated prompts, and complaints from doctors, frustrated patients and angry families.

Kate pretty much never falls behind, and she never panics. She resents the burden of documentation not because of the time it takes but because, unlike the physicians' notes, her entries don't matter; no one reads them, except possibly administrators looking to justify their jobs. She tries to remember the line about the two rules to living well: The first is, don't sweat the little shit. The second is, it's all little shit. Still, Kate tries not to take breaks or check her phone until the scheduled tasks are accomplished, and she's ahead of the curve. The older, experienced nurses don't resent this because it also means she's available to help when *they* get swamped. And the younger, newer nurses like it because they want to be like her.

But Arkin, she thinks, has upset the cool arc of her hospital days. She knows that, like him, something about her lack of family, of friends in the area, or of a pet, or home, or spouse, or kids, has freed her to float through her days. The stress and busyness of the hospital is actually a relief, topographical interest in the otherwise level plain of her life. But Arkin has reintroduced a turbulence, and she thinks now it was turbulence of any kind that she'd been avoiding, at least since her mom's death. Or perhaps she'd always been this way, had moved across the country in an act of emotional simplification, rounding off her psychological decimal points to nothing at all. She doesn't know why this is so. Arkin at least has the excuse of his mother's suicide, his father's earlier abandonment. Whatever *did* happen in Afghanistan, it was clearly a thing of nightmares, which Barnhardt's threats of disclosure have reawakened.

Kate has no such scars. Her father's death was awful, but she was seventeen when it happened—and nothing like as unexpected as Arkin's mom's suicide, with the implied rejection suicides carry. Her father wasn't ending their relationship by having a heart attack; he just *had it*. Somewhere within, Kate acknowledges that, as smokers, both her parents engaged in a literally self-destructive activity that contributed to both their deaths. Does *that* fact explain the cool-ish breeze of her emotional weather? Kate doesn't think so, and laughs at herself for the phrase. But whatever the cause, she thinks it does explain the relationship with Arkin, the connection. Whatever the cause, they both drink, they both withhold, and they both relish the risk-free attachment they've formed. Not only have they never even glancingly discussed children, much less marriage, they've neither used the word *love*. She realizes they've never, either of them, said even something as unloaded as *I like you*, or even *I like this*. Most people might manage to end even a bad date with, at worst, *This was nice*. Not them.

And yet—and this word leaps to Kate's mind—she *aches* for him. His fear, his doubt, his need, are hers as well, even without a clear sense of their exact nature, and Kate believes Arkin feels the same. That doesn't exactly sound like love. But, remembering a phrase from calculus, Kate thinks perhaps it's a first approximation of love. And she doesn't want anything to derail it, is furious at this patient Barnhardt for unsettling Arkin as he has, unsettling this new connection.

So when she sees Arkin coming down the hall, around the unit circle, and heading for Barnhardt's room, she naturally follows.

———————

Arkin comes to a brief halt at the foot of the bed, then moves to Barnhardt, who silently watches his approach. Arkin again notes the yellowing of the skin and sclera, the gynecomastia or swelling of the breasts caused by the liver's inability to clear estrogen from Barnhardt's body. The muscles in Barnhardt's arms appear increasingly atrophied, and spider angiomas are more widespread on his face and arms. Although awake, and although his lab values are slightly improved, Barnhardt overall seems slightly more lethargic, likely from progressive encephalopathy.

Arkin puts his stethoscope to Barnhardt's chest, notes the tachycardia and pounding pulse consistent with the hyperdynamic syndrome seen in cirrhosis. Although he remains on oxygen, Arkin thinks Barnhardt is more short of breath today, both from his underlying lung and heart disease as well as possible developing hepatopulmonary syndrome, a common complication of cirrhosis. The ascites appears worse, the abdomen larger; Arkin touches it and, even under the gown and sheet, he can see the fluid wave propagating across the belly. Overall, Barnhardt's condition appears to be worsening despite "maximal medical care," as common usage has it.

"Well?" Barnhardt asks, and then to Arkin's silence, "Where do we stand?"

Arkin retreats from the bedside, sits again in the chair by the window, notes again the distant water tower with its distant "Raider Pride" sentiment. Nothing has changed, not the town outside, the gray-green of the hospital room on South Eight, not the course of the patient's illness within. Only minutes earlier, he'd intubated the woman on South Seven, beginning her weeks-long arc of illness and treatment, over which little would change from one day to the next. The day before, at the range in Pennsylvania, fractions of a second defined the action and reactions of rifle marksmanship; in medicine, reactions can take a lifetime.

Barnhardt might almost have been reading Arkin's mind. "I'm dying, aren't I?"

"Yes."

"How soon could I die?"

From somewhere in his distant academic past, Arkin recovers the term *future conditional* for Barnhardt's use of "could." He chooses to the ignore the possible *if* implications of the question, and answers, "You have a MELD score of forty. That means you probably have less than three months. Possibly much less, depending on how aggressive we are in treating you."

Barnhardt is strangely, almost appealingly, docile, reasonable. "I love that. 'Aggressive.' The way you people use that word. It sounds so definitive, so strong—aggressive—but it can mean almost anything. You can manage my, well, symptoms, aggressively. Slow everything down, slow me down, help me . . . die. Or you can manage the disease aggressively, prolong *things*, help me live longer. But you can't do both. Can you?"

"No." Arkin is only vaguely aware that he has fallen into Barnhardt's pace and tone. Manipulating the rhythm and dynamics of these conversations is a technique that the best clinicians employ; Arkin can't recall a patient ever using it against him.

"Do you know how much is spent in the last six months of patients' lives, in the United States?"

"A lot," Arkin says, earning a look of—still gentle—reproof from the man in bed. Arkin hesitates before continuing and, at the same time, becomes aware of Kate standing in the doorway, intentionally out of Barnhardt's line of sight but there, Arkin thinks, for him. He turns to Barnhardt, and says, "Hundreds of billions."

"Yes," Barnhardt says, then pauses for a long moment before saying, "I want some of it."

Arkin says nothing, waiting. Though alone in the room with Barnhardt, he is deeply, even pleasurably, aware of Kate, his silent but connected partner, in the doorway. That doesn't necessarily ease the impact of what Barnhardt has to say.

"This thing you all do, Arkin, is sanctimony. You don't offer life; you don't even want to offer me, with your documentation, your sobriety rules, a *chance* at life. Even though a doctor, not alcohol, caused this. And the only alternative you do offer me is suffering, which you say you will alleviate with drugs that may make me less anxious, less nauseated, less agonized—while at the same time making me stupid, soporific, helpless." Barnhardt actually laughs, true and unforced, and says, "My balls are literally in a sling. And you *offer* to make me less *anxious* about it."

"What would you like me to do?" Even as he says it, Arkin recognizes it's the sort of closed-ended question doctors aren't supposed to ask.

Barnhardt's eyes light at the prospect of answering. "I want you to let me live. Or I want you to help me die. Now."

"I can't do that."

"Oh." And here Barnhardt begins to shift out of amiability and into something much keener and more direct: "I see. The same man who shot down innocent villagers in Afghanistan, although *he can't quite remember,*"—laughing derisively at the idea—"is unable to help a sick old man out of the world with a big shot of morphine."

Arkin senses Kate flinching in the doorway, shrinking from Barnhardt's laughter.

"Oh, Arkin, you really are something. Well, sooner or later, we all pay the price for our bad acts. I guess it's a lesson you're about to learn too."

Arkin says. "I'm not going to lie for you, document anything. Even if I did, you're not a candidate. No one would transplant you. They give organs to younger and healthier people."

"I'll worry about that. Just write the report."

"No." Arkin gathers himself, gathers his breath, determined not to fight—as if he had an argument, which he does not. He has recourse only to the familiar, the algorithm. "I'm going to order another paracentesis, get some of that fluid off and make you more comfortable. I think we can stop the antibiotics we've had you on for infection, start something called rifaximin to help with liver toxicity."

"Never mind that," Barnhardt says, almost kindly again, dismissive. "You can go." He waves his hand, orangey and queenlike. And then to Arkin's retreating back: "Ask the nurse manager to come in." And after a moment: "Or better yet, have risk management stop by."

Arkin stops, a few feet from Kate, only mildly surprised at Barnhardt's mention of risk management, the administrative team concerned with potential lawsuits, legal liability generally, patient damages. He knows what it means, what Barnhardt is both threatening, again, and offering.

Kate sees Arkin deciding not to respond, taking a breath, then walking past her out into the hallway. Kate turns and follows without Barnhardt's ever having been aware of her presence.

In the hallway, she asks, "What are you going to do?"

"Nothing."

Around them, the rush and rhythm of South Eight continues unabated, as it does on the floors beneath them, the buildings of the big medical campus around them, its doctors, nurses, aides, lab technicians, and administrators, the dedicated and exhausted and periodically vanquished brigades of health care.

"Nothing," Arkin says, and goes.

Kate takes an Uber from his apartment, where she has driven him and his car from the Riverside, again. He is still so drunk when she leaves that he doesn't stir. She has never seen his apartment, an amalgam of white walls and textured white ceiling and big box furniture. She sees no photographs, only a few medical journals, his laptop, half a dozen packaged meals from Freshly in the refrigerator. There's a phone charger and a handle of Jack Daniels on the counter, a third down; there's a twelve-pack of Lagunitas that he has neglected to refrigerate. There's a rudimentary dinnerware set, a few glasses, basic T-fal cookware that looks as though it's never been used. She guesses that altogether the kitchenware cost two hundred dollars at Target.

In the bedroom, where he's snoring faintly facedown on a poly cotton bedset, there's a dresser and bedside table which she recognizes from the Wayfair website, and nothing else. Clothes are neatly folded in the dresser, hung in the closet, with three pairs of shoes; Kate feels no special guilt at the examination of his things, although she can't think what she's looking for. The word "color" comes into her mind, but Arkin isn't colorless so much as weightless, adrift. Even as she thinks this, though, she has to acknowledge her own gliding path through life, school, around the country, to different hospitals, jobs, men.

But Kate wonders at the dimensions of her potential mistake with this man. He's smart, gentle, considerate in bed, and everything anyone could want professionally. He is also, she fears, a drunk, possibly clinically depressed, completely uncommunicative at times, and for all these reasons the antithesis of "good boyfriend." More, he has a secret, including from himself, about what happened while he was in the Army, at war. Arkin certainly seems to fulfill the criteria for PTSD, with disjointed memories, in particular in his case the "inability to recall an important aspect of the trauma." Except that he is in so many respects functioning at so a high level, he strikes her as meeting most if not all of the DSM-5 criteria for PTSD.

Which makes him an even less reasonable bet in the long-term relationship category. It makes her uncomfortable that this thought causes its own opposite and more than equal reaction in her, a rising fury at herself, and fear of loss. Kate is not sure she's ever been *in love*, but the wave of feeling rising up in her recalls no experience or understanding that she has ever had before. Arkin is still sleeping when, her fingers trembling slightly, she brushes a lock of hair back from his face, and leaves.

ELEVEN

BARNHARDT'S DEATH OVERNIGHT, though sudden, is not actually unexpected. As Arkin had told him the day before, the MELD assessment of his liver disease forecast less than ninety days to live. So while the specific cause of death is uncertain, the likelihood of it was not. People with advanced liver disease can die suddenly from heart attacks, hemorrhage, uncontrolled seizure, fatal arrhythmias. Barnhardt was properly, appropriately, not on telemetry, so an arrhythmia, if it occurred, would not have been detected by the night nursing staff and could've ended his life in minutes, even moments. The multiple underlying problems with his blood chemistry would have predisposed him to conduction abnormalities. Or a seizure, which he'd experienced before, and which, if not halted with medication, could progress to the prolonged seizure of status epilepticus, and death.

Arkin finds himself contemplating these and other possibilities as he puts off examining his own feelings. No matter the threat Barnhardt posed to him, he remained Arkin's patient. No matter the awful prognosis, with death in the near future, it was not imminent. So Arkin experiences that inner nexus of self-doubt, fear, anxiety, and insecurity that accompanies a doctor's foundational questions: Where did I fuck up? What did I miss?

When, summoned by nursing, he arrives on the unit, Barnhardt's body is still in his room. After their other morning duties are accomplished, the techs will transport it to the hospital morgue in a specially designed covered gurney, hiding the corpse and its implications from other patients and their visitors. Overnight staff has already removed his IV access, oxygen cannula, urinary catheter. A second ID bracelet has been placed around his ankle. Barnhardt's eyes are open, the sclera still jaundiced, as is the skin around them. The facial muscles appear slack, but the lower jaw has jutted forward as the masseter and pterygoid muscles have begun to stiffen from the onset of rigor mortis. Arkin touches the eyelids, where the first signs of rigor appear, and finds them rigid. Nursing reports that Barnhardt was alive at the midnight check but dead when rounded on at 4:00 a.m., consistent with the beginning of rigor now.

Arkin barely remembers the details of Barnhardt's exam the previous day. He'd seen the rest of his patients after that, then went to the Riverside with Kate. He does not remember her driving him home. He knows she did because she left him a note, a brief note attached to his car keys. He does not remember talking about that last conversation with Barnhardt, though he assumes they did. He does not remember eating and cannot recall what he drank, how much, or how late into the night. Arkin feels a not-unfamiliar sense of shame but also a gnawing, just-dawning alarm at the apparent blackout. However much he drank in the past, he has never lost hours. He has driven under the influence, of that there is no doubt, but he has never been taken home in a stupor. Much of his shame pertains to Kate's having seen him in that condition; he has no idea what he might have said or done, how he might have looked. He woke up fully clothed, so she didn't bother to undress him; he imagines she was too disgusted to bother. Kate's not working today, so he can't ask her, and doubts that he could bring himself to even if she were here.

Two techs arrive pushing the mortuary gurney, accompanied by South Eight's assistant nurse manager, Rona Diehl. "Hi, Dr. Arkin," she says, pleasantly enough; Barnhardt was nobody's favorite patient.

"Hi Rona. Any info on what happened?"

"Nope, just found him when they went to draw labs and do vitals at four. Actually, closer to five."

"Okay. Family notified? I don't remember—did he have a next of kin?"

"Don't know, but they handled all that overnight. Dr. Lewis did the cert."

The techs have maneuvered the gurney to the bedside, locked the wheels. Diehl moves to assist as the techs prepare to slide the body onto it; Arkin moves forward a little awkwardly to help, grasping the sheet under the body, and together the four of them move Barnhardt onto the gurney. Arkin is surprised at how easily the shift is accomplished, how light the body feels. He wonders if there'd still be ascitic fluid shifts in the belly but does not look to see. The techs fit the concealment canopy into place.

"Thanks for your help," Rona says to him.

Arkin nods, silent, as the body is wheeled into the hall and away.

With the death certificate already completed by the overnight physician, Arkin has only to dictate Barnhardt's discharge summary. The certificate itself, one of the few pieces of actual paper documentation in the otherwise near-empty physical chart, notes the immediate cause of death as cardiorespiratory arrest as a consequence of hepatic cirrhosis, COPD, and heart failure. That all-purpose term "cardiorespiratory arrest" is essentially meaningless, declaring the self-evident: the patient died because he stopped breathing and his heart stopped beating. To the question about smoking as a contributor, Dr. Lewis has checked the "probably" box. The autopsy box is checked "no," typical for patients dying in the hospital. As contributors, neither alcoholism nor alpha antitrypsin deficiency is mentioned, the former no doubt because it appears nowhere in Arkin's own documentation, the latter because, most likely, Dr. Lewis didn't bother to read more than a sentence or two of Arkin's notes.

The words of the discharge summary tumble out of Arkin effortlessly. He does mention a history of both alcohol and AAT deficiency, albeit in a single sentence, because why not? Whatever threat Barnhardt posed has evaporated with his death, and whatever reason he'd had to demand Arkin's hiding the history of drinking is moot. Arkin makes no mention of Barnhardt's previous treatment by the Army because he has no direct knowledge of it; his conversations with Oliver are outside of any formal medical or family context and are also not included. Even as he dictates the formulaic "Patient expired without reported distress or discomfort," he feels his own distress and discomfort begin to ease. Perhaps it's unseemly to feel such relief at another's death, and Arkin makes an unconvincing inner attempt at rationalizing Barnhardt's in terms of decline and misery avoided. While this may be true in the abstract, and in fact is true of unexpected or early deaths for many of his sickest patients, Arkin cannot sell himself on it here. He is relieved to be rid of a demonstrably bad man, an enemy even, both of himself and countless others, if Oliver is to be believed. He is glad to forget as quickly as possible any consideration he may have given to falsifying a medical record. At the same time, his stated refusal to do so, to the patient himself just the previous afternoon, also fades from his inner horizon. Like Barnhardt's threats to ruin him, Arkin's resistance, his commitment to professional ethics, was never really put to the test. (Nor was his refusal to discuss what was basically a demand for what would have amounted to euthanasia.)

With varying degrees of success, doctors do try *not* to second-guess themselves on treatment choices. One can never know how a patient would've fared with a different antibiotic, a different antihypertensive or anticoagulant; you can only ever know what happened with the choice you did make, the order you did write. While Arkin is less adept at this than many, he believes his *medical* choices with Barnhardt were correct, and he chooses not to second-guess how he'd have responded if his own history had been revealed to others. He tells himself, possibly even *congratulates* himself, that he revealed it to Kate, the one really important person in his life. He pauses only briefly at having assigned her that position. Well, and at having bought the rifle, the H&K. He wonders what Kate really thought of *that*. She seemed to enjoy their "day at the range," as he thinks of it now. Perhaps she thinks of it as a hobby of his, possibly *the* hobby, as he has no others. Possibly she thinks (more incisively, and more likely, he has to admit) that it is an attempt on his part to assert control. To assert control over at least one part of his life—in this case, over a bullet—at a particularly fraught moment. He wonders if he will continue shooting, or if he should sell the rifle, that moment having passed.

On the way to Kate's apartment, he buys takeout kung pao chicken and stir-fried broccoli in garlic sauce. It's past seven and he hasn't bothered to change from his work clothes; he also hasn't had a drink. He'd texted Kate earlier with the news of Barnhardt's death, and sees that she's opened up the small drop-leaf table in her kitchen, spread a simple white tablecloth.

"Did you want something to drink?" she asks mildly.

"I'm fine," he says. Both of them know this may not be entirely true. Kate knows what he looked like the night before, when she put him to bed. And Arkin knows vaguely that it's been months, if not years, since he passed even a single night without alcohol. He is aware that drinkers like him, even relatively young ones, can have symptoms of acute withdrawal. He knows also that the worst of these usually start more than twenty-four hours after the last drink, so he's unlikely to experience them tonight, at least; he may have some residual alcohol in his system from the previous night, keeping them in check.

"I think I need to make a change," he says, looking at the take-out containers, the plastic serving spoons they've put out; he can't quite bring himself to look at Kate.

"Okay," she says, noncommittal.

"I mean about alcohol. You should drink if you want to."

"I don't want to," she tells him, a little more definitive.

Arkin had talked himself through a few potential approaches in the car coming over, growing slightly more frantic and muddled as Kate's apartment came nearer. All those trial runs accomplished was to remind him that he hadn't had a serious conversation about a relationship, well, ever.

"I worry . . ." he begins, then stops, not remembering any of his rehearsed approaches starting that way. "I worry . . . that I'm . . . screwing this up."

Kate watches from across the table, through the diminishing steam from the cooling kung pao.

"I've been pretty . . . undependable." He imagines that Kate, too, will think this a conspicuously poor euphemism for *out of control* or, more simply, *drunk all the time*. "I want this to work," he also volunteers, possibly just in time.

Given that Kate, too, has avoided conversations like this all her adult life, she is surprised, even startled, to find herself saying, "I do too." She doesn't elaborate though. No *I care about you,* much less the code blue undeniability of *I love you*. Typically, the guy—and it's always *the guy* in movie scenes—would also avoid an escalation and instead now say, "You may not know what you're getting yourself into." But Arkin doesn't say that; Kate is too smart and too savvy, and too strong, *not* to know. She knows enough.

"I need to stop drinking," is what he says instead. "Maybe I need . . . to . . . talk to someone."

This is medicalese for counseling, and Kate nods judiciously. "Maybe I do too," she says generously. It feels like they've been talking for hours, but the takeout is still hot—or anyway, warm— and Kate decides this might be the moment to dish out the chicken, its peanuts floating sluggishly in a spicy cornstarch-thickened goo of hoisin sauce and sesame oil and a few dispirited scallion slivers. Still, food seems like a relief. "Maybe we should eat something?" as she spoons the glop onto his plate. Arkin nods enthusiastically, though he has no appetite, feels he may never have again.

"Thank you," he says, and Kate smiles fractionally, the deep womanly quarter-smile that Arkin, and possibly no man, can ever decipher. "Uh . . ." he manages.

"Yeah," she says, the smile still there, "you can go home after."

To which Arkin nods in agreement, continues nodding as he reaches for his water glass, dry mouthed.

———————————

In the morning, Arkin is curiously relaxed. He has none of the jitteriness he expected, no sweating or nausea; he has slept unexpectedly well. He stops at Cumberland Farms to pick up a pint carton of orange juice and a bagel. He enjoys breakfast behind the wheel on his way to the hospital. He dwells on the memory of Kate hugging him goodnight at her doorway, a brief kiss on the cheek. He thinks it the purest moment of friendship he has ever known, oddly (given their history) but pleasantly devoid of sexual color. It was just—and he smiles at this—affectionate.

Arriving at the hospital, he goes immediately to the meeting of the Enhanced Assessment and Treatment team. Having already eaten, he skips the rush to the bagel spread, contents himself with coffee, and busies himself with his phone and long-ignored work emails as his colleagues find their seats around him and Eva Tern begins the weekly get-together.

"So, I believe I've had a chance to meet with each of you individually? Take you through your first exposure to our next gen EMR. So first, any reactions you'd like to share with the group?"

She looks around the conference table, takes in the studiously thoughtful expressions common to experienced professionals seeking to avoid the likely and classic misstep of speaking first. Even Arkin, among the youngest here, understands the dynamic; those with the highest frustration level, the greatest resistance to change, financial problems or disgruntled spouses, whatever, will usually be the most hair-triggered generally and thus impatient to speak. They will also usually be the most senior clinicians (not administrators, who've learned the ropes and avoid getting tangled), that is, those with the most years of disappointment with the direction of their profession and eager expound on its failings.

Today's self-nominee is Stan Gundy, a partner in the big local neurology group. "Well, my concern, is this is just another loss of . . . autonomy, I guess you'd say. Even physician privacy."

"Any thoughts on that?" Tern asks of the others, and gets no takers. Everyone understands that loss of physician autonomy is a given, progressive, and a condition of technology present across the country and for every profession in it. Gundy is right to be "concerned" but wrong to waste his breath.

The "physician privacy" is a thornier issue, and is taken up by Barbara Horn, one of thirty docs in the huge local cardiology practice. Like Gundy, in her sixties, she nonetheless skips over autonomy. "I thought about that, too, the privacy piece." This gets a few nods around the table, more than a few, actually, as Dr. Horn has started off pleasantly dispassionate, and has also deployed the corporate favorite "piece" in lieu of "issue" or "problem." "I mean, your system is actually monitoring *my* physiology, my reaction time, my reading skills even. Of course everyone is different, everyone is different day-to-day; there may be sleep cycle, gender differences, cultural differences . . ."

This garners a *lot* of approval, if still silent, from colleagues, expressed in thoughtful nods of consideration. It doesn't hurt that Horn has managed to raise the specter of both gender and cultural bias, to which she adds the potential for inadequate evidence. "I'm not aware—you haven't presented—any *research* on any of this." Tern is unbothered, in smile-and-understand mode so far. But Horn's not done, in fact has used those first points as throwaways in advance of the real incendiary device: "Even more, however . . . it strikes me that you've already got the functionality; it's a short step to performance evaluation." This really *does* get everyone's attention, and Horn underlines the point. "To biometric performance evaluation, employee grading, efficiency ratings, HR decisions." Tern's no longer exactly smiling. "You haven't said anything about who actually gets to *see* this data. Unless I missed that?" Horn says with a smile.

After a respectful pause, Tern begins, "Well, Dr. Horn, you've raised a really interesting question." Her follow-up is all-purpose and irrefutable: "I'm not sure I have an answer. I'm just on the technology side. I mean, clearly, anyone with high-level software, uh, administrator access, can look at data. But, you know, well, you know, it's just *data*; really, anything we choose can be walled off. Can even be deleted after use or within a specified time window. It can require user notification. So I just don't know. I can certainly find out."

The group is silent at this. Dr. Gundy is nodding with particular enthusiasm, though, having been rescued from the irrelevance of his offering by Dr. Horn's better points. And everyone recognizes that Tern has engaged in some pretty high-level baffle 'em with bullshit tech jargon. They may even admire her for it, but Barbara Horn's ultimate if unspoken point—that they could end up being reimbursed, or even fired, based on the computer's evaluation of their cognitive and perceptual performance—has actually alarmed them. Arkin himself has wondered immediately whether his relatively youthful brain could overcome digital markers for hangover should his drinking continue (resume?). He's impressed that Dr. Horn has leapt to a subject that will appeal to everyone at the table, and notes her relaxed smile and acknowledgment of the approving hubbub around the table. It's then that the conference room door opens and Arkin's boss, Assam Massood, appears. Massood smiles shyly, apologetic at the interruption, but beckons: "Dr. Arkin? Could I just steal you for a minute?"

———————

It turns out to be more than a minute. Dr. Massood leads him out of the admin wing, down a hallway, up a flight of stairs, and down the third floor corridor to his own office. Massood says little, keeping his pace just hurried enough to maintain a non-conversational distance ahead of Arkin. He fiddles with something in the pocket of his lab coat, perhaps his phone, turning it over and over like a stress ball. As they near his office, Massood manages, "I have no idea what this is about, I don't even know why they came to see me. I mean, *I* don't know anything— as usual!" This with the sort of nervous but affectionate smile that Massood may think reassuring, perhaps routine and self-mocking in a formulaic in a sort of way, but that chills Arkin. Massood doesn't even go into the office, his own office, instead holds the door for Arkin. "Dr. Arkin, this is Mr. Breen? Mr. Breen is from the Army?"

This Mr. Breen rises, offers Arkin his hand. He's a little over six feet, maybe Arkin's height, fit, crewcut, no gray in the blondish hair, blue eyed, sport jacketed, brogganed, broad-smiled.

"Hey, Dr. Arkin, Ed Breen," and turning to Massood, "Okay if we use your office, doctor?"

"Oh yes, of course," says Massood, peering around the door he's already begun to close behind him. "I have meetings," he says cheerfully, the door clicking shut.

Breen turns to Arkin, offers a vague smile, vaguely ironic that is, shared appreciation for Massood's conveniently crowded schedule, and gestures Arkin to the other visitor's chair. "So, glad you could see me."

"Sure. What's this about?" Though Massood's introduction, *Mr. Breen is from the Army*, is answer enough.

"Well, I understand you took care of Mr. Robert Barnhardt?"

"Yes."

"Well, obviously, we have an interest." It's not so obvious to Arkin, who says nothing. "So, I don't know how much you know."

Arkin manages a half smile, an innocent shrug, feeling the muscles in his back tensing over all that he may not want to know.

"I should introduce myself," Breen continues. "I'm a special agent with Army CID. I did a little preliminary research and understand you're a veteran, rank of Sergeant E5, is that right?"

"Yes."

"So you know what CID is—Criminal Investigation Division."

"Sure," Arkin says, relaxed, though unconsciously pulling his lab coat shut, crossing his legs and arms, the classic closed posture anyone would recognize, certainly including Army investigators. Arkin manages a too-amiable: "I've been out of the Army a while, but I remember that."

Breen answers with an equally amiable tilt of his head, eyes not leaving Arkin's, however.

"What brings you here?"

"Well, a couple things, related. First, Mr. Barnhardt was still technically an employee of the US government, detailed to the Army, sort of a quasi contractor but really more than that. And in his paperwork for the Army, he listed his mother as next of kin; that was some years ago, and his mother has passed away. So he has no next of kin." Breen offers an apologetic grin as he continues. "We're it. And, probably more to the point, Mr. Barnhardt was engaged in very high-level stuff, very high-level clearance, until just a few months ago. Certainly, within the last year. And when people with his sort of clearance, doing the sort of work he did, die outside of our care, we do routine sorts of investigations."

"So, just routine?"

"Sure. I've already spoken to Dr. Massood, who will get the autopsy rolling."

"Oh. That's unusual. In the hospital."

"Yeah, I know. Again, just routine. And then, we like to clarify what was going on, who was providing care, what brought the member to the hospital. That sort of thing."

Arkin is silent at this; his attention has wandered to Massood's desk, an overly saturated family photo there, a bronzed golf ball. Eventually, he drags his gaze back to Breen, who's unbothered by Arkin's apparent lack of interest.

"So, you admitted him, you discharged him twice, including yesterday when he died. That makes you the person with all the information. Can you just give me a . . . summary?"

If Breen were shorter, less fit, less angular, not quite so well shaved and buzz-cut, this might be a lot less intimidating, but Arkin feels, well, pressed. "I'm not sure about this . . . I guess I should ask for some identification?"

Breen's ID is produced as if by magic but more probably in anticipation of exactly this sort of delaying action on Arkin's part. The facility with which he displays the bifold laminated badge-and-face credentials adds to Arkin's unease. "And . . . you probably know this, but patients, even after death, have privacy rights. I think fifty years is the rule now?" But Arkin can guess what's coming next, which Breen confirms by reaching into the briefcase on the floor beside him, sorting through a few folders, and extracting a copy of paragraph § 164.512(f)(4) of the Federal Code of Regulations. He hands it to Arkin, who doesn't bother looking.

"That's the law enforcement exclusionary clause in HIPAA," Breen says.

"And you're law enforcement."

Breen only grins again, accepts the unstudied federal reprint back from Arkin, who says, "Okay." And then proceeds to tell the whole story from Barnhardt's first arrival in the emergency room to his death the day before. He spares Barnhardt's memory nothing. He himself, considering that he was prepared to risk personal exposure and the possibility of embarrassment, not to mention professional disgrace, to hear Barnhardt tell it, is unflinching with an actual cop, leaving out only his meeting with Beth Oliver, who was uninvolved in Barnhardt's care for years.

It takes half an hour, a little more, questions and answers and clarifications included. Arkin had allotted just about that to the systems meeting with Eva Tern and his bagel-noshing colleagues but needs to start rounding out in the hospital if he isn't to fall impossibly behind with his patient census.

Breen has only a few more questions. "So you told Barnhardt"— Arkin notes that he's dropped the *Mister*—"that you wouldn't falsify his records, is that right?"

"Yes."

"And that's even though he threatened you with revealing this"— a dismissive wave of his hand—"what, some remote event in Afghanistan, about which he really never took any action."

"That's right."

Breen heaves something of a sigh, almost theatrical in its cable TV detective world-weariness. "Well," he admits, "Bob Barnhardt . . . was not a very nice man. And he seems to have been a not very nice man right up to the end."

Arkin finds himself unexpectedly relieved, grateful, and glad that he held nothing back. He wonders, forty-eight hours into it, whether his sudden sobriety has contributed to his willingness to be candid; he feels perhaps his own spiral of history with the military, begun as a teenager, may at last be winding to an end, and is pleased he was alert, present for it.

"So far as I'm concerned," Breen offers, "that's ancient stuff. Doesn't matter here. Okay?"

"Sounds good. I should get to work." He rises, offers Breen his hand.

"Thanks for your help, Doc. I'll get back to you if anything else crops up, but I think we're done."

———————

To Kate, Arkin seems a new man. Off his boilermaker regimen, he's sleeping better, eating better, has run three mornings in a row. He's no neater—Kate wonders when he last washed his lab coat—but he breezes onto the units, her unit at least, with energy and possibly even enthusiasm. The other nurses eye her with renewed curiosity. Heather Newcomb even manages a laboriously offhand question about Kate's method of contraception. Kate hopes her equally offhand reference to the latest in IUDs will quell that particular line of gossip. That she herself wonders what Arkin's reaction would be to a pregnancy is a new development. They still haven't actually *discussed* it, but Arkin seems so much happier, it's true, that Kate can't help wondering how such a discussion might go now.

Saturday night, after three workdays in a row for each, they have a late dinner on the outdoor terrace at Sunset, the big riverside restaurant frequented by the hospital's nurses and docs for a few hours of semi-relaxed after-shift mixing. It's the experience of most nurses that, with a few drinks in the bar and cocktail area, the male doctors—women doctors tend not to hang out here—will reveal themselves to be as immature as they'd always suspected. She knows from Arkin that the doctors come away saying the nurses are "nice," or "really nice," or "fun,"—which in Kate's mind constitutes magical thinking of the highest order. All the years of medical school and residency can't erase the inequality between female nurses and male doctors: the doctors have their educations, but the nurses have the power.

Kate knows that at the crowded bar inside the restaurant, both their male and female colleagues are aware of Arkin and her on the terrace. This, too, is part of Arkin's change in recent days, and hers as well, she supposes, that they're out in public as a couple, unguarded and unconcerned. And this in turn heightens her sense that Arkin is unlike the men inside, the other doctors scouting her women friends. It's not just that he never came on to any of them, or even to her (she remembers *she's* the one who did that). It's also that he seems to assign no more weight to his role as a doctor, no greater prominence on his inner landscape, than to that of veteran, or community college grad, or child of a single parent. Sitting across from her, she sees not a hospitalist or board-certified internist, but a guy working on his sobriety, uncomfortably gripping a tall glass of club soda with lime. But this, she thinks, is no more or less incongruous than the same hand operating a semiautomatic rifle at the long-distance range in Pennsylvania, or inserting a subclavian line. None of it particularly fits, and all of it matters.

"So," she says, drawing on this new sense of the man sitting opposite, "tell me about your mother."

The gray of Arkin's eyes seems to cloud and deepen, and his mouth sets into a new line, abrupt and flat. Kate waits, watching. Arkin has never, after all, really asked about *her* parents, though this strikes her now as a symptom of the same syndrome; it's time they *talked*.

After a moment, though, his face relaxes. He unclenches his nonalcoholic beverage, uses the napkin to dry his palm, wet from condensation and possibly sweat. He says, "I told you she committed suicide."

Kate nods, knows that much. She holds his gaze, holding to the moment of openness, unprotected and available herself, inviting without urging, she hopes.

And Arkin continues: "I never . . . understood. I came home from school, after practice, and there were police out front. An ambulance." Arkin looks to the bar, the busy restaurant within crowded with diners, as if finding some counterpoint in the life there to the end-of-life story he's revisiting out in the night air. "She had shot herself. There was no note. And I was seventeen, and not a very . . . mature or perceptive . . . teenager. But there hadn't been anything unusual. Every day was the same. I'd go to school about the time she'd go to work. We'd have . . . cereal together first. We'd both get home about the same time if I had sports, or I'd stay for study hall. She cooked. I'd learned to use the Weber, so she'd give me something to put on the grill. And then she'd watch TV, or read, usually something from work." His voice has fallen to a lower register, softer and unquestionably newly *sober* in tone. "She didn't drink, didn't smoke anything. She didn't date, so far as I know. Nothing changed. And then . . . that one day, she came home from work and killed herself."

"I'm sorry," Kate says. And, against all odds, the cliché comes out right, unforced and genuine. She whispers, "That must have been terrible."

Arkin's nod is nearer to a shrug than assent. "I never met my father, I don't know who he was. She never talked about him, didn't put his name on the birth certificate. Her family . . . rejected her, we didn't see them. She had a few friends from work. She worked really hard, she took good care of us. She liked romance novels, and PBS, and she'd take me to museums, shows. She liked art. She liked Matisse, the cutouts. She liked me, I think. She loved me."

Kate reaches out, touches his hand; his fingers move to hold hers, then releases them.

"I don't know why she killed herself. But I suppose, I guess, she felt her life was empty." He pauses, closes his eyes for a moment then looks again at Kate: "I think when people's lives feel empty enough, that's when they . . . go."

Later, after parking at Arkin's rental condo, they walk through the adjacent park on the Hudson, crisscrossed by trails and by boardwalks with a view of preserved wetlands, with their cattails and lily marshes lit by the light of a waxing moon. The park is quiet at night, but they can hear occasional laughter and voices from a group of teenagers down by the river. Kate and Arkin walk hand in hand, now and then falling out of sync and bumping into one another, first their hips, then arms, shoulders touching, before finding the rhythm again, and then slowing to stop to stare at the moon. They turn to each other, now not touching except for their clasped hands, both hands, as if holding their bodies apart as they kiss, almost chastely, gently, as longtime lovers sometimes will, although they are not longtime but new, still almost strangers. Out in the river a party boat motors slowly by, the sounds of music and shouts and dancing drifting across the water to join that of the kids in the park by the water, all apart from the lone couple here and barely touching, only their lips, unspeaking.

TWELVE

WHEN ED BREEN, the Army CID agent, returns, he is accompanied by a large Black man with a round head and elegant goatee, in pin-striped suit and figured tie. Breen, slim and blond, looks almost childlike beside him. Accompanied by Dr. Massood, they've found Arkin at the nurses' station on the oncology unit, where he's just done a consult on a newly diagnosed lymphoma patient. The consult centered primarily on management of elevated blood pressures during treatment with prednisolone, and Arkin has ordered antihypertensives along with a mild diuretic. The patient faces a difficult prognosis, but he and Arkin have had what clinicians like to call a "good conversation," with the patient focused on at least this one aspect of his condition that can actually be managed, one thing about which he can be optimistic, and in which he has even found some humor—a good conversation.

Arkin is checking his census list for the next patient to see when the trio steps off the elevator and Breen says, "Hey, Dr. Arkin, got a minute?" Arkin stops, notices that Massood appears to be almost hiding behind the big newcomer, whom Breen introduces. "This is Detective Sergeant Walker Jens; he's with the city police department here. We kinda need to talk to you." Jens nods but doesn't offer his hand.

"Sure," Arkin says, there being no obvious alternative. "Do you want to talk here?" He gestures to the nearby consultation room, typically used for private family meetings but currently unoccupied.

Breen nods, smiling, the only one who is, and ushers the little group, led by the big detective, who has yet to speak. "This works," Breen says. He surveys the room, its stiff arrangement of institutional seating, its forced distancing and artificial lighting. "Let me start by clarifying: I have no law enforcement authority here. That's why I've asked Sergeant Jens to come along. That's CID procedure in situations like this. Our interest, I mean the interest of the Army, is in knowing what happened to Mr. Barnhardt, as a member of our defense . . . community. Whether there've been security violations or compromise, that sort of thing. But if there're any legal issues locally, that has to be handled by local police, by Sergeant Jens here." To whom he turns: "Did I get that right?"

Jens nods, turns his gaze on Arkin.

Massood, dwarfed from the start by the others, has retreated into a far corner of the room.

"Dr. Arkin," says Jens, his voice soft but penetrating, reverberant in the small room. "First, this is pretty unusual. Obviously, the Army is a piece of that. But the main thing is this autopsy. Which I don't pretend to fully understand, but which I guess is unusual."

Arkin blanks abruptly and completely on this—in part because he's forgotten that an autopsy was even conducted, as they almost never are on hospital patients—but more because the concept of an "unusual" postmortem is so unexpected, even impossible in Barnhardt's case, with his advanced liver and lung disease and a life expectancy measured in weeks. With so many potential ways in which these could have killed him, what could possibly surprise? Arkin looks to Massood, who glances up only momentarily from paperwork he's obsessively shuffling.

"Second, I guess, from what Mr. Breen has told me, is your connection, your history, with the man. That's why we're here, to discuss all that."

Arkin says nothing, stares. He hasn't had a drink in a week, and his perspective on the world around him is still unfamiliar, altered by the too-sharp contrasts of new sobriety. But these first minutes with the police and CID feel completely otherworldly, time-delayed, as though anything he might say would be seconds behind the prompt, nonsense. He says nothing.

Jens continues, "Dr. Massood, can you explain?"

"So," Massood begins, seeming even more at sea than Arkin feels, and minutely focused on the printout he holds. Arkin registers the paperwork vibrating with a fine nervous tremor. "To summarize. Autopsy reveals the likely presence of exogenous insulin, in a nondiabetic patient."

Despite himself, Arkin feels his face and jaw slacken in shock. He stares at Massood, who continues his plunge through the dense language of the pathologist's report. "Although hyperinsulinism is not unknown in hepatic cirrhosis, the levels in this case were much greater than expected, with a concentration of almost one thousand milli international units per liter. Insulin to C-peptide ratio was also consistent with non-endogenous administration of insulin. The patient's saline lock had been removed after death, so it was impossible to evaluate his peripheral line for the presence of drugs. However, and this was particularly noted by the pathologist, apparently the line had infiltrated slightly prior to death and revealed the possible presence of insulin in the surrounding tissue. Frozen sample of serum and CSF as well as vitreous fluid have been obtained and, um, have been sent for further analysis off-site for insulin analogues. That's, mainly, it." He looks up, anxious, only slightly relieved at having completed his walk through the forest of blood chemistry.

Jens grimaces, offers his own summary to Arkin: "So, someone gave him this drug that wasn't prescribed."

Arkin, flat, just above a whisper: "It sounds like it."

"And of course Mr. Breen tells me that, in your conversation with him, you said this Barnhardt threatened you."

"Yes."

"With exposure of something way back in the Army. That he thought would hurt your reputation."

"Yes."

"Did you think that?" Arkin feels a force rising up from Jens, as if his bulk is physically expanding, although Jens has only grown more still.

"Yes. I thought it could."

"Well," Jens says, and sighs. "Where were you Thursday night? When this patient, of yours, Robert Barnhardt, appears to have been murdered?"

Massood jumps from his chair, visibly shaking, the pathologist's report fanning to the floor. "I should leave now, this is not my, this is, uh—Dr. Arkin, you can, uh, let me see your list." Unthinking, Arkin hands him his patient roster. "And these checked ones, you've seen them?" Arkin nods. "And written your note?" Again, Arkin nods. "Okay then, good, I'll see the rest for you. You're done, take the day off, speak to these men. Actually, consider yourself on leave, paid, vacation time, whatever, okay? But drop off your ID. I'll call you when you can return." And without waiting for response, he turns away with Arkin's census list, walks briskly past the others and out of the

room. He leaves a silence behind, comfortable for the two investigators, brutal and strangled for Arkin, who understands that he's
just been suspended from his job.

"So I guess we can take our time," says Breen. "Have a seat."

Arkin was not aware of having stood. He gathers the pathology
pages from the floor where Massood has left them, and sits.

"Well, Dr. Arkin," says Jens. "Sort of a tough day, hmm?"

Arkin again can only nod; words are not forming for him beyond
the random internal and nonsensical *whats* and *whys* and then again
what?

"Then let's go back to Thursday night. Can you tell me where
you were?"

At last Arkin's mind stirs, if only around the most rudimentary
of questions: "Should I be talking to you?"

"That's a thought," says Jens, as if parsing Arkin's confusion for
him. "I haven't read you your Miranda rights. You know what that
is?" Of course Arkin does. "Because I'm not accusing you, or charging
you, with anything. I'm just conducting an investigation. The early
stages of an investigation. You are not a suspect at this stage."

Arkin silently underlines for himself those last three words, as
Jens continues. "But you are of course entitled, allowed, to have an
attorney present, even at this stage. You don't have to answer questions. Would you like to have an attorney?"

Arkin's brain has at last spun up into a higher gear, one so high
in fact that thoughts and fears and doubts are rotating through so
rapidly that he can't separate them, can't discriminate. Perhaps half
a minute passes before he's able to focus, and shake his head. "No."

"All right. Then . . . where were you on Thursday night?"

"I was home," Arkin begins, ploddingly, deliberate. "My
apartment."

"Okay. Were you alone?"

"My girlfriend was there for a while."

"And that's Katherine Maddox, nurse here?"

Arkin looks up, surprised in part at his own first-time and unconscious use of "girlfriend" to describe Kate—which would have pleased him at any other time—but more, that Jens knows about her, knows her name, even at the self-described *early stage* of his investigation. "Yes," Arkin manages. "It's Kate."

"And was she with you all night?"

"No. No, she left. She drove me home."

"In your car."

"Yes." It seems pointless to deny or color this. Possibly, Arkin feels, it will help to conceal nothing. "I was drunk. Didn't want to drive. She took an Uber back to her car."

"We know, we've checked their records."

Again Arkin is surprised at how far this new investigation has already proceeded, and registers, too, that Jens had the answers to all these questions before he'd asked them. He wonders also whether Jens has already spoken to Kate, and what she may have told him about, well, everything: Arkin's drinking, his past, his fears in the face of Barnhardt's threats, anything at all. He longs to text her and ask. But of course he can't, can do nothing but glance at Breen, who merely smiles back at him, encouragingly.

"Tell me about the rifle," Jens says, seemingly confirming Arkin's fears—for how else could the police know about the rifle except from Kate? It requires the lag of a few more seconds for him to recall that it's licensed, in the state database, no secret.

"What about it?"

"What'd you do in the Army?" Jens asks, though obviously he knows, must know, from Breen.

"I was sniper qualified."

"And you served as one in Afghanistan, with the Eighty-Seventh Infantry, Tenth Mountain. As a spotter in a sniper team."

"Yes."

"And you told Agent Breen that Mr. Barnhardt knew about this, about various . . . events, various actions, that took place there."

"Yes."

Jens pauses over this, leaving Arkin to wonder how much he knows about the "actions" in Afghanistan. For the first time, it occurs to him that these may in fact be classified even now, secret, in which case Breen will likely not have discussed the details with local police. Also for the first time, and somewhat to his own surprise, he wonders if Barnhardt would have risked the personal legal jeopardy of disclosing them, to Arkin's employers for example. He thinks this simple point should have occurred to him, and *would have* if not for his overriding fear of Barnhardt, and his own underlying self-doubt.

Jens appears not to have registered any of this inner debate occurring across from him. "And how long since you last had a weapon, before you bought the . . ." Jens pauses to check his notebook. "The H&K . . . MR762A1?"

"I've never owned a weapon before."

"Not since you left the Army?"

"No."

"So why'd you buy it now?"

Arkin pauses before answering. "I don't know."

Both Breen and Jens stare curiously at him from across the narrow space separating the two rows of waiting room chairs. The word *nonstarter* occurs to Arkin, which Jens only magnifies with a succinct, "Really?"

Arkin considers not answering, considers that he may not *know* the answer, or *one* answer, but then says, "I think I wanted to see if I could still do it. It was something I used to do . . . really well."

"And could you?"

"Yes."

"'Really well'?"

"Yes. Most of what we do here is . . . really complicated. Shooting a rifle, for me . . . is simple."

"Dr. Arkin . . . did you want to have a weapon for any *other* reason?"

Arkin is suddenly, deeply, tired; he feels like he could close his eyes this instant, in the company of two criminal investigators, on this slate-hard commercial grade furniture, and go to sleep. His entire world has altered in the course of thirty minutes, and the thrust of Jens's last questions, however innocently posed, is clear. "Maybe I should stop talking to you now," he says, newly steady in spite of his shock, at last understanding.

Jens nods, placid. "Sure," he says.

"If you want to meet again, I'll get a lawyer," Arkin says.

"Okay, yeah, that's fine. Probably smart." Arkin says nothing, now. "I mean, this man, apparently, um, was, what—poisoned? Murdered?" Jens actually produces a smile at his easy use of that hard word. "And there's a lot of people in this building, and it's not a jail, or a bank; it's not especially *secure*. But you *are* the only person here who had some history with the victim. And you can't really account for your movements that night. You say you were, what, passed out?" Again, he smiles, almost brotherly—as if to say, *Who hasn't passed out?*—but then continues: "And you *did* recently acquire a deadly weapon, which obviously was not *used* here. But something else *was* used, a medication, and you're a doctor, so you would have access. So I guess it does make sense for you to have a lawyer if you're at all . . . uncomfortable."

Still, Arkin says nothing.

"Okay, thanks." With which he stands and, with a nod to Breen, leaves.

Breen, who's been silent throughout, at last stirs himself. "Tough spot," he says. Arkin nods. Breen gazes at him a while longer, considering, before: "I'm sure we'll be in touch."

After he leaves, Arkin looks around the room, the windowless room where so much bad news has been shared with so many families, so many irreparable problems and irretrievable words.

It takes him a while to gather himself, get to his feet. Leaving the room, and then the unit, and finally the hospital itself, feels like a path never to be retraced.

———————

Kate tries calling Arkin's cell, gets only voicemail every ten minutes for an hour, at which point she gives up. She has already texted him seven times. On South Eight, two floors up from the oncology unit where Arkin had his meeting with the police, it took perhaps twenty minutes for the news to reach her, and another five minutes for her to confirm with security that Arkin has left the building, surrendering his ID as he went. She would like to get in her car and drive to his apartment, but her shift runs till seven o'clock, and leaving her patients is impossible, unthinkable according to nursing law, as well as the unspoken canon of nursing practice. Unless you're too sick to move, you never abandon your group.

It is hard for Kate to imagine Arkin without the hospital. She knows she occupies some sort of space in his life but also knows that it's a newly created one, dimensionally uncertain and potentially changeable. And beyond that, she can think of nothing sustaining in Arkin's life *but* the hospital, and medicine. It strikes her that, though she's heard Arkin complain about the problems of his profession, she has never once heard him speak of leaving it. Most doctors, and nurses for that matter, do talk about retiring one day, or quitting sooner. And many doctors *have* left: for teaching positions, or pharmaceutical industry jobs, or school doctoring, or research placements, or more limited responsibilities in large group practices. A lot of younger women physicians leave to have children; some never return.

Arkin has never talked of quitting. She thinks it a strange contrast that he, perhaps more consistently critical and cynical than any other doctor she knows about what he actually *accomplishes*, is the most deeply . . . *embedded* is the word that comes to mind. It isn't that he lives and breathes medicine, it's that he *inhabits* it. She thinks it strange that she's never seen this about him before, and it adds to her worry about his suspension. She thinks back to their conversation about practice abroad, in places of need, and wonders if they shouldn't have discussed it further.

Although she's told herself she wouldn't, she tries his phone again and leaves another message on his voicemail. A couple of the other nurses watch her, their expressions a mix of concern and pity, mixed with mild alarm. Somewhere in most women is a sort of basal awareness of their male partners' fragility, their essential brittleness. Kate has never had a woman lover but occasionally longs for what she imagines (though her gay friends disagree) is a consistency of strength and reliability that women find in those relationships. She has enjoyed working with the slowly increasing number of male nurses in her world, but with rare exceptions, when the wheels come completely off, the women turn to each other.

She doesn't know where Arkin fits on this yin-yang scale of things. He is calmer than perhaps anyone she knows in an emergency, an observation shared by other nurses, who have seen some doctors actually flee the rooms of crashing patients in panic, while others merely yell and temporize and call for help. Arkin may *feel* panic, but never shows it, never stops listening, absorbs everything without overload. All pretty *female* of him, she thinks. So can he *absorb* today's removal from the hospital and his professional moorings, however temporary? She thinks not and texts him for the eighth time, in addition to the seven calls. He doesn't text back.

It's after noon, area bars have been open for more than an hour, and Kate accepts that Arkin may be drinking. She knows that in his position, she would probably be in her apartment with a bottle of Tito's, but there's the difference: she would at least make it home before she started drinking. She well remembers having to drive Arkin home the last time he drank, and worries that, without her, he would've gotten behind the wheel.

She paces into the empty break room, looks about aimlessly, turns to leave, and runs into her nurse manager, Lucy Brown, a pillowy sixty-something, mother to six, grandmother to twelve, and both tough professional supervisor and maternal presence to the twenty-six nurses under her management.

"Are you okay?" Lucy asks, at which point Kate starts crying and falls into her boss's arms. Lucy pats her on the back, and Kate can almost imagine a "There, there," as she dissolves further into helplessness.

———————

Arkin drives almost to Yonkers, on the way to New York City, before turning around and driving back north. He gets off the Taconic at the Pleasantville exit and drives by memory to Beth Oliver's house. It's been only three weeks since he first met her, but that meeting feels like it occurred not just in another lifetime but to a different person. Driving aimlessly fits that new person. For years, Arkin was either preparing for work, at work, or recovering from work; there was no other category. He has never taken a vacation, not since med school. In fact, his reason for driving toward the city was an almost numinous image of boarding a plane to somewhere—a Caribbean beach destination was in his thought picture—though he'd neglected to even stop at his apartment and pack. He'd figured he could buy everything he needed: he has a laughable combined credit card limit of over a hundred thousand dollars. In fact, his entire financial picture is laughable: his few school loans are long retired, and he banks almost everything he makes. He's rich, he thinks, walking up to Oliver's front door, and now utterly destitute. He's thinking he should have stopped to buy his own bottle of expensive bourbon, imagining, say, a fifth of Van Winkle for a couple thousand dollars. He recalls Googling the hundred-dollar Elijah Craig that Dr. Oliver served him on his previous and uneasy visit; that, too, seems like it happened to another person.

There is no answer at the door, however—no Dr. Oliver with whom to drink bourbon of any price—and Arkin returns to his car. While driving north, precise destination unknown, he recalls reading somewhere, but he thinks when he was still in school, about "abutment suicide." Apparently, a considerable number of people are thought to commit suicide every year by driving into bridge abutments at high speed, usually leaving no note, and thus no proof of intent. Apparently also, many of these suicides are committed on motorcycles, and Arkin thinks idly how pathetic a suicide-by-Honda-Civic would sound on the news. The thought evanesces almost in the moment it occurs to him. Arkin has lived through combat, has lived for months surrounded by enemy fighters, without for a moment wishing to die. He survived his own mother's suicide without wavering in his willingness—perhaps it's just inclination?—to go on living. He has seen so many patients stop living that it holds no terrors for him, but also no appeal. It lies out there; it's his future, he knows that, but he has no desire to experience it now.

So what *does* he want? Can he be facing a murder charge? It seems impossible. He pulls off to the side of the highway, having felt the car vibrating from the shaking of his hands. He clasps them in his lap to regain, yes, control. He thinks of the patient he'd seen that morning, the *last* patient he'd seen before he was told he could no longer see patients at all, how afterward he'd congratulated himself on their "good conversation."

The man's name is Coleman; he's a trim seventy-two, still working as a community college English teacher until his diagnosis of large B-cell lymphoma. Arkin thinks now about their meeting, how, in addition to the minor issue of hypertension, the patient had a written list of questions about his condition, treatment, prognosis. Not being the attending physician but merely a consultant, it wasn't Arkin's place to address these issues. But the patient, pleasantly but quietly insistent, said that "No one has really talked to me." Arkin cannot count the number of times he's heard this exact phrase from patients. As best he could, aware that most of his oncology colleagues would likely resent *any* such conversation, Arkin answered.

The patient had multiple sites of disease outside his lymph nodes, and with advanced age, disease stage, and elevated LDH level, he fell into a "high-risk" category, with around a one in four chance of living five years. He was being treated with a regimen known as R-CHOP and was already experiencing side effects of nausea, nosebleeds, bleeding gums. They discussed how he could develop insomnia, mouth ulcers, neuropathy, worsening fatigue and anemia. When the patient (Mr. Coleman, a person with a name, Arkin again reminds himself) asked about alternatives to treatment, Arkin had temporized, deferred to oncology. He'd said only, as he'd said to countless other patients in similar situations—hoping to *empower*, as the palliative docs put it—"You're in charge. *You* make the decisions; you decide what you want." Coleman had thanked him, and the two had sat in a companionable silence for a few moments before the patient said, "It's hard, isn't it? Knowing but not knowing." In retrospect, Arkin thinks the patient—educated, older, wiser—may have been speaking as much to the doctor in the room as to himself.

And sitting in his car at the side of the highway, Arkin tries to catalog what he *does* know. He knows he didn't get out of bed in a blacked out drunken state and drive to the hospital, steal insulin from a locked med room, and inject his already terminally ill patient. What's beyond preposterous?—absurd? Whatever, but yes, the thought is absurd. He doesn't *know* the police will agree, though, and doesn't know how to persuade them. He doesn't know, absent proof to the contrary, that the hospital will ever allow him to resume practice. He doesn't know if they're required to report him to the state licensing board. He doesn't know that, in the end, Barnhardt won't have destroyed him after all.

He doesn't *know* that Kate loves him. He doesn't know that she will fully believe his denials. He looks over the steering wheel at the cars, mostly hulking SUVs, speeding past him and on into the distance. It was only the night before that he and Kate walked together along the river and then kissed—yes, as lovers but also like old marrieds, although they are not that, not that yet. He wishes he had said "I love you" to her. He thinks it odd that he can't remember ever saying those words, can't remember a specific instance. He'd dated a girl he met in micro lab in his first year of med school, and they'd spent a few weekends together until she took him home to meet her parents, at which point the relationship came to an end. He doesn't remember now specifically why, but suspects that meeting the family was an "in over your head" type experience that informed them both. He does remember the girl, Sandy Paulus; she was short, bubbly, brunette with cropped bangs—*baby bangs*, she said they were called—an A student across the board, verbal. He pictures her now and tries to recall saying "I love you" to her energetic and capable face. He doesn't think he did. He can see her face, too, during sex, focused and determined, a sheen of sweat on her forehead, and knows she wouldn't have said it either, not then even.

Arkin does not think of himself as sexually, much less romantically, *experienced*. He doesn't know how to think about a succession of lovers, a trail of intimacy, how such a lived life would affect how you think about *the* girl, *the* person, if and when you met her. What he knows is that for him, in his "lived life," Kate is beyond comparison. No comparables, as the real estate people say, and for the first time in hours his mood lightens somewhat as he thinks of that, and of her. Looking back on the women he's dated, he realizes he could probably describe each in a phrase: "really bright," "really fun," "really smart," "really wild." A single adjective preceded by an affirmative, even affectionate, "really." For Kate no word is enough, even many words would be too few, and when he tries to think of them, only *she* comes to mind; he sees *her*, not the idea of her. He finds this unique and unnerving.

He's a physician, and like all physicians, he is accustomed to encountering the world in lab results, vital sign readouts, chemical names, disease categories, pathogen types, medication doses and mechanisms. Everything in medicine is about classification and naming, even if only for the sake of sanity, arbitrarily and often prematurely definitive. Kate alone in his world stands apart from this. Not only can't he define her, name what it is that draws him to her, he doesn't want to, is content with, simply with, the person herself, unto herself. So whether she believes him or not, or even loves him, is beside the point. He loves her, and that is direction enough for now. He checks the mirror and, hands steady, steers himself back into traffic.

When at last Arkin began to respond to her blizzard of texts, Kate was able to stop crying, apologize to her manager, and return to work. The texts were anything but data rich, consisting mainly of too bright, exclamation-heavy phrases such as "I'm fine, don't worry!" and "This is crazy!" and "My first interrogation!" None of these sound at all like Arkin, who usually limits himself to *yep* or *sure* or *ok*. At least he's avoided thumbs-up or smiley face emojis.

Despite having lost a frantic half hour from patient care, Kate caught up: she hung her four- and six-o'clock intravenous meds, gave the various oral doses, administered pre-dinner insulin to her two diabetics, and helped with a bed bath for the hip repair in 814. She crisply signed out to the night nurse taking over her group, a new girl still drowsy from her long afternoon nap in advance of the still longer overnight. Hospital rules forbid night nurses from sleeping during their shifts, which Kate and her friends think ridiculous. At her first job, Kate had worked nights at a hospital that scheduled nurses for thirty minutes of sleep between one and three in the morning, staggering these breaks among those on duty. That hospital, unlike this one, believed the research that showed this practice resulted in fewer mistakes, better staff retention, and fewer MVAs, or motor vehicle accidents, among nurses driving home the morning after overnights. Even after day shifts, nurses and docs would often find themselves drifting off on the way home as stress hormones from the day's work cleared their systems.

This evening, Kate is anything but sleepy as she nervously scans the street for Arkin, who'd texted he'd meet her here, outside the hospital. She thinks it a plus that he asked to get together here rather than in a bar. She thinks it odd that he hasn't asked her to his place or invited himself to hers. She thinks it confusing that she's ambivalent about that. Only slightly less confusing is that his Civic's lights now flash at her from some distance down the block, well past where nurses and others will be entering the parking garage—and where they might see Kate and Arkin talking, she realizes. It's yet another circumstance about which she finds herself confused as she walks down the sidewalk to him, pulls open the passenger door, slides in.

Arkin's twisted around in his seat to face her, his expression as over-amped and positive as his earlier texts. "Wow, something, huh?" he says cheerily.

Kate stares at him for moment before jumping, businesslike, to next-steps mode: "I'm gonna call them, hospital, police, whatever. I put you to bed; I know what your condition was. I'm a fucking nurse, and this is ridiculous."

Arkin's cheery facade fades to nothing. "It's the 'fucking' nurse part that may be a problem."

"Why, because we're fucking? We're allowed!"

"Yes, we are," he says so gently that Kate drops instantly out of profanity mode, and registers the depth of feeling in his, "And I hope we keep on doing it." He reaches out to touch her face, but hesitates, and Kate takes his hand in hers. They find themselves in an awkward and ambiguous handclasp around the console shifter and cupholders. "But . . . you need, I need you, to stay out of this. I don't want you dragged in."

"How can I not be dragged in? Even if I don't call them, they'll call me at some point."

"I know that, but it's best not to . . ."

"Protest too much?"

"Yes, right. We're friends, we're *close* friends, but you don't need to defend me. I didn't do anything, I had no *reason* to do anything. They'll ask their questions, when they're ready, and then this'll be over. We're both . . ."

He's looking for the word, and Kate supplies it: "Professionals."

"Yes, we're *professional people.* We should conduct ourselves that way; we don't need to make a scene."

"You think I'm making a scene?"

"No!" He thinks she may about to shift back into profanity mode, and he adds, "I just want to protect you. You're all that matters."

They look at each other for a while. Kate exhales, asks, "You're not coming over?"

"I don't think we should."

Kate nods in agreement, adds, "And you're not going out? Not drinking."

"No. You?"

"Fuck no," she says and moves to leave. She pauses with her fingers on the door handle, looking back at him.

Arkin can see the finest details of her face, hair, skin. For the first time, he notices little flecks of gold in the gray of her irises. For some reason, he recalls that gray eyes are the result of something called Mie scattering, the way the light refracts off the stroma, off the higher levels of collagen overlying the iris, in gray eyes. And with this recollection, a visceral self-loathing rises up in him that, once again, for perhaps the millionth time, his medical understanding of the world and the people in it, the quasi scientific cast it provides, has come between him and those people. Sitting opposite him is the person closest to him since the death of his mother, a woman of ferocity and compassion and understanding, and stromal collagen levels are what's in his mind. For the first time he considers that being forced out of medicine by the investigation might be a relief, a blessing, so that he could begin to see this woman as more than a collection of fibers and cellular functions and RNA types and pump action of the heart and expansion of the lungs. He thinks he could learn to love their aging together not as the migration of proton pairs across deteriorating DNA molecules, but the action of love, over time, and pristine.

"I love you," he says. The words come out of him as easily as the night air has enveloped the car, found its way in, found their skin with its cool touch. The words are beyond descriptive, beyond terms or even English, really, itself, they are simply out of him, the collection of him, and her for him, in sound. He says them again, "I love you."

And she says, "I love you too," the gray-gold irises shining and sweet and deep and true.

He watches as Kate walks away, down the sidewalk to the garage entrance. He sees how easily she shifts the heavy backpack slung over her shoulder. He sees how the scrubs and light jacket fit the contours of her body, taut yet relaxed. He wonders again if she's conscious of the sexual power she's wielding over him—even now, even with the trouble he faces, and their familiarity with each other, their bodies. And now with the words they've spoken. He thinks she is—and to confirm it, she gives a brief and provocative sway to her hips as she turns into the garage, and offers him a wave, a small grin, and disappears from view.

———————

"Miss Maddox?" She hears the voice even before she sees the big man standing by her car. "I'm Detective Jens. I wonder if we could have a word."

THIRTEEN

ARKIN CHECKS IN AT the counter at the Wall-Pack range, gets an amiable nod from Paul Shepherd, as always in his instructor cap and NRA polo shirt, followed by a rumbling "Hi, Doc." Arkin looks up in surprise, the big man opposite confessing with a laugh, "I Googled you," showing Arkin his phone and adding, "I think you're only the second doctor we've ever had here. What's wrong with you guys, anyway?"

"Too busy, I guess," Arkin says, not wanting to examine all the things that might be wrong with his profession at the moment.

"Yeah, that I can understand," he says, making change on Arkin's twenty. "Take lane four," he says. "What you gonna be shooting at today?"

"Hadn't thought about it. A thousand, I guess, like before?"

Shepherd nods. "Mind if I watch again?" Arkin shakes his head. "I'll spot for ya."

"Okay."

"Let's do it." Shepherd locks the register, follows Arkin out onto the range.

Arkin completes his second round of five shots at a thousand yards, all the bullets striking within a three-inch group about two inches up from the bull's-eye. Shepherd has been watching through a Celestron spotting scope on a tripod behind Arkin. "What you got for elevation?"

"Eight MOAs."

"Might wanna come down a click." Arkin adjusts his scope appropriately. "Windage spot on."

"Thanks," Arkin says.

"You just guessed it?"

Arkin manages *Mmm*, or possibly *Hmm*, anyway a confirmation.

"I mean, you're not using Ballistic or one of those range apps on your phone, just guessing the wind, shooting off a bag rather than a bench, no tripod."

Still, Arkin says nothing. Instead, he fires another group of five rounds, this time within about a two-and-a-half-inch group, again at a thousand yards, now centered on the bull's-eye. This series of five rounds were fired in about fifteen seconds, essentially rapid-fire for such a distance.

"Shit," Shepherd intones, watching the last impact. "You said you trained at Benning, didn't you?"

"Yeah," Arkin says, putting down the rifle, inserting a chamber flag into its empty breech. He sits up, ejects the magazine, reaches for a box of ammo.

"That's where Sniper School is, right? You went to Sniper School." Arkin only nods now as he loads fresh rounds. Shepherd watches speculatively. His belly overhangs his belt by a considerable amount, and it rises and falls with his breathing, perhaps a bit above his normal rate, possibly in response to what he's seen on the range just now. "I've never seen anyone shoot like this. I mean ever. Not just here, competition, anywhere. I mean, not the way you did, just shooting."

Arkin stops, puts down the magazine. "Thanks."

"Ever in a combat situation?" Arkin nods. "Me too," Shepherd says, getting a look. "Desert Storm. Sixty-Sixth Armor, Second Battalion. The Iron Knights," this last with something of an ironic smile. "I was an Abrams gunner. 'Course it's a little different being inside a tank, than what you did. We didn't lose a single tank to enemy fire. Seven we lost were to our own guys."

"Friendly fire," Arkin says.

"Yep."

Unavoidably, Arkin thinks of Kelly, although this hardly qualifies as friendly fire since Kelly was about to shoot at him. He'd never thought to wonder how that death was counted; "Enemy Action," he supposes. After a moment, he tells Shepherd, "I've seen somebody shoot better. Other guy in my team, the shooter I spotted for, he was better than me."

"Love to see that. He live around here?"

"No." Shepherd knows not to ask further, but Arkin volunteers: "He's dead." There's a longer silence between the two, companionable enough. After a time: "I told my girlfriend . . . that I was better with a rifle than any doctor in the country." This gets a smile from both. "But I think . . . I'm better with a rifle than I am a doctor."

Shepherd laughs a little at this, though the undertone, or perhaps the implications, are somewhat unsettling. "Well, they're two different things, huh?"

"Yeah," Arkin says, although it's a question whether the Army and police investigators on his case would agree. He looks off, then nods downrange, to where a good-sized doe and a single yearling have emerged from the woods and are browsing near the six-hundred-meter target array.

"Yep," Shepherd says, "they been around. Better there's nobody else shooting, 'cause I always shut down the range when they come out."

"That's good."

"When I was in basic, there were fifty of us on the line at the range, and a deer walked out. 'Bout half the guys kept on, shot the shit out of her. Thought that was really . . . kinda sick."

"The others stopped?"

"Yeah." He glances at Arkin now. "There're shooters, and then there're shooters, right?" Arkin nods. Shepherd is watching the two deer making their way across his range. "One thing about fighting a tank—you never saw anyone get killed. At least I didn't. I mean, I did shoot, I did hit my targets, these Russian tanks the Iraqis had. But we'd hit 'em from two miles usually, more sometimes. Didn't see anything, thank God." He glances back to Arkin. "Couldn't'a done what you did. Either over there, or I guess what you do now. You guys are tough."

Arkin manages a wan smile. "Thanks. And thanks for the use of your range."

"Anytime," Shepherd says and pats the younger man on his shoulder.

Arkin has reached the outskirts of Newburgh, in western New York State, when his phone rings. He puts it on speaker: "Hello?"

"This Dr. Arkin?" says the unfamiliar male voice.

"Yes?"

"This is Jim Porter. I'm an attorney at Bell Klein representing Katherine Maddox. She asked me to call you."

"What? What's going on?" Arkin hears the thin edge of panic in his voice.

"Are you in a place where you can talk?"

"Hold on," he says as he brakes hard, swerves onto the freeway shoulder. "Okay, yeah. What, what's happening? Is she all right?"

"She's okay, but she's in a . . . situation. She wanted me to let you know." Arkin mumbles some sort of an acknowledgment, and Porter continues. "So she hasn't been arrested or booked, but last night she was brought to the police station. She called us right away—our firm handled her mother's estate, and I do most of the criminal law. So I went in and met with her and Detective Sergeant Jens—I believe you know him."

"Yes."

"And I know he's spoken with you about the death of a patient in the hospital, Robert Barnhardt, under what they're calling suspicious circumstances."

"Yes," Arkin manages, struggling to slow his breathing.

"And I know that you and Ms. Maddox are in a relationship, and I understand you told Sergeant Jens that she dropped you off at home the evening this man died, that you had been drinking. And that she then took an Uber back to the hospital to pick up her car. Is that correct?"

"Yes."

"And that's what Katherine says as well. But she also, according to Mr. Jens, actually went into the hospital that night, before going home. I'm not going to ask if you know that to be the case, because obviously you weren't there, and there's no reason for her to have discussed it with you." This last is said with a sort of purpose-ful force, as if discouraging any input from Arkin on what may or may not have been discussed. Porter underlines this with, "I'm just letting you know." Arkin says nothing. "But her ID was used to go in through an employee entrance, so they have that. And Ms. Maddox does not dispute that—she stated she went in to get a cup of coffee from a vending machine and to use the restroom."

"So? So what? That doesn't mean anything."

"I don't disagree." Arkin doesn't like the lawyerly double negative, but Porter's going on: "The real problem seems to be that earlier in the day, Katherine signed out a vial of—and I'm not an expert in this so I may get the terms wrong—a vial of rapid-acting insulin. Which the police can find no record of its having been returned—I guess to the medication locker?"

Arkin is staggered, it takes him a few moments to find his voice. "I . . . don't think that means anything. I'm not sure how they handle insulins in their med rooms. But a lot of places, they're not using insulin pens, and if they had vials, then . . . it's probably pretty . . . relaxed. I'm not even sure the nurses log them back in. They may just scan them, I don't know."

"Well, I think that's what Ms. Maddox says, or something like that—again, I don't understand the details yet. And apparently there's enough . . . doubt . . . that Sergeant Jens has held off actu-ally booking her. So all we did was talk, and then she was released, about one in the morning. And they will talk again in the morning and consider whether they want to formally arrest her and bring charges. So . . . that's where we are."

"Jesus," Arkin whispers. "Is she all right? What can I do?"

"Well, that's one of the reasons I wanted to speak to you. There's nothing right now, except . . . I think it would be best if you and Ms.

Maddox did not communicate for the time being. Uh, it would be easy for the police to track any contact you had, and given that you are in a relationship, and depending on how their investigation proceeded, it could look, or they could imply, that you were somehow in league on this."

"That's ridiculous."

"I don't disagree." Another double negative, Arkin notes. "But I do think it best you keep your distance. And I have said the same to Ms. Maddox."

"And what does she say?"

"She doesn't disagree."

Arkin looks out the driver side window at the unexceptional skyline of Newburgh, a city which he recalls having read has among the highest crime rates in America. It does not escape him that both he and the woman he loves are suspects in a murder case, or "persons of interest," as Netflix would have it, and that if for any reason he were stopped, the police would likely become aware of this, as well as the presence of a high-powered rifle in the trunk of his car. A week ago he and Kate were respected professionals, their worst problem an over-keen taste for bourbon and tequila respectively; today, a criminal lawyer has cautioned them against incriminating contact with one another.

"Dr. Arkin?"

"Yes?"

"Do you understand?"

A knot grows, spreads up from Arkin's chest into his throat, throttling him, his voice, until he can barely mumble: "Yes."

"Good. Then, I would also suggest that you might want to consider obtaining legal counsel of your own. But that's a decision for you to make. Okay?"

Arkin doesn't bother answering this. He touches the red button on the CarPlay screen and disconnects.

Arkin takes the next exit, drives south on Route 300 passing a Ramada Inn, a Denny's, a muffler shop. He turns left into the parking lot of a Longhorn Steakhouse, parks, enters the restaurant, and unthinking—"avolitional," as psychiatrists might put it—walks up to the bar and orders himself a double Jack Daniels with beer back. There's a fake steer complete with long horns mounted above the bar; there's fake wide pine planking on the floor; there are fake Remington cowboy cutouts lining the backs of the dining room booths. Arkin gulps down the double, orders another, takes it and his beer mug to one of the tall table groupings, and settles himself onto a high stool's scarred vinyl. He checks his phone, finds no voicemails or texts, and no emails beyond the usual springtide of Amazon, bank, charity, and political filler. He powers the phone off, places it face down on the laminate tabletop. Powering down completely has an air of drastic departure from the norm, but he expects no texts from the hospital, no flagged results from the lab, and now no calls from Kate. For the first time in perhaps a year, he is cut off from everything outside the geometry of this moment, the circular top of this table, its cuboid stools, the cylindrical lowball glass and beer mug. He stares at his right hand, watches it as—back to the avolitional— the glass of bourbon rises to his lips, followed by the beer. He follows up with another round.

Follows up, he thinks, one of the cardinal medical practices, not to be neglected; lab and imaging results, consults, referrals, all to be *followed up* by the diligent physician. Failure to follow up puts one at all sorts of risk, as in *medicolegal* risk, another term of art in his work. It appears undeniable even to Arkin's fast-blearing mind that he and Kate have found themselves at medicolegal risk, in that one of their patients is a homicide victim, although he can't see where any failure to follow up has contributed to the disintegration of his life and Kate's.

It is a given in the world of the medicolegal that there can be any number of unanticipated causes of risk—Arkin is pleased at having thought of this word, *unanticipated*, even as the alcohol in his system has begun to blunt his semantic memory. That drinking to unconsciousness on the night of Barnhardt's death left him unable to account for his whereabouts when Barnhardt was injected with a lethal dose of insulin was unanticipated. That Kate had to return to the hospital to pick up her car was unanticipated, as was her decision to enter the building for coffee and bathroom break. That both their careers are now in jeopardy was unanticipated. That either or both of them face the possibility of arrest and trial and even prison time is beyond unanticipated, in the realm of incomprehensible. Arkin waves to the bartender for more bourbon, more beer. With what is left of his executive function, Arkin calculates that this will bring him to a total of nine alcohol equivalents. Or perhaps it's twelve.

During the time it takes him to perform this calculation, the drinks arrive, brought by a twenty-something waitress in black jeans, long-sleeve black shirt, short black apron. Her face is round, her acne incompletely Clearasil-coated, and her hair a white blond not seen in nature. Also in keeping with surrounding decor, the blue of her eyes, her overlong eyelashes, and her red and white striped finger-nails are all manufactured. "Are you all right?" she asks as she sets down the fresh drinks. Her concern, at least, seems real enough.

"I'm a doctor," Arkin answers.

Strangely, this seems not to quell her unease. "Are you meeting someone?"

"I doubt it."

"Someone to drive you?" she asks, points to the full glasses. "Because this is a lot."

"Oh yeah, someone will drive," Arkin says and downs the bourbon. From somewhere in his training, he recalls an equation called Widmark's formula, that describes how fast one's blood alcohol will rise with a given amount of alcohol in a specific period of time. He recalls that the rate you absorb alcohol far exceeds the rate at which you can metabolize it, particularly if you drink as much as he already has in such a short time. In other words, he's drunk already.

And he hates it that, even now, in trouble with the police himself, and with Kate facing possible arrest, he can still only think in terms of Widmark's formula and medicolegal risk and neglected follow-up. He hates the language of medicine, and he hates even more that it has conditioned and curbed his thinking so completely. Even the full flower of tonight's binge, even his fouled mind, take shape as an intake of alcohol equivalents, another term of art.

"My girlfriend's in trouble," he says to the waitress. "I need to get fucking drunk." This earns him some sympathy, an understanding look from behind the Clearasil and blue contacts. Arkin is pleased that he's substituted "get fucking drunk" for, say, "self-medicate."

"It's okay," he says to the waitress, and then: "Someone will drive."

———

It develops that Arkin drives. When his car hits the guardrail on the interstate ramp, the airbag fires and then deflates even as the car flips over the guardrail and down the embankment slope beside the highway, coming to rest on its roof at the bottom of the roadside ditch. Fortunately, Arkin is asleep when this occurs; he was asleep from about the time he turned onto the ramp. And he's still asleep when the police and ambulance arrive.

———————

He wakes in the emergency room of the small community hospital a mile and a half from where his wrecked car is being winched onto a flatbed tow truck. He feels like weights have been attached to his eyelids, holding them shut but also pressing down on the globes themselves, and with a single central weight driving into the apex of the nasal bone. His left chest wall hurts about four out of ten, in particular on inspiration. Arkin would like to laugh that the language of triage has survived even this latest disaster.

"Can you tell me your name?" comes a raspy baritone off to his left.

"How's my car?" Arkin manages.

"I doubt it. Tell me your name."

"My name is Arkin. Dr. Arkin."

After a moment, he hears: "You're a physician?"

Arkin exerts himself, forces his eyes open, spots an older man in scrubs and lab coat leaning against a code cart. The man has two or three days of white stubble, a halo of curly white hair with residual streaks of gray, sad and smudged eyes.

"Yes," Arkin tells the man.

"Me too. Dr. Brevard, ED attending. You know what day it is?" Brevard runs through a couple more orientation questions which Arkin doesn't bother with, ending at, "How do you feel?"

"Sleepy."

"Well, you're probably concussed, but your blood alcohol was point two eight when they brought you in. You were talking then, although you weren't making any sense. You were awake for the CT, which was normal. Your reflexes were okay, cranial nerves fine, your prolactin was normal. Chest X-ray shows maybe a hairline crack in number six on the left side but nothing major; lung's okay. You remember any of this?" Arkin shakes his head, minutely. "You understand what I'm telling you?" Arkin nods. "Since then, basically you've been either sleeping—or passed out."

Arkin closes his eyes for a moment, exhales. "Now what?"

Brevard grimaces, asks, "Where do you work?"

Arkin tells him, adds, "I'm a hospitalist."

"Really," Brevard says. "So you're a fucking colleague." Arkin says nothing. "You do this often? Drink to blackout, wreck your car?"

"No," Arkin whispers, into space.

Brevard sighs, straightens, tells him, "You're spending the night here in the ED. Call it professional courtesy. I'll come back."

———————

Three hours later, it's four in the morning, and Brevard returns. Arkin has slept most of the interim, only fitfully noting the sounds of the emergency room around him, staff talk, occasional laughter, the cries of sick babies, the groans and shouts of infected and confused oldsters, the righteous assumed anger of drug-seekers of all ages. Arkin has heard it all before at every stage of his training and practice, the helpless cacophony, the absolute unalloyed diversity of misery and helplessness, and he is able to sleep through it without much difficulty even as the alcohol has left his system.

But he's awake now, sitting up, the head of his bed elevated, a cup of coffee warming his hand, the third one his nurse has brought him. The pace of ED visits has predictably slowed at the perigee of the overnight shift, and Brevard seems none the worse for the hour. Arkin thinks he must be one of those lucky night guys who is able to sleep in the daytime hours preceding his shift, a true nocturnist.

He folds his arms across his chest, stares at Arkin. "So how do you want to handle this?"

"It doesn't matter. Whatever you think."

"If I write that you were drunk, if I include your blood alcohol number in my note, you'll be charged with a DUI. You ever had one before?"

"No."

"At a minimum, you'll have to report it to the state medical board, Office of Professional Conduct. You'll get a reprimand, censured, you've got any kind of history they might want you in a substance abuse program."

Arkin ponders this, and the fine tremor reflected in the quivering surface of the coffee in the cup he holds. "I don't care. Do whatever you need to do."

"Really?"

"Yeah." He puts the coffee down on the overbed table. "I'm not sure I want to practice, anymore. I may be done anyway."

"Oh. Okay," Brevard says, and then: "Why?"

Arkin thinks about it, and about the way he feels on the hard nonabsorbent mattress, the way his side and head hurt, the way his stomach burns from alcoholic gastritis, the way his mouth tastes of sour reflux and his armpits stink of sweat. "I'm tired of . . . the assholes I work with, the assholes I take care of, the assholes who manage the hospital, the assholes who run the insurance companies . . . and the asshole I see in the mirror every day. Mostly, I'm tired of making no fucking difference. The old ones keep getting more demented, the drunks keep getting more jaundiced, the heart failures keep getting more swollen, the infections keep getting more resistant. I have no fucking idea what I'm accomplishing, and I conceal my failure in the language of medicine that only my colleagues care about, and in my reliance on guidelines that change every time a new study comes out with a two percent higher confidence interval. I killed another soldier when I was in the Army, in combat, and I became a doctor to make up for it. Instead, I've gone on killing my own side, only more of them."

Except for a tightening around his mouth, which may represent a suppressed yawn, Brevard's expression doesn't change.

In response, Arkin is instantly, predictably, embarrassed. He rarely curses, has nothing against his fellow physicians, and pays almost no attention to the actions of insurance executives or hospital administrators. The only richly deserving "asshole" of his rant, he knows unmistakably, is himself. The rest of it, his mention of Kelly's shooting and the deaths of patients, sounded like something rehearsed alone on a commute.

Brevard seems to have paid no attention to the labored bullet points. "So . . . you're a lot, or just moderately, burned out?"

Arkin stares back at him, one dead-of-night gaze to another. Burnout, the century's over-discussed syndrome of his profession, has escaped self-inventory on his part. Of some cardinal signs—poor sleep, memory lapses, physical fatigue—he has, or chooses to recognize, none. Others—cynicism about work, alcohol abuse, and doubts of personal efficacy—have been with him since, well, residency. Against this, and without any impulse control at all: "I think I've been burned out since I was eighteen."

Both he and Brevard consider the possibility of early concussion-related emotionality, and disregard it. They stare at each other for a time, punctuated by a few muted mid-shift noises from the nurses at their station. One nurse snores faintly at her computer, asleep sitting up, nodded off. Another types away at a proficiency exam. The unit secretary is streaming an old Seinfeld standup performance on her cellphone, and the lowered volume of a Beacon Theatre audience's laughter, distant in both space and time, adds an historical counterpoint to the sounds of a BiPAP machine in the patient room next door.

"It's a fucked-up business," Brevard says. "But what the fuck else are you gonna do with your life?"

Arkin stares at the older man for a while then looks around his room, one in which old men have breathed their last, lacerated children have wept, young women have delivered their babies prematurely, and older women have cried out at the torments of dementia and drug-resistant UTIs. The walls and ceiling are an ugly, arid rainbow: drab brown, mustard yellow, lime green. It seems designed to make patients wish to die, and for the first time since his mother's suicide, Arkin wonders if he himself wishes to do so, possibly attempted it by driving away from the Longhorn earlier in a near-unconscious state. He feels suddenly, completely, sober and alert. "My mother committed suicide when I was seventeen."

The near non sequitur seems to make complete sense to Brevard, who nods, waits. "And . . ." Arkin stumbles on the next thought, its half-formed expression, and the central issue of his presence here in this emergency room, this hospital, this deepest valley of the night, and for which all the previous thoughts and words have been evasion. "There's this woman I know. A nurse I met, and I think I dragged her into this situation . . . with a patient." Brevard is silent, unmoving.

"A bad situation," Arkin says, examining an inner cascade of beliefs, nonbeliefs, questions, doubts, before: "And the police suspect ... she may have killed him." Arkin glances at Brevard, aslant, checking for reaction though unwilling to parse it.

"Killed him, as in the hospital?"

"Yes. Someone did."

"You think it was her?"

Without hesitation Arkin says, "No," shaking his head, emphatic, certainty growing in him with each moment, each motion, congruent with dawning wonder that he ever questioned it. "She ... it's not that she *couldn't*. She's ... stronger than me, completely ... dedicated." These words strike even Arkin as bordering on fatuous and yet feel entirely right, accurate. "But ... she wouldn't. *Because* she's strong and expects me to be strong, she wouldn't ... *have to*."

"And that's why you got drunk and wrecked your car? Because you believe in her? Because the police are wrong?"

"I guess because I got her into this."

"Well, that's fucking courageous."

Arkin feels a quivering across the muscles in his abdomen, like a starter motor building revs, which he recognizes as the beginning of anger. Having lived through his mother's death, and Kelly's, and months of threats of enemy fire, and actual fire, and the rigors of his training both military and medical, and the loneliness of his existence overall, it has never yet occurred to him that he may be a coward. And yet here, tonight, he has drunk himself into a stupor, into an ambulance and room 3 in the local ER, and into further jeopardizing his already-jeopardized career, when all that was *really* required is that he stand by Kate Maddox, the girl he loves.

Stress-induced nausea rises in him. He lowers his head, closes his eyes, takes some deep breaths to fight it down in hopes of avoiding the bedside emesis basin, and tells Brevard, "You're right." He takes another deep breath, hears how freighted it is with the possibility of sobbing, fights this down too. "I fucked up." Brevard looks at him for a while longer, until Arkin repeats, the mix of clarity and conviction growing stronger: "I fucked up."

"Okay, then. I'm not mentioning alcohol. I'll edit the lab results out of my note. I won't fill out the DUI form."

Arkin looks to him now. "I don't want to get you in trouble too."

"You still want to quit medicine?"

"No," Arkin says reflexively, but possibly honestly as well. "I don't know," he blurts.

"Then you've got more to worry about than a DUI. Plus, the cops'll be happy—saves them hours of work." Arkin only nods. Brevard straightens, a note to be written as the end of his shift approaches. "But doctor . . . you practice as long as I have . . . you learn to forgive. You learn to forgive yourself. Everything you said about our bullshit jargon and guidelines and half-ass inadequate research . . . ?"

For a moment Arkin wonders if this older man, experienced older doctor, is about to tear up himself.

"Forgive us. It's all we've got."

Arkin meets the man's gaze, possibly his thirty-year-hence doppelgänger, registering this new notion of forgiveness, alien and yet unburdening and comforting in its simplicity.

"And if you can't forgive, then you should get out."

———

Arkin arrives at his condo via taxi about 6:00 a.m. By then he has arranged for his car to be seen by an insurance adjuster and has reserved a rental replacement at the local Hertz office, a ten-minute walk. He is sober, shaved, showered. Prior to all this, troopers had come to the ER to interview him, to receive Dr. Brevard's exculpating report, and to give Arkin the personal items retrieved from the wreckage of his car, including his phone, laptop, rifle case, and gun bag.

He recollects his conversation with Dr. Brevard, now, with shame. Fatherless, he lacks what he imagines is several decades of correction by an older male authority figure, and imagines, too, that this may explain what he considers a staggering lack of insight about himself, his motives and actions. One thing, he tells himself now, that he likes about medicine is the aspect of mystery it embodies, particularly when encountering a patient for the first time. It has always interested Arkin how many (perhaps most?) of his colleagues enjoy making snap diagnoses. How often ED docs would interpret an EKG printout with a glance, only to have their interpretation reversed by the later cardiology read. Almost without fail, a hospitalist teammate's confident take on a CT scan will later be contradicted by radiology. It interests him that his colleagues are rarely shaken by these sorts of reversals. They say they understand errors are a part of practice, which they are, but their persistence in making rapid and self-assured mistakes suggests they'd rather be fast and wrong than acknowledge and wade through confusion.

If Arkin has a strength as a doctor (which he feels at the hungover and concussed moment is questionable), it's that he accepts the confusion and complexity of examining largely unknowable humans with semi-complete science to reach a destination on a grid of mostly arbitrary diagnoses. He relishes wading through the layers of possibility and uncertainty, reading articles on UpToDate or Medscape or PubMed to arrive at the most elegant and descriptive diagnosis available. He knows there're other docs that feel this way, and he has met a few.

So it shocks him now, alone in his anonymous apartment, child-less, suspended from his job, virtually friendless except for an equally itinerant nurse he's known for barely a month, to think how little energy he's expended in understanding himself, much less the two great mysteries of his life: why his mother killed herself, and who *he* killed at Mata Khan. He has the brief, sickening realization that his enjoyable investigations of the mysteries of medicine are a shabby displacement for the personal research he's avoided. *All these years,* he thinks, *half my life over,* he thinks, *and I learned nothing.*

And it's with this thought marinating his concussed brain that his eye falls on the Plano case, with its H&K semiautomatic rifle nestling undamaged within. He struggles to focus on minutiae—the additional calls he needs to make to his insurance agent, the rental car pickup, a trip to a dealer to shop for a new car—to no effect. He can recall the feel of the clicks and motions of the breech mech-anism as a magazine slides into a rifle. He can imagine charging the weapon, rotating it into the new and foreign position, muzzle upward, pointing at the submaxillary triangle under his chin, just above the hyoid bone, aimed slightly posterior so as to direct the bullet through the center of the cerebrum and an exit at the apex of the cranium. He wonders briefly at the possibility of lingering activity in the frontal lobes after discharge, but thinks the disruptive pressure of sixty thousand pounds per square inch in the exploding cartridge . . . precludes this. He would feel nothing, he thinks, and know nothing.

Somewhere in the still observing clinical compartment of his brain is his memory of learning in medical school that suicides are fundamentally impulsive, and he remembers specifically a review study from the '90s in which suicide was attributed to something called "aversive self-awareness." He thinks about this as he walks over to where the rifle case leans against his Target-sourced dinette table set, how in this framing suicide is made possible by a "cognitive deconstruction" in response to a sense of failure, which blunts self awareness and emotion. It brings, and he remembers the phrase, "irrationality and disinhibition" that allow for the impulsive, dramatic act that is suicide. Arkin feels almost like laughing aloud at this textual counterpoint to the feel of the rifle itself, in his hands now. He takes a loaded magazine from his gun bag and positions it at the magazine well at the bottom of the lower receiver.

Here, he forms a new working hypothesis, that the prospect of *failing* to kill oneself is experienced as an additive incentive to continue with the act. He wonders if anyone else, any researcher, has *ever before* considered this possibility, and briefly toys with the idea of writing a paper, or perhaps a letter to an editor at some psychiatry journal. He would first have to search PubMed for the original reference, then read citing articles, and then provide context: his own suicide, of course. That whole concept, his experience of the story he's just told himself, produces such "aversive" feelings in him that he snaps the magazine into the H&K and charges the weapon, all in one smooth and comfortably practiced movement. It has the reassuring feel of a confident and rapid diagnosis.

He holds the rifle at port arms, one of the central parts of the *Manual of Arms* he first learned in basic training, the rifle canted diagonally across the chest, one hand (the left) just forward of the upper receiver, the other (the right) on the buttstock behind the pistol grip. He realizes, and experiences this as more than a little ludicrous, that he is standing at attention, as one would on the parade ground. Of course he is not on the parade ground, but nevertheless his heels are together, the toes pointing out at a 45-degree angle. The legs are straight, but the knees are not locked. He stands straight, chest up and arched, shoulders square, chin drawn in. Absorbing this picture, experiencing it from within, he thinks that has never in his entire life felt himself so perfect an object of mockery as he does in this moment. He can't think of a moment when he felt so ridiculous or, for that matter, so inept. His thirty-second-old theory that the prospect of failing to commit suicide promotes it, falls completely apart. He forms a new theory: that feeling like a fool is a condition of living, and that contemplating suicide is a reminder of how truly foolish a man can feel.

He relaxes his laughable position of attention, lowers the rifle, and ejects the magazine and then the round in the chamber; it clanks uselessly against the "ornate seatback scrollwork" of his fake bronze dinette chair from Target. He replaces the H&K in its case. He retrieves the loose round and reinserts it into its magazine, which he puts back into his gun bag. He sits at the dinette and looks across the room at an empty Jack Daniels bottle, the last of which he'd poured out into the sink on arriving home this morning, after shave and shower, but before possible shooting.

The question of outright *cowardice* aside, it interests Arkin to consider how much of his life has been conditioned by fear: fear of being killed or injured in combat, fear of humiliation in his profession, fear of making mistakes with patients; he presumes that fear of connection (with all the sub-fears that may underlie it) explains his lengthening bachelorhood. He registers that fear of life itself may have prompted him to unpack and load his rifle moments before. He registers again that it was only fear of foolishness that kept him from the trigger.

Against this, sitting in his empty and soulless apartment, Arkin tells himself that he *did* face the dangers of combat, *did* jump out of planes, *did* go through med school and residency, *does* practice medicine, and *does*... (here he pauses)... love Kate, and *did* lower the rifle. If whatever his fears are, his actions belie them, perhaps he can allow himself, permit himself, to lay the fears aside.

He checks his watch; Hertz will be open now. On the way out of his apartment, he stores the rifle in his front closet and drops the bourbon bottle in the recycling.

FOURTEEN

KATE SITS IN THE waiting area outside the open-plan office space in which Detective Sergeant Jens has his desk; through the glass partition separating her from them, she can see Jens talking with another detective, white, short, balding. They look like a parody of a parody of *Miami Vice*.

The elevator opens, and Jim Porter, Kate's first-ever criminal defense lawyer, comes into the waiting area, sits opposite her. He wears a pin-striped suit over a shirt that looks as if it's been slept in; his gray-streaked hair is uncombed, and the huge two-wheel briefcase he totes looks half his size. He yawns, sighs, and greets her. "Good morning, Miss Maddox."

Kate manages a *Hi*, a nod; the bright white of the LED lighting combined with lack of sleep leaves her feeling washed out, emotionally flattened, but with an incipient wave of bitterness roiling somewhere just beneath her diaphragm.

Porter seems not to have noticed. "We'll be a while yet. I spoke to Sergeant Jens on the way over; there's a problem with the video." Kate merely nods again as Porter opens his briefcase, begins shuffling through files, background paperwork, something.

Kate wonders what that must be like, a day filled with legal research, brief-writing, case conferences. She can't help comparing the thought of it to her own work life, which feeds a concomitant rise in the bitterness in her, laced with fear it's about to be her *former* work life. Some old Joni Mitchell song—it seems to be Kate's day for dated pop culture parallels—runs through her mind about not knowing what you have till it's gone. "Big Yellow Taxi," she remembers it now. She remembers, too, the current of joy that ran through her in the early days of nursing school—in particular, her first clinical experiences in area nursing homes. These experiences consisted entirely of the most basic care functions. She'd bathed people, at times in bed, but at times in showers, Kate gloved and dancing around the stream of water as best she could while holding upright her naked, frail, quivering charges. She'd helped them to the toilet, wiped their bottoms, women front to rear; she'd helped tremulous old men retract their foreskins before peeing; she'd sprayed and combed the old ladies' hair; she'd shaved the old guys; she'd cleaned and inserted pessaries for prolapsed uteruses. She'd inserted urinary catheters for incontinence, rectal tubes for diarrhea, changed diapers by the hundreds. And, strangely, she'd loved all of this, the humble, intimate, uncomplicated humanity of it. As her education and then her career advanced, the tasks became vastly more complex: she'd learned to titrate powerful medications in the ICU, manage A-lines, spot and interpret telemetry abnormalities, defibrillate patients in arrest, and more. But her delight in the simple tasks of nursing has never left her, and it's this, she thinks, that she would miss most if she could never work again. She feels the bitterness spiking once again, now mixed with anger at finding herself in a police station, lawyered up, her professional life at risk. She resents the doctors in positions of authority at her hospital who, this morning, have placed her on leave during the police investigation. She resents that her suspension was communicated via email to her union rep (and then from the union rep to her via text), without the courtesy of a face-to-face or even a phone call. She notes that Arkin (though the finger of blame was less steady in his case, she has to admit) at least got to actually *see* his boss when he was suspended. Though she has never been much troubled by the rigid doctor-nurse hierarchies in health care, the chasm in experience strikes her as dramatic. Changing diapers and wiping bottoms and bathing the paper-thin skin of the old ones is a humanizing experience doctors simply never have, and she thinks this shows in the way they treat each other, treat the nurses, and ultimately treat their patients.

It's in the midst of this silent harangue that Arkin walks into the waiting area and sits down next to her. Porter looks up in curiosity and then in alarm when Kate tells him, "This is Dr. Arkin."

"You're not supposed to be here," says Porter, getting no reaction from either Arkin or Kate. Kate sees a bruise on the left side of Arkin's forehead, notes how he's holding himself stiffly, wincing slightly with inspiration—her assessment skills aren't suspended— how his eyes are pouched and rimmed gray with tiredness. Still, he seems calm, focused, sober.

"I called the unit; they said you'd be here," he tells her. "I want to pay for this," he says, and turning to Porter, adds, "whatever this costs. If you need to bring in someone else, do it."

"I'm not working for you," Porter says.

"That's all right, doesn't matter. Anything she needs. This is my fault," he says, turning back to her. "She's only here because . . . of us. But she's incapable of harming a patient, for any reason."

Kate manages a smile, relaxing into it, this vote of confidence. The truth of what she'd do for him is likely a lot more complicated than Arkin thinks, but whatever else he is, he's a guy, and men are best shielded from the truth about women's potential ferocity. She reaches for him, touches his arm, finds his hand and intertwines their fingers, hers tough and strong from the work she does, his a doctor's softer hands, long fingers, a surgeon's hands, someone might have said in a different age. "You really shouldn't be here," she says softly, to which Arkin only nods once, not moving. "Are you okay?"

"I had a rough night, but yeah," he says with, for her, startling conviction, "I'm fine now." He turns back to Porter. "I mean that. I have money; I'll spend it."

Porter notes that his client continues holding tightly to Arkin's hand and, knowing the potential costs of defending a criminal case, as well as his own billing targets at the firm, nods in agreement.

"Good," Arkin says. "Can I stay?"

"You can wait here," Porter says.

Arkin nods, gives Kate's hand a squeeze, and Jens looms in the doorway.

"Hey, Dr. Arkin, how you doing?" Not waiting for an answer, he tells Porter, "Ready for you and your client now."

———

Arkin watches Kate and her lawyer follow Jens into an interview room, sees the door close, an "Interview in Progress" sign illuminate over the lintel. He imagines them settling themselves around a table, a digital recorder there on the scarred laminate, possibly a camera somewhere as well, over Jens' shoulder. But he recognizes that, aside from streamed police procedurals, he has absolutely no idea how any of this works. The one thing he does know about legal issues is that they're expensive and, after deducting something for the cost of a new car, he figures to have about $180,000 in checking and his 403(b) to spend on Kate's behalf. He can max out his credit cards and borrow more. The thought of doing so, of spending *everything* for her is strangely liberating, as though money and career and the regard of his colleagues are all receding into the background of his previous life, or anyway his pre-Kate life. And pre-Barnhardt life. It occurs to him that he hasn't thought of Barnhardt at all since the moment he'd turned in his hospital ID at the security desk. He wonders what Barnhardt might have thought of the havoc his death had caused, in particular to Kate, and then recoils at the realization that almost certainly he'd have enjoyed it, tormenting a young woman, a professional, reveling in her vulnerability. Arkin can only dimly recall the innocence with which he first encountered Barnhardt in the emergency room those weeks ago, the collision of past and future embodied in the imminence of that moment, and his own stupefying naivete and denial.

"Well, hey, Doc," Ed Breen says from the doorway. Once again he's in civilian clothes, jacket and tie, and Arkin wonders briefly, inconsequentially, what his actual rank is in Army CID, enlisted man or officer.

"What are you doing here?"

"Well, Sergeant Jens asked me to come in for an update, maybe sit in on an interview or two? Lotta traffic on the thruway though; guess I'm late."

"They already started."

Breen looks beyond him to the closed interview room. "He in there with the nurse?"

"My friend, yes," Arkin corrects him. "Kate. Katherine Maddox."

Breen nods, untroubled, seats himself. "So how you doin'?"

Arkin only nods, distracted, mentally in the interview room with Kate, imagining her, hands folded; imagining Jens with a yellow pad for note-taking; imagining Porter asserting or clarifying or delaying, whatever lawyers do.

Breen interrupts with, "You know you're out of this, right? You're off the hook?"

Arkin surfaces reluctantly, silent.

"They spoke to the bar owner, the bartender. The police did. They confirmed that you were drunk, really drunk. They found two other customers who were at the bar who had to help your . . . friend, the nurse, get you to her car. You weren't capable of killing anybody. Police confirmed your car was in the hospital lot all night, and they even checked with cab companies and Uber and Lyft and . . . you didn't go anywhere—they know that. I'm sure they'll be talking to your boss, the one I met? I'm sure you can be reinstated pretty much whenever you want."

Arkin does take this in, nodding to himself, although just now the prospect of returning to work seems fantastic. "I'm more concerned about her at the moment."

"Well, that's understandable. Her situation is . . . complicated."

"No, it isn't," says Arkin, his conviction, the certainty of it, registering with Breen.

After a moment, he says, "Our Robert Barnhardt, he certainly was the center of a lot of . . . drama. Even after he died, he's caused your friend some trouble, and of course you."

Arkin reverts to a silence, watching the still lit interview room sign.

Eventually Breen resumes. "You know, he lied. I mean Barnhardt: his business, his job, was lying, but this went the extra mile. That whole thing about your shooting unarmed villagers in Afghanistan, in Paktia Province? That he was gonna expose?"

Breen's got Arkin's attention now; he feels the muscles in his thighs and belly and chest all contracting, pulling him forward into a kind of curved and focused arch.

"That was a lie," Breen says. "He made that all up."

Now Arkin's silence isn't chosen, it descends on him like a gelatinous wave, settling thickly around his head, almost blocking sound. Breen's words feel like that: simple viscid noise, not possibly *real*, but . . .

"Yeah," Breen continues, "It took months because, well, that's just the way they did things, or the way he did things. Pressuring the villagers. Hold onto the bodies, claim the investigation's still in progress, let tempers cool. Eventually you pay them, return the bodies, lots of ceremony, everything just right. Not our finest moment."

Arkin just stares at him, a fine twitch starting below his left eye, head throbbing again.

"You were already out of the Army by then, back in college."

Finally, Arkin struggles to voice his question, the only one he can formulate. "What do you mean, *It was a lie*?"

"You didn't shoot anyone," Breen says, quite casual, his ease in stark and bizarre contrast to what Arkin's feeling as his world and history unravel and reknit. "You were carrying an M4, 5.56 millimeter, new NATO round, right? Basically a 223 Remington? I read the report."

Arkin can't move.

"And your sniper teammate, Kelly? He was shooting the old NATO round, 7.62. That's all they found in any of the villagers, when they did their postmortems."

Arkin only whispers now, "He told me there were no autopsies."

"Of course there were," Breen says with a laugh, which he smothers, remembering where he is or perhaps where *Arkin* is in what he's saying. "Everybody on all sides in Afghanistan fired 7.62s, including Taliban, especially in their AKs. They had old Lee Enfields, which are 303s, and some machine guns that fired 7.62 by 54 millimeters, which is larger than the AK rounds; they even got a few Russian sniper rifles that used that same round. But what they *didn't* have was any M4s or anything else that shot the 5.56."

Although Arkin knows quite a lot about rifle cartridges, the numbers are eluding him somehow, indecipherable, which Breen seems to sense.

"The point is, if unarmed people were *only* killed with the 7.62, you could argue, Barnhardt did argue, that maybe the shooting was done, could have been done, by Taliban. I mean, your friend Kelly shot people, yeah, he couldn't pretend it hadn't happened—you reported it. But maybe the other side was shooting too. At least Barnhardt could argue it and negotiate a lower payout. If *you* shot villagers, though, there'd be no argument. But you didn't."

Still a whisper, ghostly: "Why didn't anybody tell me?"

"Why would they think about it? No one said you did. You were already out. Barnhardt was a *fixer*. He made things go away, and once they were gone, they were gone forever. After that, he didn't care."

It takes long moments for the muscles in Arkin's torso to relax, for him to sit back on his bench, eventually find air to speak. "But I fired my weapon. I know I did. That happened."

"So? I read all the reports. You were running down a hill, full speed, your weapon is set to burst mode, right, which they still had in those days? For suppressive fire?" Arkin barely nods, or shrugs, or shivers, and Breen continues: "So you touch the trigger three times, that's nine rounds gone, like that," emphasizing it with a snap of his fingers, in turn awakening a memory in Arkin, which Breen seems to have already anticipated. "And then what did you do? When you stopped, when he turned?"

Arkin can't exactly visualize the past, but—possibly from the shock of Breen's words and the destruction of his own central doubts—he can feel it, can feel his body unbalanced on the slope of that hill down into Mata Khan, can feel the hot sweat under his camo gear—and can *feel* his finger on the M4's selector. Softly, so as not disturb the tenuous grip of this moment on that distant one, he says: "I switched to single shot."

"Of course you did—you didn't want to miss, and he was about to kill you."

Arkin stands, then sits, then stands again, as though detached from even his physical geometry.

"Maybe you should get some air," Breen suggests, a little taken aback himself. "Maybe you should take a walk? They'll be in there for a while."

Arkin looks vaguely toward where Jens and Kate and her lawyer are still meeting, although for now he is disconnected even from her, having lost the thread of that threat to another long past. He gets himself to the door, through it, and then away.

"So, explain to me about the insulin," Jens says.

For the third time, Kate describes the process for taking multi-use insulin vials from the common stock drawer in the med room's automated dispenser. How the medication is drawn up and a label printed for the syringe, which can then be scanned prior to administration. She senses that the details are actually of limited interest to the detective: "So you admit you took insulin vials from this, what do you call it, Pyxis machine?"

"Of course," Kate says. "I gave insulin to, I don't know, two or three patients that day at least."

"You always give it?"

"Almost always; half our patients have diabetes. More sometimes."

"But not Mr. Barnhardt?"

"He wasn't my patient!" Kate says for more than the third time, although the distinction, central to nurses, is meaningless to Jens.

"But you *could have*, right? I mean, you would have an insulin vial in your hand, for someone. You had access to syringes; there's a box of them, right?"

Kate is tired of explaining what is and isn't controlled access in the med room.

"And there's no way of measuring what's in that insulin bottle; they're just replaced whenever you run out, by the pharmacist, that's what you said." Kate nods wearily. "So you could take some insulin for one patient but then put *more* of it into another syringe, and stick *that* one in your pocket, and no one would ever know. Isn't that right?"

"Miss Maddox, don't answer that," her lawyer says to her, then turns to Jens. "You're asking my client to do your work for you. Can we move on?"

"I'm just trying to understand procedure here, that's all." Jens looks back to Kate, expression open and unthreatening, hands and arms spread benignly.

"Yes," Kate says. "Yes, once the vial is out of the Pyxis, you could draw up another syringe, *anybody* could, any nurse giving insulin can do that. It's not morphine or Dilaudid, it's not a controlled substance, it's not an antibiotic or a pill with a set dose—it's just insulin."

"Which in this case was used to kill someone."

Kate stares at him for moment before: "I have no idea. I don't even know how to think about that. We give insulin subcutaneously on our unit; they do insulin drips in the ICU, but you're talking about injecting it intravenously. Some huge dose—I would have no idea how much, how fast to push it, what insulin to use. It's crazy."

"Someone did."

"I doubt it," Kate says, a little louder than necessary before controlling herself, recalling some long-ago training about "professional communication" in nursing. Perhaps it will be more productive to think of Jens as a patient, potentially dangerous but for now just cantankerous and slow to understand. "And I don't believe any nurse on our unit ... could conceive ... or consider ... *diverting* insulin ... much less harming a patient with it." This last has been delivered so methodically, and with a just discernible degree of condescension, that Jens seems persuaded to shift focus.

"Of course, a doctor can just write a prescription for insulin, right?"

Kate stares at him.

"Then you wouldn't have to get it from your medication room."

As if to a child, almost, Kate says, "Any doctor. Any nurse practitioner. Can write a prescription. For any medication. At any pharmacy."

Jens leans back in his chair, folding his arms across his chest. "So let's *talk* about Dr. Arkin."

At that moment, Arkin himself is out on Main Street in front of police headquarters, half a mile north of the hospital where he was working until a few days prior and, if Breen is right, can likely resume . . . whenever. Directly to his front is the city's lightly used semi-luxury hotel and convention center. More prominent in Arkin's thinking is that the Riverside Bar is about a five-minute walk west, through the city's recently designated "Italian District" and just past the Amtrak Station; he turns in that direction. The Riverside will just be opening, and with Arkin's recommitment to sobriety only hours old, part of him is, well, screaming for a drink (the word *amygdala* floats to mind, seat of primary emotions, pre-med anatomy).

His higher mental functions, such as they are, are on hold. For years he has lived with the incompletely suppressed presumption that he murdered innocents in an arid mountain village almost seven thousand miles from here. He remembers how he once checked the cost of the twenty-four-hour-plus trip from New York to Kabul, then researched travel from there to Khost and on, finally, to Mata Khan. At the time, the pandemic was in full flood, which made travel impossible, this timing likely somewhat providential given Arkin's uncertainty about his motive for such a trip. Did he think to make amends or, perhaps, simply to look around in hopes of understanding what really had happened?

And now he knows: a lot of people died, but not at his hands. He flashes on how this parallels his life in medicine: a lot of people die whom he *hasn't* killed. It's faintly amusing that the one patient he might have wished dead, and who by any *objective* standard is better off that way, actually *was* killed. Only not by Arkin, but possibly, unbelievably, by Kate in order to protect him. Comedy knows no bounds, heavily buttressed by the same death's having, if only indirectly via Breen's involvement, lifted the stone of guilt Arkin has been carrying around since those days at Firebase Salerno. It is this impulse to laugh that he feels he should address at the Riverside Bar.

He reaches the pedestrian bridge passing above the tracks leading to the Amtrak and Metro North train station, built in 1918 and modeled, someone's told him, on Grand Central in New York. A less apt comparison, he thinks, would be hard to find. It reminds Arkin instead, its drab and cavernous waiting room in particular, of aimlessness and loss. But he can't help remembering how, on the day he'd met Kate, weeks earlier, he'd stood outside the hospital and contemplated coming to this very station, taking the train south to New York, and disappearing from the life he was leading, had led, beginning (he supposes) at that moment of indefinable death and unknowable mortality in Afghanistan.

Arkin pauses on the bridge now. The gleaming rows of bourbon bottles at the Riverside are exercising their sultry pull on him. It occurs to Arkin that much of his adult life has been characterized by running: running *down* the hill in Mata Khan, running from the reality of his mother's suicide, away from the absence of his unnamed father. He'd run away from the sometimes dismal implications of his profession, from his own drunkenness, possibly from his job, and, now, away from his connection to Kate, his responsibility—since he does see it this way—for her predicament. Running *to* the bar.

From his vantage point, he looks north up the Hudson to where a former railroad bridge, now converted to pedestrian walkway, crosses the river. It reaches a height of more than two hundred feet, and Arkin recalls a conversation with a psychiatrist colleague who'd been interviewed about the potential for suicides from such a span shortly before it opened. He'd thought that potential was considerable and, indeed, so many people had jumped from it since its completion that a dedicated suicide hotline phone had been installed mid-span. Arkin thinks about how he'd loaded his H&K this morning with the same thought in mind. But why, he wonders, should obliteration be so appealing *now*, when the central burden of his life, complicity in the murder of innocents in wartime, has been lifted? He doesn't need to run anymore, a small thought that nonetheless thunders across his consciousness. He doesn't need to run, he doesn't need to shoot, he doesn't even need to *practice medicine*, he also thinks, astonished, as his brain lumbers back into something like normal executive function. And, he realizes, he doesn't need to drink.

He puts his hands on the bridge railing, on the rust and metal and the grime of the past, braces himself, breathes, then turns right, uphill, away from the bar, and back to Kate.

———

Breen is sitting where Arkin left him. "Better?" he asks.

"Yes, I am. Thanks." Breen waves this away. "So, tell me again, why do you suspect Kate?"

"Well, it's not really me, I just represent the Army's interests. It's the police; for them, it's a case. So far as I'm concerned, Barnhardt . . ." here he trails off, his meaning obvious enough but better unvoiced.

"I understand that but you're here, you're involved. So explain it to me."

Breen studies him for a moment, considering, before: "Okay, let me show you." He leads Arkin out of the waiting room and to a work area adjacent to Jens's desk; there's a computer, monitor. Breen finds a piece of paper in his pocket, types out the temporary username and password the police have provided. "I've been given access, just to the case materials, but to help with my report when the time comes."

Arkin can see dozens of file names scrolling past, among them, he guesses, the report of Barnhardt's autopsy, interviews with administrators, nurses, more.

Breen finds a folder named "Hospsurv," opens it, clicks on the file it contains. "This is the hospital surveillance video from that night, about twenty minutes of it. They're using the best new compression codec, called H.264—lets us look at simultaneous video from lots of cameras, good quality."

"And the hospital let the police have this?"

"Sure, why not? I probably shouldn't show it to you but . . ." He glances over at Arkin, pauses a moment before: "We're both *Army*, right? So maybe I should." He turns back to the computer. "Anyway, I have the password. So here's that night, starting about 12:30 in the morning."

The monitor screen fills with a grid of two dozen windows, the videos in each synced to a digital timestamp in the lower right-hand corner. "There're lots of cameras, but it's a big place so they don't store everything, some video for just twenty-four hours, others for longer, like these."

Arkin can identify most of the video locations, public area hallways, three cameras covering the interior of the pharmacy, the cafeteria, gift shop, all the hospital entrances and parking areas.

"So here's your friend," says Breen. He points to one of the windows in the bottom right of the screen, where Arkin sees Kate walking through pools of overhead light to one of the employee entrances. The timestamp says "12:34 a.m." She uses her ID to swipe the outdoor card reader, enters the building, and is picked up in the next video window, in a nonpublic hallway. "So she gets a cup of coffee, just as she says she did." On video, Kate's in a vending area, can be seen in rear three-quarters view as she uses her ID again to buy her Green Mountain. "But now, instead of leaving, going back out to her car, she stays in the building." On screen, Kate leaves the vending machines, checks her watch, and then turns away from the exit. In the video frame, she moves away from the camera, walking down the hallway to a bank of elevators, one of which she enters. "And that's where we lose her."

"Her lawyer told me she went to use a bathroom."

"Why not use one on the first floor?"

"I don't know—who cares? Maybe she didn't want to use a public bathroom. Where did she go?"

"We don't know—that's part of the problem. We don't have elevator footage, it's not saved past twenty-four hours, and we can't see the annunciator, so we don't know what floor she went to."

"Can't you see where she got out?"

"Well, that's the problem. These are employee elevators, and they open onto parts of the patient floors that aren't recorded for privacy reasons."

"What does she say?"

"She says she went to the second floor, which is a cardiology area. I guess they do . . . ?"

"The cath lab, yeah."

"Which is also not recorded because patients are there. But there's an employee locker area, lounge, restrooms—that's where she says she went."

"Okay, yeah, I guess I knew that," Arkin says. He watches the various video screens, ongoing activity on most, the hospital a busy place even after midnight with foot traffic in the main lobby, cafeteria, registration area, information desk. Other employees come and go at the entrance Kate used. All the while, the time stamp continues to run at the bottom of the screen. At 12:44, on the employee hallway video, Kate emerges from an elevator, moves toward the entrance she'd used earlier, and leaves the building. The exterior camera again picks her up, this time walking away from the hospital and toward the employee parking lot. She disappears out of frame; the rest of the video windows continue as before, routine comings and goings around the hospital's public spaces for another thirty seconds or so before going black.

"And that's what we have," Breen says. "She was in the hospital for almost ten minutes to get a cup of coffee and use a bathroom." Arkin says nothing, staring at the now blank monitor. "Seems kind of a long time, ten minutes. She could have gone anywhere."

Arkin looks at him at last, only half-focused, says, "Go back."

"What?"

And Arkin repeats it, though somewhat dreamily. "Go back on the tape. Thirty seconds." Which Breen does, Arkin's demeanor strange, yes, but convincing in its strangeness. All the video screens resume running as Kate leaves the building, passes through the same pools of light as she heads for her car, leaves the frame. "There, stop," and Breen freezes the twenty-four synced windows. "There," Arkin says, pointing to one of the screens, the hospital's main public entrance and lobby. It's a big area, and the camera angle's a wide one, so the figure Arkin's indicated is small in the frame but recognizable. "Can you enlarge this?" Again, Breen obliges, selecting that window, expanding it to fill the entire monitor screen. After a moment, Arkin says, "I know her."

Breen studies the figure, a well-dressed middle-aged woman in a lab coat, stethoscope around her neck, ID held aloft. "I know her," Arkin repeats. Breen restarts the video, the figure waves her ID breezily toward the security guard at his station, who gestures her through his gate and on into the building.

Breen sees nothing out of the ordinary. "She's some doctor, right? On call, overnight duty, come to see some patient. So what?"

Arkin is muted, nerveless almost. "She doesn't have any patients in this hospital. She's retired. But she is a doctor—she was Barnhardt's doctor." He turns to Breen again. "Fifteen years ago, in Afghanistan."

———————

Without knocking, Breen opens the door to the interview room, comes in. Kate watches as he bends, whispers in Jens's ear. Kate can see his lips moving, partially visible behind his concealing hand; she hears his voice but not the words, only a low, urgent whisper. Jens glances at him, then to Kate, saying, "Miss Maddox, can you excuse me for a minute?" And to her lawyer, "Mr. Porter, that okay with you?" Porter nods, and Jens is led out by Breen.

Porter stifles a yawn and Kate says, "I could've killed him." Porter stops mid-yawn. "He deserved to die. If Arkin asked me . . ." and lets the thought hang there, Porter gaping, startled. "But he didn't. And I didn't."

Porter looks to where the digital recorder is still running, red "Record" light blinking silently. The same is true of the camera behind Jens's now vacated seat. Kate only smiles, and Porter's anxiety is not improved by a voice.

"Hey." And Arkin's there, peering around the doorjamb.

"You shouldn't be here," Porter says, loudly, possibly for the benefit of the digital devices in the room.

"There's been a development," Arkin says, unbothered. "Maybe you should come out."

Kate, and then Porter, follow him out into the main office area, away from recorders.

"What is it?" Porter asks, with a glance at Jens and Breen, now at Jens's desk, studying the computer there.

Arkin's focused only on Kate. "The night you went back to the hospital, they have video of you, like ten minutes in the building before you went back out to your car."

"I know," she says. "They say I went to the unit, or could've, and injected him."

"Did you?" Arkin asks, but with a half smile that alerts and warms her, lifts her mood from the prevailing drabness of the moment, the surroundings. She shakes her head, mirroring his smile. "I know," he says.

"Why? What is it?" Porter asks.

Arkin turns to him: "Maybe you should go talk to the police. And the Army." And then, returning to Kate, "I think we're done here."

FIFTEEN

IT'S A REGULAR WORKDAY for both Kate and Arkin. It took five days for Kate to be reinstated after the video surfaced of Barnhardt's former doctor entering the hospital the night he died. The bureaucratic complexities of nurse staffing were more ponderous than those of physicians, for Massood had called Arkin the very next morning to tell him he was back on the job. Arkin opted instead for some time off, to be with Kate until she could return too.

They'd driven north, out of New York and into Vermont, stopping first near Manchester for a night at a skiers' inn, near empty at the time of year, and for dinner at an expensive little restaurant highly rated on travelers' websites. It was run by a wife and husband team who'd traveled widely, working at and then running restaurants around the country. Kate and Arkin ate empanadas and lobster risotto and cubanos, sharing everything and marveling at how the owners' travels had shaped their menu. They drank a glass of wine each, then stopped and had espresso with dessert.

In the morning, they'd driven farther north, to a state park where they hiked for two hours up onto the gentle slopes of the Green Mountains. They drank Gatorade and ate PowerBars in a clearing that gave a view of Dorset Mountain to the northwest and Equinox Mountain to the south. They talked again about the proprietors of the restaurant they'd visited the night before, and how their work travels had shaped their lives. Kate had already requested information from several international health care organizations, including the International Committee of the Red Cross, the International Medical Corps, Mercy Ships, Doctors Without Borders, others.

After this, they'd driven further north. They'd hiked in the higher mountains around Stowe and toured the Ben & Jerry's factory in Waterbury. The tour included a tasting of freshly made ice cream, in their case a flavor called Chocolate Chip Cookie Dough. They joked about how their trip seemed to revolve around food, but it was also about hiking and making love and not talking about the hospital or what had happened to them there. They did not talk about Arkin's past, about past crimes not committed, or the crime that may have been committed more recently.

Back in the hospital, the memory of their car trip fades. Kate returns to South Eight with a box of maple sugar candy for her fellow nurses, which all say they shouldn't eat, then do. To say she is welcomed back is an understatement, not just because she's liked but because the volume of *What the Fucks?* directed by the nurses toward the hospital administration reflects their anger that one of them might be suspected, even momentarily, of hurting a patient in their care.

Of course, no one yet knows what actually happened to Barnhardt. None of the nurses know the name *Dr. Beth Oliver*, though at least one of the night staff, a CNA, had seen a doctor entering Barnhardt's room on the night he died. The CNA hadn't recognized her, which in itself was not unusual since hundreds of different clinicians in lab coats may visit the hospital and its patients in the course of a week. The hour was a little more unusual, but not unheard of: dozens of specialist and hospitalist doctors and nurse practitioners are on duty or available on call overnight, and outpatient providers come to the hospital, too, after their workday to see patients; in any event, Oliver's visit went unremarked.

———————

Equally inconclusive are Barnhardt's final autopsy results, as Massood reads them to Arkin in a welcome back session over pre-rounds coffee. The details and problems are legion: there are no antemortem samples available for comparison, IV lines were again noted to have been discarded before the body was transported to the morgue, and though insulin was found in some tissue samples, the off-site lab had considered the more accurate CSF and vitreous insulin levels "elevated but nondiagnostic" for intentional overdose, although "such cannot specifically be ruled out." Both Massood and Arkin recognize in these phrases the familiar professional formulation for "We think this happened, but we wouldn't swear to it in court." Both find the report's discussion of lactate, C-peptide, and 3-β-hydroxybutyrate immunoassays difficult to follow, possibly over their heads altogether, and anyway, again, nonspecific.

Massood is obviously, openly, thrilled with the outcome, jubilant at Arkin's "return to the fold," as he puts it. Arkin had never especially connected with his director, but sees in his mood now a reaction that goes beyond relief at difficult conversations (and staffing problems) avoided, but rather a sense of shared vindication. It reminds Arkin that on some level, all doctors, all the time, live in dread of the next accusation, and Arkin is touched at the sense of camaraderie and affection Massood shares.

The buoyancy sustains Arkin only until his first patient encounter of the day, with a thirty-seven-year-old man the hospitalists have been consulted to see for "medical management" after he was admitted by cardiology overnight for NSTEMI, or "non-ST elevated myocardial infarction." The problems Arkin's to address include smoking, obesity, and poorly controlled type 2 diabetes. These are straightforward, common enough in young heart attack patients; his father's presence and attitude is less so.

"So are you the one to arrange for the transfer?" interrupts the older man, early sixties, gray at the temples, CrossFit slim, and wearing a suit even Arkin recognizes—Brioni, Zegna?—but anyway as costing more than Arkin spends on clothes in a year.

"I'm Dr. Arkin. I'm internal medicine, not cardiology."

"Don't care," says the other. "My name's Belden. I'm on the board at Presbyterian—that's where I'd like my son to go." Arkin nods, notices the boy in bed—well, not really a boy, he's thirty-seven after all, but boy-seeming, sullen, silent. "I've been here for an hour already. I'm told my son needs a catheterization. Cardiac catheterization. I understand it's not an emergency, so I want him moved to a higher level of care."

"Well, this is really something you should discuss with the admitting cardiologist."

The response is blunt and immediate: "Nope. I just want it done."

Arkin typically might have been inclined to let all this go, but the man's tone, his use of "higher level of care" (which is *not* applicable even to the august New York Presbyterian in this routine case), and possibly the more recent encounters with Barnhardt and what *he* represented of the power elite, keeps him in the room. "Are you a physician?" Arkin asks.

"No."

"And you're aware that you may have to pay the cost of the transfer out of pocket? That insurance won't pay for the ambulance?"

Belden's answers are growing no less abrupt. "That's fine."

"And you're aware that under these circumstances, Columbia Presbyterian is under no obligation to accept the transfer?"

"I'll take care of that," the man says and Arkin briefly, prudently, closes his eyes, throttles the anger rising in him.

"That they rarely have beds available for this sort of routine issue. That they'll say you have a great cardiology group up there, a fine cath lab, and no reason to transfer." To this, the father says nothing, apparently has nothing further to say at all. Arkin stares at him a moment then turns to the son, the younger Mr. Belden, in bed. "And how do you feel about it?"

The patient looks at him in surprise; possibly he is unused to offering an opinion after his father has expressed his own. They look at each other for a moment, the slightly older, much softer man in the bed, scared and resentful at having had his first heart attack, angry at his father. Which he shares with the doctor standing at the foot of the bed, a little younger, taller, slimmer, but still a contemporary, and an ally.

"I'd like to stay," says the patient.

"Okay," Arkin says. "So tell me about yourself. Let's start with the diabetes, how long you've had it, what you take for it. Let's do a quick exam." Arkin moves toward the bed, the elder Mr. Belden stonily silent, on his way to the door. Arkin slips the stethoscope from around his neck as his cell buzzes; he checks it—and reads the one line there: "Can we meet? Important. Breen."

———————

Arkin has texted back his suggestion of the physician's lounge in the basement, arrives first, leaves the door open for Breen. He picks out a private corner, though at this hour there's no one in the lounge anyway. Stacked around are copies of the *Lancet*, *JAMA*, the *BMJ*, the *NEJM*, *Annals of Internal Medicine*, and more. It's appealingly retro, to many of his colleagues, that the hospital continues to spend thousands of dollars a year for subscriptions to print versions of these famous medical journals. And displaying them here in the lounge suggests that doctors will have time to sit and read, which is rarely the case. More frequent use of the lounge relates to the presence of its hotel-sized automatic cappuccino machine, the yogurts and puddings in the fridge, the packages of cookies and a not-so-fresh basket of fruit, all of it free.

Arkin flips open an old copy of *JAMA*, starts in on an article comparing "the risks of overcorrection in rapid intermittent bolus (RIB) and slow continuous infusion (SCI) therapies in patients with symptomatic hyponatremia." Almost immediately, he remembers having read the article online and that it turns out not to make much of a difference. He can't really recall a study that concluded everything they'd previously thought about some practice or procedure was wrong, and *Here's the right way—do it now!* Possibly he missed it.

He doesn't miss Breen's arrival though—"Hey Doc,"—or behind him, Beth Oliver.

Breen says, "I believe you know Dr. Oliver?"

"Yes," Arkin says, uneasily. He stands, remembers he's holding the *JAMA* issue, tosses it down.

"Hello," she says, to which Arkin can only nod. Today she's in jeans, a white shirt, a tailored black jacket. Her hair is pulled back into a simple ponytail; she wears no makeup. Altogether a different look than in their previous encounters.

"Can we sit?" Breen asks. Arkin gestures to the empty room; they find a table, chairs. Breen takes a moment, then starts. "Dr. Oliver asked for this meeting. And she asked me to arrange it because, for reasons you can probably imagine, she is not welcome in Corporation hospitals at the moment. Is that right, Dr. Oliver?"

"Yes," she says, composed, unbothered.

"But she did want to talk to you. We've just now concluded our business with Sergeant Jens at the police station, but I still did have a visitor pass and access here, and was happy to walk her in." He turns to Oliver. "Does that describe it?"

Again, only, "Yes."

"So," Breen says. He leans back in his chair, both in posture and attitude absenting himself from their little group.

Oliver takes a moment, then begins: "You've had some trouble, I understand, Dr. Arkin."

"Yes. Some," he says, noncommittal, still adjusting to her presence here.

"I'm sorry for that. I wanted to explain myself, at least in part." And after a moment, "You know I'm not being charged by the police."

"Yes. I heard that. And I've seen the final autopsy and lab reports. They were . . . not helpful."

The ghost of a smile appears on Oliver's face. "That depends on one's perspective, wouldn't you say?"

"Yes," Arkin says, almost under his breath.

Breen gets up from his chair, wanders over the fruit basket, even farther away from the conversation occurring between the two doctors, carefully elliptical as it is.

"But I'm sorry for your trouble, and I thought you might like to know a little more about the man who was at the center of it."

"Barnhardt."

"Yes," she says, and then, "I told you he was a bad man. And that we were all scared of him. And then you told me what he was doing to you, trying to do, and to your career. I admit it brought back so much of what I had experienced. So the other night—to explain, Dr. Arkin—when I considered how the past had come back into my life, and yours, I thought I'd come and see him again."

"You'd come to see him before."

"Yes, but you were there that time, you came in, and I felt this needed to be us alone, just him and me."

Arkin is determined not to read anything into Oliver's expression (which is neutral) or into her silences (which are arid). He knows there are words being left unsaid, which he prefers, he thinks.

"So I thought I'd try again," Oliver says, "Late, when no one would disturb us."

Breen is now leaning against a wall, relaxed but distant, *enabling*, Arkin thinks.

Oliver continues: "What do you know about MSF, Doctors Without Borders?"

"I, uh, I have an application packet at home."

"Do you?" Oliver says, mustering the whisper of a smile at this news. "Well, I knew them pretty well in Afghanistan. They were doing important work, I thought, with the local population, who we weren't allowed to help, not really, and who were suffering with so much fighting and illness in their country. It was a terrible time, and MSF was great, doing great work. And then . . . a few weeks before I first met Mr. Barnhardt, their hospital in Kunduz was fired upon by an American airplane, something called an AC-130 gunship. Do you know what that is?"

"Yes, I do." He looks over at Breen. He knows, too, Arkin thinks.

Oliver says, "Well, that . . . history . . . is part of what I came to talk about with Mr. Barnhardt, the other night." Neither Arkin nor Breen speaks; it seems neither wishes to interrupt. "You see . . . when our plane fired on that hospital, we killed forty-two people. Eighteen staff members, twenty-four patients. Some of the patients burned alive in their beds. Three of those were children. And there were many different explanations offered for how this could have happened, because Doctors Without Borders had provided coordinates for their hospital, and it was clearly on a protected list. At first, we said Americans had been attacked. But that wasn't true, so then we said we hadn't been attacked, but that Afghan forces had asked us for air support, and the hospital was mistakenly hit. And that didn't work either. Eventually it was attributed to a whole series of mistakes, communication errors and misunderstandings, electronic problems, "fog of war," they called it. They denied that it was retribution for treating injured Taliban fighters. Although some Taliban fighters may have been inside the hospital at some point in the past, when they occupied the city. In any case, no one actually ever said who was responsible for the order to attack. An order that was confirmed multiple times, including after the men in the airplane questioned what they were firing on, and why. This all happened—you can look it up."

Arkin glances again at Breen, who is motionless, waiting for what comes next. "Your patient, and mine, Robert Barnhardt, gave that order."

Arkin closes his eyes, takes a deep breath, then another. He can visualize the AC-130, how its huge side-mounted howitzer could devastate enemy positions as the plane circled at a distance; he tries not to think about what it could do to a hospital compound.

"That was part of what I came to discuss with Barnhardt the other night." Her gaze has deepened, darkened. "That's the man who was threatening to end your career. You understand?"

"Yes," Arkin says.

"And that's the man whose diagnosis I missed. Shortly after the bombing he ordered, that killed so many." Oliver stops, her gaze deeply inward, not back in time so much as down into it, before she resumes in a near whisper: "It is difficult to say . . . how my repugnance for a particular patient . . . might have affected my clinical judgement or . . . behavior. Which in this case condemned him to years of suffering."

This thought, and the word *condemned*, seems to sustain a silence all its own, so that Arkin is actually unaware of how much time may have passed before she continues. "I believe I wanted to . . . describe . . . that possibility to Mr. Barnhardt, as he reached the end of life. How I may have been responsible for what he'd experienced. So I drove up. I wore a lab coat, carried my old ID so I wouldn't have to explain my presence after visiting hours, because I did want privacy." Finally, she looks at Arkin, an arctic outline of hard truth forming around her mouth. "But he was asleep. So whatever . . . final reckoning . . . I hoped to accomplish, either for my own action or his, in the bombing of innocents . . . was left unsaid. With his long illness at an end," she adds, with a certain muted delicacy. She looks back to Breen. "And I understand that it was only a few hours later that he was found to have expired."

"That's what I understand too," Breen says.

Oliver nods, then nods again as if in the affirmative to some question that only she has heard. She stands. "Well, I just wanted to see you, and share that," she says to Arkin, and then to Breen: "Thank you for letting me do that, Mr. Breen." Breen's half smile is remote, conveys no meaning, nothing at all. "I've always enjoyed working with the Army," she says, and walks past him and out of the lounge.

"You good?" Breen asks Arkin. "You got it?"

Arkin stares at the man for a moment and, as though saying goodbye to not just this one agent of the military but to the whole it, and all his history in it, says, "I got it."

SIXTEEN

ARKIN AND KATE HAVEN'T exactly moved in together, but they have packed away their furniture and books and kitchen utensils and most of their clothes in a shared storage unit near her apartment. Both have terminated their apartment leases. Arkin has sold the car he bought after wrecking the Honda and is now in another short-term rental that he and Kate are sharing. Kate has donated her car to Make-A-Wish. Arkin has sold the Heckler & Koch rifle, the gun case, his ammo and spare magazines, all to a shop just across the river. He'd thought briefly of keeping them, but the nearest gun storage facility was an hour away, and in any case whatever impulse he'd had to start shooting again seems to have receded. He guesses that he'd fired perhaps two hundred rounds from his expensive new rifle but considers it a bargain, having shown him what he needed to know about the person he was and had become.

Kate had done the bulk of the research on their work options, including the somewhat murky issue of which organization would let them be together, and how secretive they'd need to be in pursuing same-country assignments. After the conversation with Oliver, Arkin had formed a preference for Doctors Without Borders, but

Kate had learned that International Medical Corps would more easily accommodate their desire to be together, and that's where they'd applied, formally separate, informally as one. They'd each taken written tests, interviewed, met with a hiring and HR panel, provided stacks of references. Ultimately, their separate tracks joined when both applied for placement in Mali, in West Africa, and had been accepted. Kate had actually been signed on as a nurse manager, a career advancement of sorts. Both had given notice at the hospital on the same day.

Twenty of the South Eight nurses had treated Kate to a going-away party at a restaurant called the Brewing Company north of town, where they'd all drunk a lot of craft beers and eaten chicken wings and pizza. Some of the nurses cried—possibly, and though they would miss Kate, in considerable part at the romantic nature of her departure to faraway adventures with Arkin. They giggled and teased Arkin, who felt out of place and said little, but who also blushed periodically, including at some of the suggestions for "sex in the wild," as one of the women put it. Being nurses, they were able to expand on this theme without shame, and explicitly. Kate, normally a "rugged bitch," as one of her girlfriends put it, was almost radiant. When she and Arkin were teased about marrying eventually, she made pretend gag gestures, then laughed and found his hand under the table.

Arkin's farewell is more sedate. The hospitalist group secretary has arranged a cake, which he and his colleagues have eaten around their conference table late one workday. A few of the off-duty physicians and nurse practitioners have come in for the occasion. Some express curiosity about his decision to leave the group, hospital practice, the country. The curiosity is muted though, as Arkin had expected. The men and women gathered around the table, he knows, are among the most highly motivated and focused people in the world. They've been through years of education and training; they've amassed huge loans; they continue to study religiously; they navigate extraordinarily stressful situations routinely. They are not inclined to question their choices of career path; those paths have consumed them for years already, with years more of literal toil ahead. Their interest in what Arkin's doing is an order removed from their interest in the next hour, the next patient, next month's work schedule, and Arkin thinks this is as it should be, for them.

But not for him. He thanks them, smiles more than he does in the average week, shakes everyone's hand, hugs a few. Massood watches from down the long table, with the inward grace that comes, Arkin thinks, from being the boss, older, born on another continent, slightly less buried in day-to-day clinical responsibilities while steeped in the ambiguities of management and corporate politics: he's wiser than the others.

"When do you leave?" he asks.

"Next week," Arkin says. "We're just waiting on visas."

"Have you ever been to Africa?" Arkin shakes his head. "Me either. I always wanted to go. I'm jealous."

Arkin smiles at him, their shared exposure, however brief, to the world of criminal investigation and suspected, still possible, lethal dose homicide, having forged an unexpected connection.

Massood returns the smile. "I didn't want to be a doctor," he says. "We are from Pakistan, where my father was very important in business, in textiles. He owns mills, cotton; I think now he has five. At first he wanted me to join him; I didn't like that idea. Then he wanted me to study law, or engineering; I didn't like any of that. I went to college in Miami. He wasn't happy, and when it was over, he said I would have to join the military. Which I also didn't like.

So my last *option* that would be acceptable was medical school, but I hadn't applied and it was late. But there was one school in the Caribbean that had late acceptance, and I interviewed. My grades were all right; they said they would take me." He looks at his hands, pensive or simply out of awkwardness, Arkin can't tell. "If I could write a check, at the table, that minute, for the first year's tuition. For eighty thousand dollars. Which I could. My father would cover. So I went to medical school and I became a doctor."

In Massood's eyes Arkin sees a mix of sadness and regret and perhaps the remnant of some early and no longer recognizable dream, no longer even nameable. After a moment, Massood says, "I never wanted to, and I hate so much of it. I hate the suffering, and the futility, and the sadness. I hate our failure to share our fears with our patients when we should, and our impotence when they sense our doubts, and our evasions. I hate that it costs so much to treat what they have so often brought on themselves. So I hate medicine." He pauses for a long moment, then looks to Arkin. "But you love it. Everything I hate about it, you love. Not because I'm wrong, but because you want to do better, you want to fix things, you want to make it right. Even with this man Barnhardt, you refused to lie, you refused to go along, you tried to do right."

"I don't know about that. At all."

"Oh yes. And now, you're going off to some place where you can do more. Do better."

Arkin says nothing, and in fact he hasn't thought about his departure in these terms and doesn't believe it. He's following the advice of the first person he's ever loved, which seems like plan enough. "Thank you, but I don't know. We'll see."

"Yes, we will," says Massood, his mood lifting. "Congratulations."

On the last day of work, Arkin sees a typical mix: five pneumonias, three heart failures, three COPD exacerbations, two cases of likely viral colitis, four of cellulitis, two bacteremia, two infected joints, one recovering DKA. He discharges six of the twenty-two patients, three back their nursing homes, two to rehab, and one to her home, where she lives with her son, aged seventy. That woman, Nora Singleton, ninety-two, was one of the first patients of the day, as the hospital likes to clear discharges as early as possible to make room for the later admissions.

Mrs. Singleton's son arrived using a rolling walker himself, which he pushed aside so that he could sit on the side of his mother's bed, hold her hand. He looked up at Arkin with tears in his eyes, and said, "Thank you, Doctor, thank you, thank you."

His mother patted his hand reassuringly, and winked at Arkin.

Kate drives up to the hospital's main entrance, Arkin waiting there at the end of his final shift. He has left his hospital-provided lab coats on a rack in the office but carries a shopping bag full of miscellaneous items from his locker: spare stethoscope tube and earpieces, a pulse oximeter, an old opthalmoscope and otoscope set he's had since medical school, sepsis cards, stacks of paperwork he'd never completed. He'll discard the paperwork but plans to take the rest to Africa. Such practical markers of his near future remain disconcerting.

Kate looks at him from behind the wheel of the rental. "So? How'd it go?"

"Totally . . . weird," he says, which gets an appreciative look. He's become more open these past weeks, she thinks, more prone to self-disclosure, as the professional in her might put it. "But . . . routine too," he says, and then, "Can you park for a minute?"

He puts his shopping bag on the passenger seat, and Kate finds a nearby "Patient Pick Up Only" space. Arkin waves to the security guard at the door, who waves approval in return, Arkin still known, still one of them for these last hours.

On foot now, Kate and Arkin cross over a grassy divide, walk past the ER ambulance entrance. Nine of the twelve bays have paramedic or EMT ambulances, and another one is driving up as they walk on. They look in the ambulatory ER entrance, jammed with people awaiting intake at the registration window; there're women with infants, toddlers, a nosebleeding teenage boy, and many elderly. Arkin experiences an enormous and unworthy feeling of relief—for the first time in years—at not seeing these new arrivals as potential patients. They will never be his responsibility, never Kate's "group"; they are only, just, *people.*

Kate and Arkin continue on, past huge supply delivery bays, past a sheltered picnic table area sometimes used by staff for lunch breaks on nice days. Across the highway on their right are apartment developments springing up along the Hudson, lights coming on now in the late summer twilight. Rounding the corner of the building, at the top of which is South Eight, Kate's old unit, they see spread out before them the huge new hospital rising on the site of a now demolished medical arts building, an old parking lot and helipad. The new building will be state of the art, four hundred private rooms, a thirty-bed ICU, and more. There will be high-speed fiber optic internet for patients and staff; there will be new food delivery systems allowing patient menu selection and delivery to any room within ten minutes. The current main hospital building will house a medical school.

They stare at the new building for a while. It's been designed so that every room will have a view of the Hudson, floor-to-ceiling glass, forty-inch TV screens.

"You sorry?" Arkin asks Kate.

"No. Not really. You?"

Arkin shakes his head.

"Might be nice, someday, brand-new building, high tech, everything clean."

"They won't have that in Africa?"

Kate only smiles at this. Beside them, the old hospital seems almost in living rebellion against what the new building represents. They can hear its ventilation system, they can see shadows moving against the windows of the big obstetrics unit just over their heads, they can hear not-so-distant sounds of sirens coming and going. They can hear voices from nurses and aides and paramedics working at the ambulance entrance bays. Below them, yet another ambulance speeds up the highway ramp toward the hospital turnoff behind them. On South Eight, and in units throughout the hospital, nurses are preparing for new, late admissions.

There are 280 patients in the hospital—or were when Arkin checked at the main desk before he walked out for the last time. On any given night, like the one ahead, perhaps ten will die. *Will take their last breaths,* Arkin recalls the cliche, while a dozen or more newborns will take their first. A third of the hospital's patients over seventy have, or will have, or are possibly slowly recovering from delirium, which means that at least fifty men and women inside the old building are at this moment are wondering where they are, or who they are, or are forgetting their children's names. Some of these will have received too much opioid pain medication, while there will be those who received too little. Other patients will have received too many antibiotics, or unnecessary ones, or altogether wrong diagnoses and unnecessary lab tests or imaging. And many, many dozens more patients will have been managed and also comforted by their nurses, bathed by their aides, saved by their doctors and nurse practitioners. For every patient in pain or tears, there will be another patient thinking, *I'm getting better* or *Thank God* or *They say I'm going home in the morning.*

Arkin finds that even now he cannot imagine how different Africa will be, but can dimly guess how remote all *this* will seem, likely all at once. He puts his arms around Kate, who hugs him closer to her in return. He can feel her heart beating, a steady rhythm, around sixty beats a minute, fit, strong. He can feel the slow squeeze and release of her lungs. She can feel the larger muscles in his arms around her and the obliques and lats under her hands. She can feel his heart beating, and his breaths flowing, and the warmth of his cheek on her forehead.

ACKNOWLEDGMENTS

Thanks are owed to Bethany Brown and her team at The Cadence Group, found by the luckiest of accidents, who've guided the publication of this book almost from the day of its completion. Kim Bookless has been peerless in copyediting and proofreading, as has Gwyn Flowers in designing the book in its entirety. Thanks also to Olivia McCoy and Kellie Rendina of Smith Publicity, who illuminated the daunting landscape of independent book marketing and publicity.

I owe profound thanks to the early readers who provided crucial advice and support as *South Eight* emerged and evolved. The essayist and editor Aki Busch, novelist/painter Minnie Warburton, and the novelist and filmmaker John Griesemer each shared insights that saved this writer, and his book, again and again. Marjorie Atlas, playwright turned educator, provided not just writerly advice but sisterly understanding. And my friend Jared Zelman, MD, did me the honor of enjoying *South Eight* enough to perhaps overlook medical missteps I may have made; if any such exist, they belong entirely to its author.

In a very real sense, *South Eight* was shaped by the hundreds of healthcare professionals who have educated and inspired me over the past fifteen years. I hope that in some small way it has given readers a sense of the wisdom and endurance of our often-overlooked patient care techs; of the supreme commitment and expertise of my friends in nursing; and of the brilliance and courage of my physician colleagues in the face of extraordinary daily challenges. The word *hero* is often used to describe all these, and it is entirely appropriate, if insufficient. Many, many thanks to you all.

ABOUT THE AUTHOR

After serving in the Army as a drill sergeant, Larry Atlas attended Bennington College, earning both bachelor's and master's degrees before declining admission to medical school—and moving to New York to begin a successful career as an actor, playwright, and screenwriter. Among his produced plays are *Total Abandon* and the award-winning *Yield of the Long*  *Bond*, which premiered at the Matrix Theatre in Los Angeles. He worked on multiple studio film projects, including *Sleepless in Seattle*. He conceived and implemented the first nationwide online actors' casting service and then later coinvented and patented the first navigable nonlinear video architecture. In midlife, on impulse, he went to nursing school and then worked for four years as an acute care nurse while earning a master's degree as a nurse practitioner at SUNY Stony Brook. He worked for a decade as a hospitalist NP and now practices at a subacute rehab. He has taught at Hunter, Bennington, and Vassar Colleges and is former captain of the skydiving team Spaced Rangers. Larry lives in Upstate New York with actor-turned-therapist Ann Matthews and their dog, Ruby.

CPSIA information can be obtained
at www.ICGtesting.com
Printed in the USA
BVHW051408230822
645283BV00006B/477